Dedalus European Classics
General Editor: Timothy Lane

WHERE THE GRASS
NO LONGER
GROWS

GEORGES MAGNANE

WHERE THE GRASS NO LONGER GROWS

translated by Jerome Fletcher

Dedalus

Supported using public funding by
**ARTS COUNCIL
ENGLAND**

Published in the UK by Dedalus Limited
24-26, St Judith's Lane, Sawtry, Cambs, PE28 5XE
info@dedalusbooks.com
www.dedalusbooks.com

ISBN printed book   978 1 912868 83 4
ISBN ebook   978 1 912868 98 8

Dedalus is distributed in the USA & Canada by SCB Distributors
15608 South New Century Drive, Gardena, CA 90248
info@scbdistributors.com   www.scbdistributors.com

Dedalus is distributed in Australia by Peribo Pty Ltd
58, Beaumont Road, Mount Kuring-gai, N.S.W. 2080
info@peribo.com.au   www.peribo.com.au

First published in France by Albin Michel in 1953, republished by Editions
Maiade in 2016
First published by Dedalus in 2022

Printed and bound in the UK by Clays Elcograf S.p.A.
Typeset by Marie Lane

THE AUTHOR

Georges Magnane (1907 – 1985) was the pen name of René Catinaud, born into a farming family in Limousin, central France. He went from there to the Ecôle Normale d'instituteurs in Paris before completing his studies in Oxford.

As well as being a teacher and novelist, Magnane was a journalist (he covered the 1948 London Olympics for Sartre's *L'humanité*) a pioneer of the sociology of sport in France, a translator (notably of Updike, Nabokov and Capote), and a scriptwriter for theatre and film.

THE TRANSLATOR

Former real tennis professional and elver catcher, Jerome Fletcher was Director of Writing at Dartington College of Arts and Associate Professor of Performance Writing at Falmouth University. He has published novels and poetry for children, translations, and experimental digital texts, as well as performance works. Along with Alex Martin, he has produced several titles for Dedalus including *The Decadent Cookbook*, *The Decadent Gardener*, *The Decadent Traveller* and *The Decadent Sportsman*.

He now lives in France near Limoges.

FOR APHRA

WITH ALL MY LOVE

ACKNOWLEDGMENTS

The translator would like to thank the following who have provided invaluable assistance and feedback. Dr Thomas Bauer, Jean-Christophe Chaumeny, Prof Thomas Docherty, Marie-France Houdart of *Editions Maiade*, Edward Klein, Pierre Sourdoulaud, Barbara Bridger, Alex Martin. And especially Amy Lewis.

FAMILIES

The BRICAUD family:

```
                    Etienne = Julie
                            |
     François    –    Jean = Annie    –    Francis
    (deceased)          |
                     Gaston
```

The LAMBERT family:

```
          Maître LAMBERT = wife
                         | (deceased)

            Georges    –    Philippe = Susanne
           (deceased)                  |
                              David    –    Daniel
```

The LAVARENNE family:

```
          Joseph = Maria
                 |
               Albert
```

PART 1

CHAPTER 1

Not for one moment did Jean Bricaud think that the war would arrive at his door – the door to his peaceful house built a short distance from a peaceful village at the edge of a valley where it had taken millennia for a passage to be hollowed out through the most ancient earth. It was the toughest, the most solid of houses, better protected than any other against the vagaries of volcanoes, plague, war and famine.

On that June day in 1944, it was only some time after Jean had heard the rumble of lorries that it occurred to him anything might be wrong. The news of the German debacle that he listened to on the radio every evening came as no more of a surprise to him than the loudly trumpeted announcements three years earlier of their headlong push towards the East; it was none of his business. He had done what he could for his family, for the refugees, for the starving townspeople who approached him; he had filled each day to the brim with exhausting work. So, if there were those who wanted to play with thunder and death, that was their look-out. He wasn't joining in their game. He didn't have time. Yesterday's winners are today's losers?… that was fine. He gave them a round of applause. He lent a helping hand as and when. But best not to pester him and waste his time. A small contribution, that was ok. A big one, that's going too far.

He was turning over the hay on his own. He'd never get it done. It was already past lunchtime. That empty feeling which had begun in the pit of his stomach was steadily spreading now. He was feeling it in his shanks and even more in his right forearm with which he gave the rake a quick flick when needed.

In this shimmering open space, crackling with grasshoppers and sparkling with heat, he was feeling a bit lost. And angry. If it weren't for the anger, he would have already called it a day. The hay could wait, what with weather like this. Annie and his mother went to the market in Verrièges every Saturday. Fine. No problem with that! What with all this ration book stuff, his mother was no longer up to it on her own. At seventy-seven years old it wasn't easy to comply with all this red tape. But then, it was good for maman, good for her to need Annie now and again. She'd often said that her daughter-in-law wasn't in the house just for decoration. They don't mince their words, the old folks… but Gaston! That boy had no reason to wander off to Verrièges. The cocky sixteen-year-old, built like an eighteen-year-old, was old enough to pull his weight, otherwise he'd never amount to anything, useless lump! As soon as he noticed how his uncle Francis had pricked up his ears, he immediately started yelling; "What is it, Francis? What do you reckon's going on? Maybe they're the

Maquis' cars. We ought to go and see." Francis came straight back at him. "Oh, you think so, do you? It's the Jerries. Lorries and light tanks." Jean had hoped that would settle the question. Not a bit of it. Francis immediately dumped his rake in a ditch (it was still there, with Gaston's next to it, the tines full of hay, they'd been in such a hurry. Idle buggers!) He'd said: "It's not normal for there to be so many. I'm going to see what they're playing at." My arse! Jean knew very well what Francis had in mind – a nice little rendezvous at the lake with his Juliette, the mayor's daughter. Never liked her, that one. She's got a way of looking straight at you. I've never seen her lower her eyes in front of a man. In my day the girls were never like that, even in town. Everything's going to hell, and fast.

Needless to say, Gaston had followed his uncle. Jean daren't say a word. If he started, he'd say too much and end up breaking something. He couldn't bear it – all this talk of planes and cars and motorbikes, talk which Francis had brought with him from the town and which he blew through the house like a wind. Jean had had a motorbike too, of course, but he'd paid for it with his own money, every nut and bolt, from selling on the sly anything he shot or caught with his rod. Mind you, it wasn't the same. He'd never taken this stuff seriously. For Francis it was a passion, even if he wouldn't admit it, and if he continued to encourage Gaston, he'd turn out even worse than his uncle. All their mechanical crap! It was obvious what was going on in 1940, when all that stuff flowed out along the roads and lanes. It was like the town was suppurating, stinking, growling, screeching; from time to time it let out a jet of flame and a fart. Must have been something poisonous in the belly of the town! All their transportation, all their planes, their heavy guns and what have you, they were invented to finish things off when they realised the pox wasn't up to the job. It's war, right! And Francis, his own brother, followed all the latest inventions. Even put his own shoulder to the wheel. One day he was going to patent some type of motor. He often talked about it. Of course, that was his role, him being an engineer. "Yes…" Jean had explained the previous day to that miserable, short-arsed tutor who wanted to show off, "…my brother's an engineer. Not just any old engineer. Came top of the class at the Polytechnique, in case that means anything to you, M. Poulard? And is he proud of that, eh? …we would be, in his shoes. And we are, as you see."

It was nice to have a phenomenal brother, and flattering for sure, but it was no reason to remain on his own in that murderous heat. Rivulets of sweat were forming on his forehead. Now and again they ran across his eyebrows although their course was mostly down his nose, from where large droplets regularly fell onto his wrists and shoes. "Lorries and light tanks… it's a lot of crap as far as I'm concerned. I wouldn't get off my arse to take a look at the finest piece of engineering in the world."

Then all of a sudden he had a thought which, for a moment, dried up the source of his sweat: he had heard the lorries arrive in Verrièges, but he hadn't heard them leave. What's that all about?

He quickly searched in the little pocket under his belt where he put his watch. Hang on, hang on! It was nearly two o'clock. Something odd was going on, surely. The women were always home a good hour before this. What is it? What's up?

He stood for a moment, rooted to the spot, holding his rake at arms-length, its tines pointing upwards. The sweat began to run again, cold and viscous. It took Jean some time to realise how absurd this was: in the midst of this heat, he felt cold. Cold, in June sunshine. Cold in the meadow most sheltered from the wind. Moreover, the row of oaks in front of him were as motionless as a picture in a book. Not a breath of wind stirred in them. Neither earth nor sky breathed. The moment hovered over him, held steady on immense wings.

Jean stood motionless, blinking, torn between a desire to leap into action, to set off, and an equally immediate reflex to do nothing. No. No. Absolutely not. If he carried on working, if he forced his actions and his behaviour to follow their everyday arc, he would drive away any bad luck, he would maintain the continuity of his life.

That was what he was thinking. He was already picturing that first movement where the end of the rake would slip under a tuft of scrunchy grass, but he knew this was turning into a rout. It was like in a legend: far removed from the event and yet at the same time plunged intimately into the very heart of it, he contemplated this field, these trees, the fine scattering of hay, and he found there a desperate beauty totally alien to him. Even his recent surly fatigue was becoming dear to him, because it felt like a fragment of treasure lost forever. He would have given anything for that desire for anger to rise in him again. He would give it a try anyway. Come on. Quickly. He had to give it a try. No time to lose.

He took off across the hay. He ran as lightly as he had as a ten-year old. And he really felt like he had returned to that ferocious age when everything was possible and when slaughter and death framed his daily imaginings. Except that, at ten, death held no real fear for him. Death was a mere formality like any other, a bizarre comedy that you weren't allowed to laugh at. Now he had learned real fear. Now he shuddered to feel that energy again in his legs driven by that constant, light-hearted terror of yesteryear.

With a modicum of force he pushed open the gate, still rotten after twenty years but holding together. It squeaked like it had always squeaked, with a sniggering, obliging tone. He had slowed down to hear this friendly caricature of a voice. At the same time, through an open window he heard the sound of his mother and father squabbling. This was also familiar and reassuring to him; indescribably reassuring.

Jean wanted to afford himself one last moment of childish cowardice, of happiness… he went into the house looking angry, as if nothing had happened, and actually convincing himself that nothing had happened. How good it felt to be a little boy again to whom nothing could happen! In much the same way as the gentle, faded gaze of his mother had a calming effect on him, so too did the pitiless, piercing eagle eye of his father. Ok then! Get angry, get angry with me then, tell me off for making a noise or being late! Get really angry so that I can feel the true heat of the sun a bit, so that I stop shivering and feeling myself slide towards that black abyss.

But when he came in the old couple suddenly fell silent. His father, who was hunched over the newspaper, rustled the pages and looked guilty. His mother decided not to put down the lettuce leaf she had been cleaning.

'Why are you shouting like that?' Jean asked in a scolding tone. 'You can be heard a hundred metres off.'

'Oh, nothing,' his mother said. 'It's him, banging on as usual. He doesn't know what he's talking about.'

Jean wanted to put on a gruff tone. But he couldn't.

'Show me the paper,' he said.

Before Jean had even found the page where his father's long, hard nails – those grooved nails which he sometimes cut for him – had dug into the paper, he had understood: he had been reading the infamous denial put out by the occupation authorities. That morning, the postman had talked to him about it when he passed him on the road. Then a neighbour had left the patch he was weeding and crossed two fields, his own and Jean's, to come and ask him what he thought about it: 'They haven't really done that, have they? It's not possible. That's what you think too, isn't it? You realise they're saying this is getting closer every day. They set fire to Tulle, left Guéret in ruins. Now the shooting's moved to Argenton; and the first ones to be gunned down were the gendarmes, for not being fanatical enough. Still, it's unbelievable. This denial, what do you think?' Jean said nothing. He had not read it and he didn't want to read it; any more than he would have wanted to listen to an account of the massacres in Tulle and elsewhere.

And now…

His father looked up at him. Jean met his gaze and for the first time realised that he had an old man in front of him, an ancient old man, who in turn was looking for some support. At ninety-three, he might have expected it… all the same, now was not the time. It seemed like a betrayal.

'I've got to go and see,' he said abruptly.

At once, his father and mother stood up. His father's shaking hand groped along the wall for his stick.

'Stay here you two. What's most important is that I'm going to bring them back.'

His voice was so lacking in confidence that he did not expect to be obeyed. In fact, his father muttered something, found his stick finally and set off towards the gate with a sprightly step which Jean had not seen in forty years, not since he himself was struggling to put his first steps together. This did not surprise him. He had given up being surprised, surrendering in the face of the inadmissible. He was on the verge of panic.

Mechanically, he looked for the identity disc for his bicycle. He could not find it and he continued on his way. As if he really needed an identity disc! Just the thing to waste your time on at a moment like this! He held back a roar of anger and dashed towards the bike shed.

He had gone through the gate and was set to kick it shut, as he usually did. His mother gestured to him to get going.

'I'll shut it. Go. Quickly.'

Jean turned round just long enough to shout: 'I told you two to stay here.'

'Go quickly. Don't worry about us.'

CHAPTER 2

Jean had just taken a corner too fast. The back wheel of the bike had skidded violently but he had rediscovered a reflex from the time when he was riding in small regional races – all his weight on the outside pedal – the right – and his left leg bent, his foot halfway off the pedal ready to make contact with the road to start a rapid headlong gallop before the inevitable tumble. However everything was brought under control, and already, through the leaves of the chestnut trees, Jean could make out the weathervane on the church. He took a deep breath and hurried on, head down. He was going to find the lot of them, knock back a drink, return home in triumph, and get back to work. There were six hay carts to load and unload. Three for Gaston, three for Francis. Payback! They'll see!

He slammed on both brakes at once. The front one was better than the back, less worn. The wheels gripped the gravel which jingled musically in the spokes before rattling to the ground. The bike ended up sideways across the road. Jean jumped off, stumbled and only just kept his balance.

Face-to-face with a machine gun, he blinked. He did his best to feign alarm, because deep down it came as no surprise to him. When he left the farm he had abandoned any possibility of being surprised. Given what he could see, he came to the gloomy realisation that the road was completely blocked by a German light tank and a lorry, the one he had almost crashed into. Some cars were parked on the verges. A little closer to the lorry a line of men and women stood in single file motionless in a dusty ditch, a fixed and empty look on their faces. They all created an impression of great calm as if, at the moment they became aware of their powerlessness, they had totally removed themselves from the world.

Jean stepped forward.

'Halt,' shouted the man with the machine gun, a massive bloke with red cheeks and an oddly vague and sleepy air to him.

Jean was expecting this. But he was ready to do anything to avoid joining that line of people with that look of frightful patience about them.

'I have to get through,' he said calmly.

The German shook his head and Jean noticed then that he was smiling. This smile made him seem very young, cheerful and easy-going. Mr happy-go-lucky! Jean was sure that, wherever or whenever, he could get what he wanted out of a man like this.

'I've got to get through,' he repeated. 'My family's in there. Almost all of them – my wife, my son, my brother…'

Once again the German shook his head. His smile became even more cheerful, but his finger stiffened on the safety catch of his machine gun.

At that moment, another German, an officer for sure, came up and said a few words. The smile disappeared from the soldier's face. He saluted and stepped back a few paces.

'What do you want?' the officer asked.

'To get through,' Jean said.

'You are not allowed through, Monsieur. Do you live in Verrièges?'

This one was not smiling. On the contrary, he looked extremely serious. However, there was no hostility in his look. He had fine features and spoke French without an accent, almost perfectly, with maybe just a little too much effort.

'No,' said Jean who was feeling at ease. 'I live a couple of kilometres from here. But my family…'

The officer interrupted him, without rudeness and with a sort of urgency which seemed well-meaning.

'Yes, I know. I heard. But there's no point insisting. Your papers please.'

Jean took a ration book and old hunting licence out of his pocket. The German gave them back immediately.

'Good. Now, on your way, and tell yourself you've been lucky.'

'Lucky,' Jean repeated, astonished.

'Yes. That you don't live in Verrièges.'

A glimmer passed over the man's clear face and Jean no longer found his expression reassuring. The other one's brutish mug was less worrying than this crystal-clear expression, as clear as the surface of water reflecting unknown stars.

Once again Jean felt the sweat turn cold on his brow and in his armpits. He already knew he would not get permission to go through.

Besides, the German officer had turned away and headed off.

Among those lined up in the ditch was M. Chabaud, the watchmaker from Donzac. Jean barely knew him. Even so he automatically went towards him. Where was he to go now he couldn't get through? Here or elsewhere, what did it matter?

The watchmaker called to him, in an almost hateful voice.

'Are you off your head? Get out of here quick! The officer who was here before that one, he began by shoving everybody in the ditch. Then he sent anybody from the commune off to Verrièges. *He* wouldn't have let you off the hook.'

The moustachioed face of this little man struck Jean as horrible. How come he hadn't noticed before that M. Chabaud had the face of an evil maniac? Wouldn't have let you off the hook...? What hook, eh? What did he mean? What was he implying?

'You shouldn't believe everything you're told, M. Chabaud,' said Jean impatiently. 'What do you suppose they'll do with the people from Verrièges? They can't arrest everybody.'

The watchmaker shook his head.

'No, they can't arrest everybody. And I don't know what they want. Nonetheless, if I were you I'd have taken off by now... it's not as if by lining up with us here you'll be doing anything for those on the other side.'

This time the little moustachioed man was making a good point. First of all, don't get nabbed. There were other ways into Verrièges. The Germans couldn't know all of them.

'Goodbye, Monsieur Chabaud. Thank you.'

CHAPTER 3

Jean left the main road and spent a long time cycling around the side roads, where the dried mud formed whitening crusts, then along the paths so narrow that the twigs whipped his face and scraped against his cotton trousers. A hundred metres out from Verrièges, he abandoned his bike and began to crawl the length of a hazel hedge through the tall grass that Peyraud, the tailor, had not yet cut. He had to cross a sunken lane and make it to the edge of a stream where the thick willows would provide cover as far as the first houses of the town. This was the only tricky moment in an otherwise perfectly calculated route.

The path was no more that a couple of metres wide. Jean was about to cross it in a single bound when the throbbing sound of a motor approached at high speed. Hidden in his hazel bush, Jean saw a motorcyclist go past an arms-length away. He was wearing camouflage, dirty green with splashes of brown and grey.

This was the moment…

He jumped across the lane, grabbed onto the bank then gripped the undergrowth of the hedge. The hole he had spotted was right there. He had already found his balance among the hazel branches and was about to jump, when a man on the other side of the hedge rushed at him head down and knocked him backwards.

Jean had managed to hold on to a branch of the hazel tree. The man who had shoved him back took hold of his sleeve and gave him a warning: 'Don't stay here. They're after me.'

A machine gun opened up and they heard above their heads the furtive rustle of bullets through the leaves. Once back across the lane, they tumbled quickly down the slope that Jean had so carefully climbed without disturbing the long grass that had hidden him. As he leapt across a deep hole that he thought was narrower, Jean stumbled. His companion fell on top of him with all his weight. They rolled over and over until Jean's shoulder smashed into a stump.

He felt such intense pain he thought he was going to faint. Not now! The motorcyclist could be coming round the corner of the meadow. Jean took off running again. With each stride he felt like he would dislocate his shoulder, but he kept on running. A couple of times, he heard – or thought he heard – a burst of machine-gun fire. He ran even faster.

His companion always managed to stay within a few metres of him, although he was only short. When they found some cover, Jean took a moment to look at him and recognised him immediately. It was Daniel Graetz, the Jewish lad from Lorraine who worked over at the Pradet's farm.

As soon as he stopped, his shoulder hurt so bad he had to lean with his back against a tree.

'Have you been hit?' asked Graetz.

'No. It was in the meadow just now. I smacked into the

stump of a poplar. I even knew it was there – that bloody old fishpond. It's nothing. It'll wear off.'

Daniel Graetz was breathing heavily and a fleck of foam was forming at the corners of his mouth. His eyes shone like those of a hunted animal.

'How did you manage to slip through their fingers?' he asked.

Jean liked this tone of complicity. It reduced his anxiety for a moment. He had a sense that he was solidly in the world, free and light, and that he had let slip an intolerable burden from his shoulders. The relief was such that for a moment he remained silent, wondering if he was going to let Daniel believe that he had in fact just escaped. But lying was not his strong point; already the weight of other lives pressed down on him, lives which counted for more than his own, of which his own was no more than a reflection.

'No,' he said. 'I haven't *come* from Verrièges. I wanted to *get* there. All my family's there.'

The boy's bewilderment stirred no emotion in him. He had expected it. He now understood that his long journey had been worse than useless. He had wasted his time. He should have... what? He didn't know what he should have done. What was little Graetz saying?

'...my father's there, and my cousin too. But they won't take the old man far: sixty seven and crippled with rheumatism. And Armand, my cousin, has got one leg in plaster. They'll stick them in a camp. But I'll be more use to them at large than if I let myself be sent off to the salt mines, or worse...'

Jean looked in Daniel's direction but could not see him. He's right, he thought. What he says is sensible. I'm the one who's not being sensible. I've behaved like a crazy kid.

Daniel Graetz had already said goodbye and was moving off among the trees with long, supple strides, his elbows by his side.

Jean went off in search of his bike.

CHAPTER 4

After he had exchanged a few words with the tall, thin peasant with unsettling eyes (a clumsy hand had penned 'Bricaud Jean' in his ration book), Colonel Wolfgang Rehm had himself driven back to the Place du champ de foire in Verrièges, the spot he had chosen to assemble the populace.

This 'Jean' had the very look and bearing of a fierce resistance fighter in the *maquis*. Napoleon, during his disastrous expedition to Spain, must have come across such men; gaunt but ferocious, tireless, scornful of the rules of war, dangerous even to their dying breath.

When talking to him, Rehm had had a moment of hope. With an adversary such as this, his mission might take on some meaning.

For Jean was more than an adversary: he was a true enemy. Against him, against men like him, the war reverted to its original meaning and became a vital function: destroy or be destroyed.

Walking the dusty ground back and forth, Rehm experienced a sense of extreme pleasure in conjuring up the page of his 'log book' in which he would record this meeting.

In fact, he had not had much opportunity to write in this journal, a journal he had such high hopes for. Erich, his older brother who lounged about in the offices of the Majestic hotel, had made fun of him mercilessly when he claimed that the war would provide him with a richer harvest of experiences if he saw it up close, as a soldier. 'Poor Wolfgang, the war can't enrich anybody and it's not worth getting to know. The only attitude worthy of a man is to ignore it as much as possible. The duty we owe ourselves, those of us who are and must remain intellectuals, is to shout this as loud as we can and to demonstrate it by all the means at our disposal.' He had a way of saying 'Poor Wolfgang' which made the younger brother want to strangle him violently. Because in fact, it was him, Erich, who was the poor man, the poor innocent, the poor German forever fooled and duped; duped by vocation, it seemed, and happy to be so. The smugness with which he recounted the successes – or what he called successes – that he achieved in the salons of Paris with his policy of 'collaboration' made him want to slap him. Or rather, no! The best response in such a case was the formula Hermann Goering had come up with: We had to remind these unbearable apes who dressed up their sneers and self-importance in the name of humanism that when they ceased to follow blindly and without hesitation the orders of the Leader, the Man of Destiny, they were nothing but stray beasts like any other human being. In this respect, Goering displayed a surprising level of genius. Rehm remembered with hilarity how big Hermann had completely undermined some piss-weak little industrialist to whom he had made an excellent proposal at the expense of the Jews, and who had then come up with some convoluted response in the name of his precious conscience. "Come on, come on," Goering had exclaimed. "Your whole body rejoices when you let out a big fart." Now that's healthy! We must love this vulgarity that comes from strength. I have to. I want to. We can do whatever we like.

Wolfgang Rehm lit a cigarette and exhaling great lungfuls, surrounded himself in a cloud of blue smoke. Having severed all ties with common humanity, he felt like a god floating in an azure sky. He refused to stoop down to the exhalations from this miserable earth, unworthy of him and his peers. All was well.

To kill time, he tried to take an interest in the work of the soldiers who were pushing the inhabitants of Verrièges in front of them with the same gestures that sheep drovers used.

Most of the interpreters spoke with Alsatian accents which offended the colonel's delicate ear: 'Get along, get along! Quickly. Everybody to the Place du marché,' they growled forcefully between their teeth. Why did they insist on calling it the 'Place du marché' when Rehm had made it clear it was called the 'Champ du foire' here? Bah! So what!

The serious opponent was Jean. Rehm had clearly sensed this when they exchanged looks. Until that precise moment he was faced with a peasant who could have been from anywhere. Sly certainly, and crafty, and cunning, but couldn't care less about anything except his wallet and his immediate possessions. Then there was this shock, this spark. Jean's voice had changed, his attitude had changed, everything about him became harder, more complete. Rehm thought he had seen him grow disproportionately. More than a man, he was becoming a hostile principle. He was the Enemy.

Instinctively Rehm had straightened up. A shudder went the length of his spine. If he had had fur, it would certainly have stood up on end like a dog spotting a cat. But evil was more difficult to reconcile than the hostility between dogs and cats. To calm animals down all you need to do is separate them – they forget very quickly. But neither time nor space could overcome human emotions. The soul was profound in a different way to the instincts, despite a certain primary biology. Even if this already vast world were ten times bigger, it would not have been vast enough for the soul of a Wolfgang Rehm and that of a Jean Bricaud to co-exist.

In the wake of this encounter, Rehm realised more clearly that he was destiny's representative. History was on the move, and he was the instrument of the supreme will. His gaze misted over at this thought. Although a modest executor, he would at least be beyond reproach: "Regardless of how simple or brief, my act will be an act of perfect obedience. It will have the purity of the purest metal."

The small remaining doubt he felt a while ago when he was ordering the positioning of the encirclement unit, Rehm now saw as no more than the remnant of an all-too human sensitivity. He wanted to shrug his shoulders. Certainly, there was still that slight trembling, or rather a sort of internal vibration, that he could not control. But it was a question of a purely physical state, some slight visceral event. Anyway, it was an individual, personal reaction and therefore of no consequence.

When he arrived on the outskirts of Verrièges he had expressed the correct judgment on the situation. Thus he had spontaneously placed himself in a historic perspective. He had examined the village with a cold eye, with Olympian serenity.

He needed to rediscover this internal strength, this eagle-like view which allowed him to take in the cosmic significance of the event all at once.

Rehm thought about his Journal again. He did not hide the fact from his close friends (and among these he counted lieutenant Greven who at that moment was directing the women to the right of the square and the men to the left) – he did not hide the fact that this Journal was his ultimate resource. For him, writing took on the value of a ritual. A latter-day Antaeus, he reinvigorated his soul by plunging it at regular intervals into the wellspring of his political faith and most cherished myths. He would note down in his Journal his calm and profound certainty, the conviction he held that he was accomplishing a mission. He already seemed to be re-reading: "The most difficult thing is not throwing oneself into the teeth of danger. The rarest, most authentic heroism is moral by nature. In these times it often consists in bringing to a successful conclusion, with confidence and pride, tasks which are deemed to be cowardly and ignoble."

The method would, once again, prove to be effective. Having returned to his old self, Rehm deigned to cast a suitably wise and impartial eye over the inhabitants of Verrièges. He attempted to take a scientific interest in these men with their dark eyes, almost all of them short in stature, sharp and nervous in the way they moved their head or hands, and yet whose tread was heavy, as if they were always carrying some unseen burden. "Heredity," Rehm diagnosed, "or rather, heritage. They're oppressed by a very elaborate culture but one that deep down is false. It enfeebles them and finally overwhelms them. Instead of directing themselves towards grandeur, they tend towards humility, softness and the dark warmth of the flock." This backward population, stuck in a rut, one which was evidently attached to dull, meticulous traditions, had for a long time been condemned by itself to death. Nothing spoke in its favour. Absolutely nothing. Such perfection of nothingness took on exemplary value. This was the first time Rehm found himself in the presence of living beings whose life seemed to him so unjustifiable. Even the peasant houses, so striking in the majority of regions, here seemed to him dismal and surly. On the road, whenever he rounded a bend, his sense of town planning – in his judgement a highly refined sense – had constantly come up against the unexpected appearance of scattered hamlets, disorderly and without any overall plan. Perhaps the decadent French mind would have dressed this disorder up as 'imaginative'. But to Rehm's eyes, in the view of a man who regarded himself as an envoy from enlightened regions, these were nothing but signs of inferiority. The squat houses, basic, barely distinguishable from the blocks of granite whose dull colour they had retained, seemed to be heaped against each other. This gave them an attitude of irredeemable hostility which did not escape the German's notice. As for supposing that in this way they retreated into some sort of secret, he rejected such an idea with scorn. The inner life had to shine through in some form or other when it was present. But no. No. Here it could not, it *must not* exist. What did these flat facades reveal, with their narrow, routinely symmetrical windows, unadorned, without flowers or green plants? Nothing more than poverty of the spirit and a refusal to obey. This peasantry was without culture, without ideals and without soul: simple, raw material for the race of Masters and Creators. This was the race Rehm belonged to, certainly in his own eyes; and in the eyes of his soldiers as he wore all the appropriate stripes and recognised insignia. He was the Man of Order. Put more simply and without useless tautology; he was the Man. For without order there would be only *men*: in other words, countless diversity, a freedom which would open up below, above and around him; everywhere, like the most appalling of chasms…

The eyes of that man back there on the road, that Jean, was something Rehm could not get out of his head. (He had let himself be taken by surprise, which was a mistake…) Those black eyes, those sharp eyes, threatening – no, not threatening. Worse. Worrying, like a threat which is beyond them, forever staring towards the future, towards a destiny… but in fact, almost all the men here – this one, that one, the other – had such eyes. So, he had fallen into a trap.

Again, that detestable shiver ran the length of his spine and he noticed that he was no longer managing to maintain his expression of Olympian serenity. Ah well, never mind. He would do without the serenity for the time being. Meanwhile, his anger did not suit him either. We'd see…

He uttered a series of ferocious shouts. Being able to make so much noise came as a joyful surprise. A succession of growls and hiccups like muffled explosions rose in his throat and kept increasing until they settled into an almost continuous outcry. Rehm became one long roar directed upward like a flame. It felt to him like an air-raid siren was tearing his throat. Well, too bad; for his throat and for his blood vessels swollen and throbbing on his forehead. All the soldiers ran around in a panic – the men and women too.

'Schnell! Schnell! Quickly! Quickly!'

What boundless joy! One old woman fell flat on her face crossing the street and two girls tried to pick her up. Blows from rifle butts rained on their backs. They dragged the old woman who was screaming. She lost her dentures. A girl put them back in her mouth. A kick sent her sprawling and her raised skirt exposed her pearl-white buttocks. Another woman was pulling and pushing the old one who was trying to express her anger. Look at her, on the ground. A whole heap of women on the ground. Dresses up, a great festival of thighs and buttocks on show. Splendid! Quite splendid!

CHAPTER 5

'Lambert, I'm pleased with you. I thought you were trying to be a smart alec when you first arrived, but at heart you're a good lad. Your parents will be happy with your work.'

David wondered what had got into little Father Valade that morning, coming out with such a speech and in such a solemn tone. And he thought in a hot flush of joy "It's because Papa has spoken to him. The war's going to be over and Papa knows it. I'm going to be in Paris with Maman and Papa. I'll never leave them. Never again."

All the same, he was very fond of M. Valade. To begin with he had found him quite funny, this awkward strapping bloke with a slightly crooked nose whose nostrils were covered with thousands of droplets of sweat when he shouted. 'He's got a conk like a watering can, this nitpicker,' he said. And the other boys looked at him with wary embarrassment. So he came back at them: 'Oh come on! You know he's not a nitpicker. Why didn't you say so? I wanted you to come right out with it. I don't like kids who don't say straightaway what they have in mind. People around here are devious.' Then he had realised that his classmates were not so devious. They just burnt on a long fuse and were happy to let the loudmouths sound off. They used to say: '…let him go off on one', a phrase they usually reserved for a hunting dog that barks its head off when it picks up a fresh scent. Nor was M. Valade, over-scented and pomaded on Sunday mornings, the clumsy simpleton that he had first thought him to be. He realised this on the day poor Paruquot had called him 'a little yid' (on the grounds that his name, David, was not commonly used in the area). M. Valade had not got really angry. He had simply gone very red. But he had gone red in such a way that all the boys had felt deep down, as well as in their throats, a very precise sense of profound awkwardness and regret. It's the pain you feel from upsetting your mother or somebody who is dear to you…

'I never thought I'd hear such a word in my school.'

He spoke without expression in his voice, all the time avoiding looking in Paruquot's direction.

'I never thought anybody in any school in our country would hear such a word.'

The effect was that from that moment on, 'the Parisian' was adopted personally by each and every pupil, including Paruquot.

Yes, David Lambert was very fond of M. Valade. As indeed were all the others.

When the teacher stepped out of the room to answer an energetic bell the pupils didn't respond. They were on to their second maths problem but, in this heat and after the news that the English radio had been whispering recently, their hearts were not in it. Already, that morning, M. Valade had postponed the maths problem until the afternoon because he had some urgent business to attend to and break had lasted more than half an hour.

Perinaud, who was by the window, suddenly leapt onto the table which he referred to as his 'lookout post'.

'Shit! It's a kraut, lads!' he announced.

He ducked quickly as if to dodge a bullet.

M. Valade returned, very pale.

'You will gather up your stuff and leave in perfectly good order.'

The pupils did not move. Nobody raised a finger to ask to speak. Instead of obeying, they stared at the schoolmaster. And the question that they asked thus was so insistent that M. Valade immediately explained: 'By order of the occupying forces.'

For several seconds, there was still no movement, coupled with an unusual silence. A German appeared at the doorway. He was a big, swarthy-faced man with deep wrinkles. It was one of those faces that belongs to a professional funny-man, both naive and mischievous, which children find irresistible.

'You children are going to make your way to the square,' he said in very good French and with a smile that reduced his eyes to two dark slits. 'You're going to have your photo taken.'

David heard some stifled laughter and murmurings: 'He's got a funny-looking mug. Or rather, a nice mug.' Their faces had cheered up already. They shone, taut from health and the inextinguishable hope of their age. It certainly wasn't for the pleasure of taking their portraits that the krauts were assembling them like this. So, what did they want from them?

In the time it took him to buckle his schoolbag, David came up with a great scenario: the Germans, in order to break through a *maquis* roadblock were going to push the school children out in front of them. Suddenly, at the most dramatic moment, one of the children shouts out. 'Everybody down.' And the Germans are mown down by bullets, just like an ambush in a Western.

All the same, it was certainly true that he had a decent mug, this Kraut. David took another look at him, for the pleasure of being able to say later: 'There are Jerries with good mugs. I've seen one.' He looked up and the smile froze on his face. It wasn't a nice-looking face any more that he saw in front of him.

The German's tanned and wrinkled face no longer expressed the grimacing but infinite good-will of the clown. It did not express spite either. It was just a bored face. Profoundly bored, bored to the point of total absence. It was nothing more than a sort of mask, an accessory. David had always been afraid, very afraid, of those adults whose faces suddenly no longer reflected their souls, leaving them like boundary markers or posts or road signs. As a result of this inexplicable, inconceivable phenomenon, anything was possible. Grown-ups should always be viewed with suspicion. Even more so where the Jerries were concerned.

David grabbed Fernand Hourtaud by the arm; Fernand was his neighbour and best friend on that day.

'What's up?' Fernand asked. 'Feels like you're shaking.'

David did not tell him that he had also started shaking, and that he had gone pale. On the contrary, he quickly turned his head away and confidently asserted: 'No. I'm not shaking, but I do know the Jerries, and I don't want to be led off like this.'

Fernand nodded, respectfully, without asking for an explanation, and David at once felt himself filled with a sort of light. He was strong, he was sure of himself, he was ready to face any dangers.

'Good', he whispered. 'We're at the back, which is good. Get down on all fours, under the table. I'm going to hide behind the map cupboard.'

Bent double like a Sioux, glad he was wearing espadrilles which made no sound, he reached the corner of the room where there was just enough space for his skinny body. Several of the others saw him and looked away immediately so as not to give him away, like in a game of hide-and-seek; they were good mates and as there was an enemy, there was a game to be played. And it had to be played.

Now what? He wasn't going to abandon his friends. It was time to catch up with them. The last ones filed out in front of M. Valade and the interpreter. He would not be noticed. 'Do I go or not?…'

David Lambert saw Fernand right at the back of the classroom slowly manoeuvring to put as great a number of benches and tables between himself and the eyeline of the German interpreter.

All at once his hesitation vanished. He had been told many times to beware the Krauts, and above all somebody had made him understand that whenever he heard mention of death or heard death approaching, it was his duty to get away.

Now, at that moment, he seemed to hear the oncoming hoofbeat of death, still far off, but hellbent. And he shuddered like the hair was standing up on his head.

In fact he knew this was only the rapid beating of his heart.

But he was determined to pretend that he had just received an unmistakable warning.

The classroom was empty. Fernand approached David.

'So,' he asked hastily, 'do you think we did the right thing not following the others?'

'I'm sure. Absolutely.'

Fernand smiled broadly.

'I think you're right. You know why?… 'Cause just now M. Valade saw that I was hiding, and we looked at each other, both of us, very quickly, right in the eye. And straightaway he looked elsewhere, to not give me away. So he thought I was doing the right thing.'

'He's a good bloke.'

The two kids, one behind the other, crept to the far side of the playground and climbed the wall with ease, it being no more than a metre and a half high.

They crossed the school garden quietly, hopped over a low wall, crossed another garden and found themselves on the side of a sunken lane that they knew well. All they had to do was follow it for less than five minutes and they would be out in the country.

They were about to head off along it when a machine gun opened up so close to them that they threw themselves flat on the ground among the long grass and cabbage stalks with their remaining yellowish leaves.

At the same time, a husky and lugubrious voice announced over a loudspeaker: 'Attention! The populace is warned that anybody trying to go anywhere but the Place du marché will be shot. The soldiers have been ordered to fire without warning.'

Fernand approached, red in the face.

'All the same,' he said. 'What if it's true that they only wanted the children for a photo… what do you think?'

David saw that he was shaking. He knew that he too was shaking. But his sense of certainty remained intact. They had to flee. Perhaps this certainty was unreasonable, but it was obvious and irresistible. He seemed to be drunk on it.

'I think we've got to get out.' He said dryly.

'Okay.'

To the right of the garden there were rows of beans on poles. The two boys crawled towards them and found a shelter where they could survey their surroundings better.

Suddenly, they elbowed each other at exactly the same moment, such that they almost fell over: they spotted a German soldier.

Standing on a pile of wood, machine gun in hand, was a huge fat bloke, a giant almost. His face was sun-burnt without being tanned. Seen as it was in profile, it was impossible to detect the slightest trace of brutality or cruelty in it. On the contrary, he expressed a sort of serenity. The German was there, perfectly vigilant, convinced he was in the service of the Good. Perhaps, given his apparently strained and willed immobility, he even felt he was posing, under the intense gaze of the sun and deep-blue sky, as some sort of statue of the absolute Good.

'Bastard,' young Lambert said between gritted teeth. 'You can see how much he'd enjoy shooting at us.'

'You know,' said Fernand. 'If we could just run forty yards or so down the lane we'd get to the rye field at Marty's place and we'd have a chance of getting out without being seen. If we run very fast he might not spot us.'

'Not a chance,' David interrupted. 'A machine gun at that distance! We'd never get away with it.'

Fernand bent down to have a closer look at the hedge on their right.

'So,' he suggested. 'All we can do is wait 'til he moves away a bit. There's a sort of stile there, in the hedge. It'll take ten seconds for us to jump to the other side. The garden over there is on the edge of the rye field'.

David agreed. He felt weirdly tired and it was a relief to leave that sort of detail up to Fernand. He was considered resourceful, young Fernand; a poor student but a good climber, runner and jumper, good at finding birds' nests, good fisherman, etc…

To defer to Fernand was to put his trust in the countryside itself. The countryside was hot and dense like the fleece of a fabulous beast. Such sweetness and such strength in those thickets, those fields and those rivers. A heavy, suffocating heat seized the boy's heart. Since the beginning of the war, he had never been on holiday, not a single day of real freedom. He went to work on the farms on Thursdays and Sundays to get himself known and to help his mother find some fresh supplies for the food parcels. Ah, those food parcels, he wouldn't forget *them*…

He had been so happy in the middle of the week when his father had arrived, smiling and filled with hope. 'We'll be leaving soon, together, don't you worry. If it's not this time, it'll certainly be the next.' Of course David had believed him. He always believed what his father said. He was so well-informed, so careful and so quick to make fun of all those impatient ones who had been saying 'It'll be over tomorrow' for the last two years. His father couldn't be mistaken. And he had promised that before they went back to Paris they would take a holiday together, a proper, long holiday.

Already the two boys were getting used to the situation. The German with the bronze complexion no longer seemed so daunting.

They were taken aback when they saw him jump off his pile of wood at the same moment as the muffled sound of running footsteps came from the sunken lane. Then very quickly some raucous shouts covered by the crackle of a machine gun. Then a cry, brief but so intense, so heart-rending, that it encapsulated all human rage and despair. A second burst of fire cut it short.

Beside himself and overwhelmed by panic, David stood up to rush towards the lane. But Fernand got hold of him and brought him down with a deft trip.

'Are you mad? Just calm down.'

'It's my father. They've killed my father. I want to go and see.'

Fernand kept him pinned down and whispered: 'You're imagining things. There's no way you could recognise the voice that cried out.'

'Maybe you're right. I was thinking of my father just now and…'

Fernand let him go. Everything was silent and calm. The Germans had left the man they had slaughtered in the lane. Further off towards the centre of the village, intermittent and random machine-gun fire was heard.

The two boys moved off on all fours. David noticed that Fernand was now pale and that he was looking at him with a suspicious gentleness. Obviously he was feeling sorry for him. He knew that he had not been mistaken, that a son could not be mistaken about such a thing.

And David, stunned, was wondering why he had no urge to cry. It seemed to him that he would never cry again.

Within him there was no longer a space for hate, nor for fear. With immense astonishment, he was waiting for the moment when the world would come crashing down.

CHAPTER 6

'They're an odd family, the Bricauds,' Valade the teacher had said. 'Don't you think, M. le maire? A mixture of the best and the worst there.'

'Yes. I don't remember who was telling me – oh, it was M. Boiget the old headmaster – he said they always – how did he put it? – have their head in the clouds a bit and the ability to make words rain down from the sky. It's true you find this even in the worst of families. Grandfather Bricaud was criticised by everyone in these parts for being a drunk, then he took refuge in the forest and frightened the children because of the tufts of hair that grew out of his ears. But in a discussion he was capable of tying priests, doctors, and yes, even teachers, in knots.

M. Valade was in no mood for humour.

'Anyway, the younger son, Francis, seems to be up there with the best of them. Besides, he's a friend of mine.'

Mme. Ducros, the mayor's wife, remembered these re-assuring sentiments every time she saw her daughter's gaze linger on Francis a little too long. He was certainly intelligent. A bit too intelligent perhaps. People said he could not settle to anything. A dreamer then, not a go-getter.

At a moment like this, Juliette should have snuggled up close to her mother... here's somebody who avoids the company of men and ends up being noticed as a result. All the same, she shouldn't go around with her mouth half-open like that. And those swooning eyes! Good Lord! What manners! After coming across a smile like that you couldn't trust your daughter any more. My daughter! Already a stranger to me, and yet she was my little girl just a while ago, such a little while ago, such a little while.

Mme Ducros felt very calm. She had never listened with more than half an ear to the stories of German brutality. These stories had been told piecemeal or in tirades, more or less mixed in with contradictions and embroidery. How could anyone think that these strong men, these soldiers, would take any pleasure in seeing old Minotte for example crawling in the dust clinging on to her daughter? She was playacting, wanting to draw attention to herself. Besides, that officer seemed so distinguished!

Two events, both of which had taken place almost simultaneously, further increased Mme. Ducros's confidence: the arrival of the schoolchildren as smiling and chatty as ever, and the arrival of her husband who had been detained at the mairie.

Discreet but uniformly flattering murmurs spread among the crowd, on the women's side as well as the men's: 'It's M. le maire. M. le maire's here. He's looking determined. He must know what they want of us. He's not going to beat about the bush.'

Mme. Ducros had never been more proud of her husband

than she was at this moment. He was a man who knew what he wanted and would get straight to the point. With the double safeguard of this capable man and the crowd of angelic-looking children, there was nothing to fear.

Mme. Ducros looked around wearing that pleasant smile that had made her so popular, but she saw that she was surrounded by hard faces, showing the strain of a painful wait, mouths open, black and eager. Brutish. A mouth like that was brutish. Mme. Ducros shuddered. For the first time since the arrival of the Germans was announced she felt frightened.

Quickly, she looked towards her husband. He walked with a slow, dignified gait. It was he who demanded that she take her time, to show by her lateness that she was entitled to special respect. Very calmly, he spoke with the solicitor. The men that he had called together – the doctor, the priest, the Legion president, the owner of the brasserie, and other notables – immediately adjusted their pace to his.

The distinguished officer had moved off some distance and turned away as if he was not going to lower himself to get involved in such an insignificant matter. It was a colleague of his, older but obviously of inferior rank, who made his way towards M. Ducros.

'Are you the Burgermeister?' he asked in a rougher than usual voice, as if he was trying hard to sound stern.

'I beg your pardon?' M. Ducros shot back dryly, in a tone he used to put the bothersome and the stupid in their place.

He pulled himself together at once and added: 'Yes, Monsieur, I am the maire of this commune.'

The German, who had large eyes, bushy black eyebrows and a big nose, stared at him for a moment then stated slowly:

'We know there are weapons dumps here. We know this from a reliable source.'

His accent and his affected coarseness turned these phrases, where every word was given weight, into something like a caricature, like particularly bad theatre. But Mme. Ducros had no desire to laugh at it as she saw that her husband had gone pale.

The German did not give him time to respond. He took two paces back and signalled to a tall soldier with a sheet of paper in his hand. An interpreter no doubt. He spoke in perfect French: 'Now listen, all of you. We know there are weapons hidden in several houses in this village. If you hand them over, your houses and possessions will be spared. Only those hiding the weapons will be arrested. Those who have weapons must say so immediately.'

Silence fell. It was such a profound silence that the buzzing of the summer insects – known in these parts as the 'beeyard' – grew to an obtrusive level. The vague squeaking of the German officer's boots could be heard as he paced back and forth looking bored, as if waiting impatiently for the conclusion of this pointless formality.

Finally, a man came forward; Rivaud the tobacconist. Mme Ducros felt the wind knocked out of her and she realised that she was standing there with her mouth open like the farmers' wives.

Rivaud did not seem afraid in the slightest. Never before had he looked quite so much like a smirking rat. At that moment, every ounce of rattiness and smirkiness in him came together with almost indecent intensity in his bluish face, ill-shaven as usual. What was striking was the seriousness of the little man. He had no desire to play the fool. He was very pale. He was compelled by duty. He felt bold, heroic even. It was by a truly scandalous twist of fate that he remained trapped in his condition of ironic clown. He had never looked so much like a ratty rat.

Mme Ducros felt bad about entertaining such uncharitable thoughts. She was reassured however by the great friendship she felt towards poor Rivaud. She wanted to embrace him, to thank him for this courageous act which would perhaps put an end to all this anguish.

Rivaud was taking his time to decide. One moment he was looking down at his feet, at the ground, the next he raised his long, slightly twisted nose towards the two Germans – the NCO with big eyes and the tall, thin interpreter. Twice he passed his index finger behind his ear in a gesture which everybody recognised. Mme Ducros realised it was a gesture that she was familiar with although she had never been aware of it, and that she would miss it when Rivaud was executed... she felt her eyes brimming with tears. She wanted to throw herself onto her knees and beg for the life of this inimitable, this irreplaceable tobacconist who resembled a smirking rat.

The officer was getting impatient. He was marking time on the spot.

'I've got a rifle at my place,' Rivaud said at last, wrinkling his nose.

Everybody understood that the German was struggling with a violent impulse not to throw himself at Rivaud and beat him black and blue. It was obvious that the tobacconist, for his part, had misunderstood. He thought he was at fault. He expected to be arrested, even shot. The officer understood this too, because he spoke to him in a gruff manner, like you talk to a child when you want to hide your anger.

'What calibre is it?'

'Nine millimetre, I think'

'Ah! You think… well, go away. We're not interested in that.'

He ceased to even register the existence of Rivaud who immediately disappeared anyway. He gave a signal to the interpreter and said: 'Since nobody's turning themselves in, we'll conduct a house-to-house search of the village.'

Then he turned to M. Ducros and in the same impersonal tone:

'Monsieur le maire, you're ordered to select ten hostages. If you're ready to do this, please lead us to the mairie.'

M. Ducros remained perfectly still.

Again, there was silence, that extraordinary silence which suddenly revealed the muffled rumble of storm insects. Even the thin, chirping voices of the children who had been arrested in good order were totally extinguished.

Was the peaceful life of Verrièges also to be extinguished like this, and its destiny about to unfold?

It was clear that M. Ducros already knew what he was going to say. He had not hesitated for a second. If there was any delay in his response, it was in order to give his words their full weight.

'I'm responding on behalf of all the inhabitants,' he declared firmly but without emphasis. 'If it's absolutely necessary for you to take hostages, for my part I can only put one name forward. My own.'

The German officer went pale and without saluting he

turned away.

He issued a few brief orders, then returning to M. Ducros he stated in a slow and emphatic tone:

'This was your wish, M. le conseiller-maire. From this moment on Verrièges no longer registers on any map of the world.'

PART 2

CHAPTER 1

The entire village had been taken prisoner.

It was at the Lavarenne's however, Jean's closest neighbours, that he found out his mother had succeeded in getting in. She had passed the barrier (where he had had to turn back) with no problem and walked straight through under the nose of the man with the machine gun without looking at him while shouting to the people lined up in the ditch: 'What d'you think they're going to do to an old woman like me? They're not going to eat me.'

And the German had lowered his machine gun.

At the Lavarennes' farm, less than half a kilometre away, everybody was accounted for. It was an extraordinary stroke of luck. The two families, the Bricauds and the Lavarennes, took it in turns to do the weekly household shopping. That Saturday it was the Bricauds' turn.

The young daughter-in-law, Germaine, as sweet as ever, had offered to bandage Jean's shoulder. He had hastily refused and left, saying that first of all he had to feed the animals. He preferred to keep his distance from those who had been lucky. What's more, he noticed something akin to dread in the look his old friend Joseph Lavarenne was giving him. His misfortune was written on his face, that was certain.

Back home, he did not feel strong enough to go into the cowsheds. He dropped down on the threshold of the hay barn without paying heed to the cows who, having heard him and recognised his smell, were lowing softly.

Négrou his dog came up and rubbed herself against his knee. He put out his left hand automatically to stroke her.

It was then, when he saw this outstretched hand, that he realised he was shaking. He had never seen such a pronounced shake, even in an old person. Not even in Grandad Mazaud, the old innkeeper who had been dead for years. On the day he noticed the shaking he had said to him joking: 'Take a look at this, my lad. This is how I sprinkle sugar on my strawberries.' Today the memory of old Mazaud's eyes, weak and dull, came back to him, as deep as wells and vaguely mocking.

Jean on the other hand was neither old nor an alcoholic. He was shaking out of fear then; nothing else. With bizarre detachment he thought: 'I'm scared to death' and he found it odd that he was feeling so frightened and yet so calm. When he was told in 1939 at the beginning of the war that he would soon be firing at the Germans, he had felt a similar calm. Besides, no German had come his way and he did not have to fire on them.

Jean looked at the empty house. The door, which he had not thought to close behind him when he hurried off, was gaping open like a hungry mouth. The house was waiting. The house, the door, the windows, the furniture, all those familiar objects, half-human, neither sentient nor totally animal, continued to wait patiently, obstinately, steeped in an almost intolerable stupidity.

Jean would have been relieved to see them shaking like him, or even falling apart, collapsing in a heap. False witnesses! Worthless traitors who dare not admit that they would go over to the enemy at any moment. Once the destruction of a being had been decided, everything was the enemy as far as he was concerned. He was becoming a stranger in his own country, in his own house, a stranger to himself, to everything.

The bitch continued to press against his knees. She was not rubbing herself as usual. She was snuggling, seeking refuge.

As if she had sensed that her master was not offering his usual protection, Négrou began to whimper louder and louder. Jean understood that he should have been stroking her more attentively. But even that, that familiar gesture, seemed unbearably false. He pushed Négrou away. Instead of moving, she planted herself in front of him. Her whimpering began again, louder this time, and very quickly it swelled like a huge bubble.

Then the bubble burst and the long, lugubrious howl of a desperate dog rose into the motionless air. Jean stood up ready to give her a beating. He noticed to his great surprise that his threatening appearance rather reassured the dog. Calmer, she looked straight at him wagging her tail. 'There you are, back to your usual self,' her brown eyes said. 'Everything's all right again. You can get angry if you like.'

At the same time, from the other side of the grindstones, a double howl, cavernous and powerful, started up like a delayed echo of Négrou's. It seemed to Jean like the blood was freezing in his veins and every hair on his body was standing up. This howl, supernatural in scale, could only be an omen, a warning from another world.

He stood for a moment stretching up towards the sky and shaking like he was going to shatter. Then he understood: his hunting dogs… it was just his two hunting dogs; Vicki and Nita, who were calling to their friend Négrou. But their call was so heartrending that Jean could not bear it any longer. He ran straight to the hunting dogs' pen.

His eyes were filled with tears, but he was driven by a murderous fury. 'You filthy bloody creatures. Just shut up!'

He grabbed hold of a pickaxe that was standing against the vine and wrenching off half the hinges on the door to the enclosure he rushed upon the two dogs who, looking up, went berserk trying to outdo each other in the racket they made. He started to strike out like a madman, holding the pick clumsily in his good hand.

The two dogs: Nita, a black-and-white Auvergne pointer, and Vicki, a jet-black cocker spaniel, threw themselves frantically against the fencing, wild-eyed, their tails between their legs. They were now howling at their shrillest. Petted as they were by everybody, this was the first time they had ever been beaten. And it never even occurred to them to escape through the wide-open door.

Nita received a blow which knocked her sideways, but she got up again limping. Then the heel of the pickaxe hit Vicki on the back of the neck. With a strangulated yelp, the pretty little dog collapsed on her side, her paws limp.

Jean threw aside the pickaxe. He was about to fall to his

knees next to Vicki and burst out sobbing. But no. He mustn't give in to that. If he let himself go, he'd be good for nothing.

He stood there, as if rooted to the spot, his beloved dog lying stretched out at his feet. He did not move, even when Vicki who had only been stunned by the blow got up and crawled towards the corner of the enclosure where Nita was already cowering. The relief in seeing that the dog was not seriously hurt glowed in him briefly and then was forgotten.

Nita and Vicki, terrified by his stillness, gave off little whines.

They trembled uncontrollably and their long ears twitched in a grotesque manner. Jean shut their pen and made his way back towards the house. That was the last time he would stroke his animals, and the last time he would talk to anyone. He would never again be able to do anything natural.

The sun, the familiar shadows of the hayrick and the bread oven, all those things that prolonged the illusion that nothing had happened, that life could just carry on, induced a dumb fury in him. It was a farce.

And the farce was well and truly over. Fate... people talked about fate when they no longer understood what was going on. Or rather, on the contrary, was that the moment when they began to understand? Jean stumbled along, more in disgust than through weakness. What's the point of walking even? He was sorry he had learned to walk, to breathe, to eat...

So fate, his fate, was there somewhere. It would take on the form of a face perhaps, of the silhouette of a human being. That is how it should have presented itself. However, all that Jean sensed was the usual blaze of summer, and the gentle murmur of the trees and the muted buzz of insects drunk on sunlight.

Right! Something had to be done. There was always something to do. If he couldn't find it, it was due to his heaviness, his slowness, his weakness. 'Papa!' He had spoken the word under his breath. He always asked for his father's advice, even on matters that the old man knew less about than he did; just the sound of his voice produced a surge of strength and courage.

Unfortunately, for the first time today, this very day, he had seen in his father's eyes a cry for help and – most distressing of all – old age.

Come to think of it, where was his father? Jean had not even asked if anybody had seen him. Had he completely lost his mind? He ran back to his neighbours.

CHAPTER 2

Old Etienne Bricaud continued his trek towards Verrièges. It was an interminable trek. He wheezed, he moaned, he muttered under his breath, now speaking to one person, now another, as he was thinking about everyone; first and foremost his son, Francis (his favourite because he had him very late in life, a few months after the death of his eldest son, in 1914, and it had seemed to him then that his youth could start over). He was also thinking of his daughter-in-law, a bit of a simpleton but a good sort. And there was Gaston.

He was thinking of all of them of course. But in the end the older ones could look after themselves…

He was deeply worried about a young lad who was not related to him either closely or distantly – young David Lambert. He was the son of Francis' best friend, M. Lambert. And even if old Etienne hadn't met him by chance in the village, he would have liked him. Twelve years old – that was the age when he thought children were totally delightful, for the second time. At first, he liked being played around with by the tinies who were beginning to laugh, pulling his moustache, recognising him and calling him by his name. Then a sort of shadow fell between the ages of three and twelve. In those years kids were like little monkeys, good for nothing except playing up to the women in order to take them in and get sugary desserts and 'flognardes' out of them. But at twelve, these devious little animals took a huge forward leap which turned them into human beings in whom the strange sun of self-consciousness began to rise.

Little David, yes, this scrap of a man, as the others said, – for he wasn't big for his age, oh no – was much more than a scrap of a man. He was a man. Much more of a man than so many of those big blokes who said yes or no just to be like everyone else, or to be different from everyone else, which made them dumber than an ox...

Twelve. He was twelve. A fine age! Old Etienne was how many times this age? More than six times. Yes, a lot more. Back when he was six times twelve he would go out hunting at five in the morning and not get back 'til nightfall, a bit slower than the others but no more tired.

Now... well, now things were different. He had to stop and breathe deeply until he nearly fainted. Etienne noticed that he was stumbling, and with much effort, he took a few more steps to sit down in a spot where the embankment was high enough for him to get up again without effort.

What a bloody miserable state of affairs! Etienne was not cut out for getting old. He could not resign himself to it. He was not in favour of this law of nature. He was totally against it.

He had just walked much too quickly and without the aid of his stick. It was when he thought about young Lambert, that all at once, he found himself released from his old age. But it could not last.

His straw hat weighed heavy on his head, but he dared not take it off because of the sun. It was actually a very light hat: he only wore it during very hot weather and it would outlast him. He had bought it one day in the summer of 1914 – on a day exactly like this one, crushed under a blinding sun. And like today, death was in the air...

My son, my son François, my eldest, my big boy was leaving. And today, it's the other one, the younger one, over there, who looks like him. They didn't want to call him François like the other one. They were afraid it'd bring him bad luck. But I like the name Francis too.

Then there's the other one, Jean's son. I sometimes forget his name, that one. Yes, of course. It's Gaston. And I can say it easily enough when I want to. It's just that I don't always want to. He seems so far away, over there, on the road, him. He doesn't understand anything and doesn't want to understand. It's what M. Boiget says: it's a different century... not Francis. Francis is almost as young as him, but it's not the same with him. He has a way of looking at things that sheds light on them, even old age, even the stories of very ancient men that he sometimes tells.

He's a son to me, of course, but even so, he's not entirely my son. My real son was François. He came along when I was still young so that every morning I woke everybody up with my singing. I woke the whole world up. I felt strong and brave enough to scoop him up in my arms, to carry him and to warm him up. I needed a son so badly at that time. I'd married late and always in a hurry, so I'd never really dared to believe I'd have one. It seemed too much like a dream. Then he came along. Just like that. He was easier than all the others, never cried as much, hardly ever got messy. At school he learned what he wanted to and how he wanted to. He worked without having to be told and he was strong in a fight. He laughed. How he laughed! The other one, Francis, was sharper at school and I had people singing his praises. Even got his picture in the papers – twice. But he wasn't as well-built as my François, nor as full of life. He certainly can't laugh like him.

In the war it wasn't bad luck that killed him. They kill who they've decided to kill. They kill the ones who live too fully. They can't bear being outshone.

For me, as a farmer, hope and youth have lasted a very long time. I was a late developer. When I was getting to sixty, it felt like I was still growing. True, I wasn't getting any taller but I could work harder and harder, and bring enjoyment to the people around me. It was my second growing-up, and it made me happy. Yes, I can safely say that up to sixty I felt I was still growing. Right up until that particular afternoon in August when the old gamekeeper, Martial, brought me the official news from the mairie.

I'd seen him go into our neighbours', and I knew it was to do with their Pierre, their big, happy lad. When they were kids he couldn't bring himself to leave François' side; didn't even go home for supper. Poor Pierre. Tears came to my eyes.

Except the old gamekeeper also came to the gate of our house. He came with his head down, all sad, shuffling along like he was being pushed from behind.

Then all at once my tears dried up, and I knew I'd never again feel tears running down my cheeks. I'd gone over to the other side. I was there and I'd stay there. On that side of life, there are no more tears, not even tears of laughter which can also flow like a spring.

Martial shut the gate behind him. He didn't manage to slide the bolt, his hand was shaking so much. And me, I just dried up on the spot. I was drier and more brittle than the squeaky, cracked old gate. The blue paper fluttered in Martial's hand. But my hand was steady when I took hold of it. Never since have I shaken. Never since have I cried. That day people said of me: 'Bloody hell, he's hard, the old man.' It's often been repeated since, and I like that. It's just about the only thing I do like any more. And on top of that, knowing deep down I'm even harder than they think.

Old Etienne slowly got his breath back. He began to see clearly again. He could easily make out the stone on the side of the road that had made him stumble. With the end of his stick he sent it rolling into the ditch.

He took childlike delight in the feeling that his eyesight had become clearer like that. He looked around him and recognised the cottage belonging to Noémie and Sidonie, the two old girls who made a living from little sewing jobs and from their field which he had often sown and harvested to help them out.

The past which had enveloped him like a mist had just dissolved into light.

What were they doing to the little one, down there? And his other son, Gaston…? No, that wasn't his son. Nor was Francis. Hang on, yes, he was. Francis was his son for sure. He was getting everything confused just now. Hah! Deep down he wasn't confused about anything. He had become a father one day and then all those he loved were his sons.

He wanted to be with them. He'd go. He'd get there, by day or by night. Hup! There we are! Old Etienne on his feet. That little one... that little one... if you're near him, nobody will dare touch him, surely.

CHAPTER 3

David Lambert was nestling, or rather lying prostrate, among half-blackened cabbage leaves which smelt of death.

He wanted to throw up, and he tried to convince himself that it was because of this smell, because he knew full well that his upset came from the desperate effort to deny his pain. He denied it ferociously, through gritted teeth, and made a great resolution. 'I will never cry again. I will be dry and hard, as long as I live. My whole life, every minute, I will avenge him. And my lifetime will be too short'.

Fernand nudged him and with a movement of his head indicated the spot where the German with the tanned face was standing just now. They could only make out the mottled top of his helmet which in any case was moving slowly away.

'Now's the time to jump over the hedge,' said Fernand.

'You think?'

'I'm sure.'

'Right. I'm going first then,' David suggested.

He was already crouching, ready to leap.

Fernand held him in an assertive grip.

'No. I'm better than you. Watch the way I do it.'

With no more noise than a soft rustle, Fernand got up, took hold of a large hazel branch in both hands, threw himself upwards, his legs at right angles, and making use of his momentum, a twist from the waist carried him over the hedge.

David, still crouching on his heels, was on the point of endeavouring to copy him. But with a loud rustling, Fernand reappeared. He was hurrying, recklessly this time, to get back over the hedge. He opened his mouth to talk to David at the same time as a burst of machine-gun fire crackled on Fernand's side of the hedge.

A look of intense, otherworldly surprise appeared on the boy's broad, red face, then he disappeared, swallowed up by the undergrowth

David threw himself backwards face down. He heard footsteps running along the sunken lane. It was the German who had been mounting guard on the woodpile. He exchanged a few words with the soldier who had fired. Jovial words. Then belly laughs.

They were laughing.

David buried his face in the thickest of the bitter grasses. He was suffocating. He was about to let out a scream. It was too much. Much too much all at the same time. There was no point in remaining hidden any longer. Regardless, he'd be captured and killed like a hunted animal. The need to run tingled in his legs. It would be a straightforward end…

He tried repeating his oath; 'I will be hard. I will get revenge…' But the words seemed empty of meaning. Who was his vengeance for if everyone he loved died one after the other?

A sudden sob gripped his throat and tears filled his eyes.

Not yet! He wasn't hard enough for hate yet. 'Maman,' he whispered. 'Maman...' He conjured up the sweet fair face of his mother who perhaps still knew nothing; the mother who would need him so much.

CHAPTER 4

Suzanne Lambert had tried in vain to spot her son, David, among the schoolchildren who had just assembled on the same side of the square as the women. Then she remembered that he must have asked permission to go to the Lavarenne's farm that afternoon to pack his suitcase for the journey home. So perhaps he had not got caught up in the thing.

She was holding little Daniel, her seven-month-old, which meant she had not been able to go to the aid of old Marie Montagnol – known to the folks round there as la Minotte – when those brutes had knocked her down and kicked her around like a bundle of rags.

Ever since then Marie Montagnol had been slumped on a bench, crying and crying. Sobs and gasps shook her large frame so forcefully that her soft, unhealthy body seemed on the point of falling apart. Her daughter, Amélie Bernaud, a solid farm girl with an extraordinarily shiny, dark expression, propped her up against her shoulder. To those who asked her where she was hurting, the old woman gave no reply. All she did was shoot frantic, fluttering glances around her.

Complaints would have been less worrying than this

obstinate silence; the old woman seemed to have rejected human language completely as if it was something unacceptable, as repellent as the brutal treatment of her.

Even old Julie Bricaud, la Minotte's closest friend, had to leave her quietly in her corner unable to get a word out of her.

Instinctively Suzanne Lambert had moved close to old Julie and decided not to leave her side.

Old Julie had an oddly calming voice; an ancient voice that Suzanne sometimes believed she had heard even before her childhood, in a previous existence.

Julie still refused to believe in the possibility of any calamity. Her certainty was so serene that Suzanne soon shared it. She even surprised herself by adopting her usual tone of voice; that of a woman whom the world constantly sought to please.

'Even so, they have been a bit heavy-handed, leaving us stuck out here like this. My husband and I have travelled down from Paris to spend two days with the family, and this is how they're making us spend our time.'

Old Julie patted her lightly on the shoulder. She repeated that all this nonsense would come to end any moment now, and that above all she should not worry about it.

But Amélie Barnaud with her strong arms still wrapped around the flabby shoulders of her mother, muttered under her breath: 'Yes, yes, yes… believe that, mère Julie, believe. Believe it if you want to.'

Suzanne felt that these words were aimed at her. Amélie Barnaud's dark eyes latched onto her. It was by no means a malevolent look, but it was one without illusions, unapologetic, rigidly impartial. Faced with this woman with massive shoulders, thick, ruddy hands, whose prematurely grey hair attracted attention like an involuntary confession, Suzanne became aware, with an unease that bordered on a feeling of guilt, that her delicate whiteness had something of the artificial about it and was unreasonably luxurious. The moral (and perhaps physical) world where one such as Amélie Barnaud felt most at home would have succeeded in killing her in a matter of moments.

Suzanne led old Julie a little way off and confided in her: 'I don't like being near that woman. She has the look of a she-wolf about her, and I feel she enjoys seeing that I'm afraid.'

'Oh, no, no,' Old Julie replied at once. 'There's no better woman than poor Mélie. Nobody's more obliging or more courageous. She's got plenty of worries on her plate. She's the only one in the whole house who works. Her husband was killed in 1940. Her mother's not up to it – as you can see – and her girls are just kids. Simone, the older, is seven and the other one is four. Think about it! The younger one, Ginette, has never been very healthy, always hanging round her neck. They're no good, those girls, from what I've heard: she's struggling to cope. Look at the two of them, clinging to her.'

Suzanne looked. A tall, skinny girl held on tight to Amélie's arm. She squirmed and whined while she looked about her with a lively, sly expression. The smaller sister pulled at her mother's skirt with all her might, sometimes revealing the very white skin above the black cotton stockings held up by garters which made her thighs bulge a foot above her knee.

From time to time and without one muscle in her face moving, Amélie would let fly with a slap; a real, dry-sounding smack despite the extraordinary calmness with which it was delivered. People said the only one she loved was her son who was sixteen and already in the *maquis* – a 'clumsy oaf' and 'a hothead' according to village wisdom. Such a woman, in Suzanne's eyes, lacked the maternal instinct. She simply carried out a function; perhaps she was even happy to endure it. 'A she-wolf.' Suzanne immediately regretted having repeated this word in her head, because now it gave this simple peasant woman mythic status.

'Oh, you're right,' she said forcing herself to adopt a lighter tone. 'She must be a very capable woman. After all, given her situation it's hardly surprising she shows no great liking for those women who seem to have nothing to do.'

Old Julie preferred not to offer her opinion on the subject. She noticed that baby Daniel was waking up and when she stroked his chin with her rough finger, he burst into laughter.

Several heads swung round towards them. Daniel had a remarkably piercing voice.

Even the German officer – the one with the face of a medal and a gentle look, the one of whom several women had said: 'That man can't mean us any harm', that was until he started foaming and screaming like a madman – this haughty officer who seemed in command of the whole detachment, stopped wandering back and forth looking bored, and looked towards the baby.

'He's looking at us,' said Suzanne trembling. 'Mère Julie, he's looking at us. We must hide in the middle of the others. He wants to hurt us, I'm sure.'

'No, no. Not at all. There's no man so evil that he'd want to hurt a little child. Stay where you are and pretend you haven't seen him.'

Suzanne thought Julie was right. But her heart was pounding in her chest and despite herself, her gaze met the German's. 'Don't come this way. Don't come this way', her inner voice kept repeating, putting every ounce of will into this interdiction. And for a moment it seemed to her that her gaze possessed magical powers, because after taking a few steps in her direction, the officer came to a halt.

He turned away. Then he came back towards her and seemed to take a renewed interest in little Daniel. But she felt sure it was her he was looking at...

CHAPTER 5

Colonel Rehm was concerned.

So far, the reports from the SS soldiers charged with searching the houses – in particular the house of M. Le Maire who had been formally accused in an anonymous letter from an informant of hiding a stash of parachuted weapons – had come back negative. They had found nothing. Not a thing.

His comrade, Lieutenant Ernst von Greven, had simply shrugged his shoulders, saying: 'What difference does it make? We need to set an example. Let's get on with it. We're pressed for time.'

Greven was very young. Barely twenty-four. He looked more like twenty and seemed destined to retain that adolescent face burnt by pride and fury.

Nevertheless, he complained about the slow progress of his career and at every turn he rushed headlong towards extreme solutions. Rehm knew that all it would take was one false step, not even that, a moment's hesitation or a scruple, for him to permanently lose the respect of this subordinate who was more daunting and demanding than any superior officer. He had been like that ever since the war had taken a turn for

72

the worse: invariably it was the most reckless who gained approval from the top brass.

Thus, the colonel made an effort to maintain a rigorously neutral expression. He called a sergeant over; Otto Strauss, who had gained a flawless reputation fighting against the *maquis* in the Savoie.

Strauss screwed up his thick face. Early wrinkles made it look like a closed fist. Then he shook his head for a while: 'No, no!' he declared. 'I don't like that one bit. These people wouldn't be behaving like this if they were hiding something. If you want my opinion, we won't find anything because there's nothing to find.'

'All right then!' Greven retorted impetuously. 'Let's just strike camp and walk straight into the next ambush.'

Of course, Sergeant Strauss was careful not to express an opinion, but Rehm clearly felt that he saw no other acceptable solution. He, himself...

He settled for telling Strauss to continue the search with the utmost thoroughness. Then he told Greven that he would communicate his decision in due course. This was delivered in such icy tones that for the first time since he had become Rehm's companion, the young lieutenant shifted his ground.

The colonel was exasperated. He did not know which irritated him more: the requirement to take Greven's opinion into account, or the lack of results from his searches. He would have taken great pleasure in discovering that the inhabitants of Verrièges were as guilty as they seemed.

As for wiping them out for the sake of it, he did not care much for that. Nor did Strauss, nor most of the soldiers; their cruelty, instinctive and deep-rooted as it was, only really came to fruition in the sunlight of a clear conscience. And for the time being, their conscience was him. Once he had given the order, they could be sure God was on their side. They could pillage, ransack, burn, inflict the worst torture, all in the name of virtue.

Only Greven seemingly possessed the horrific innocence of a wild animal. He had grown up in an Age of Iron. From his first years at school all trace of humanity in him had been obliterated. A soul had been fashioned for him which was extremely simple, without hidden recesses or shades of grey, rigorously sterilised on a daily basis with the flame-throwers of a heroic ideology.

Rehm told himself that he ought to envy him, and he sometimes did. But more often than not he felt a highly unstable mixture of repulsion and attraction. It would have been more straightforward, and in all respects more satisfying, if he had felt either contempt or admiration for him. Nonetheless, he could not help but feel a quick thrill of enthusiasm every time Greven's ferocity was unleashed ('As pure as a black diamond' he noted in his Journal) any more than he could prevent an almost immediate and opposite reaction: a sudden lapse into scepticism. His belief in the grandeur and power of his personality was only ever short-lived. This was partly down to the highly seductive physique of young Ernst. A tall, thin boy, supple and perfectly proportioned. His complexion, although he was blond, was deeply tanned such that the pale blue of his eyes – a 'glacial blue' he wrote in his Journal – stood out strikingly. The first time Rehm had felt bathed in that blue light he was transported. It seemed to him like he was hearing a very high note, held by dint of clarity almost, but sustained indefinitely and tirelessly. He had come to the immediate decision – at the same time accusing himself of brutality and unfairness – that the boy was too handsome to be entirely a man. And then several weeks later after he had established a cordial relationship with Ernst and could call himself his friend, he had found him one evening in a state of nervous collapse. It happened in the bedroom of a hotel, quite luxurious but nothing special. Ernst had just taken a bath: as it was very hot, he was wearing nothing but brown woollen underwear. He was sprawled across the bed, and sobbing. At first Rehm had wanted to leave. But Ernst begged him to stay. He started talking. He was the victim of the most blatant, most awful injustice. He, who was all gentleness, was obliged to kill, ceaselessly, excessively, without hope of ever being able to stop. He offered men, all men everywhere, his love and protection, and men responded with distrust, hatred and betrayal. Men were not worthy of his generosity. There was only one recourse: to kill enough of them so that one day the survivors might place themselves in his hands. Then and only then would they understand what happiness, what ineffable joy, he brought them. In the meantime, he had to carry out his mission as executioner unswervingly. The degree of self-pity he felt and the exalted level of admiration to which the spectacle of his own greatness of soul raised him, caused his tears to flow unchecked.

The following day he was as precise and abrupt as ever. Perhaps a little more so even. Not the slightest trace of unease in his attitude towards the colonel. No doubt he had forgotten all about the outpourings of the previous day. Indeed he was obviously prepared to deny, with an innocence which his angelic expression rendered convincing, that any such scene could ever have taken place. As things stood, Wolfgang Rehm did not know if he was fond of him or felt sorry for him. At least he was sure that he had rarely met a man who had such a mind of his own and was so dangerous.

He feared him, and he could not come to terms with that. In the circumstances, the most embarrassing thing was that Greven felt pretty much the same way about him.

Meanwhile, the round-up of the populace continued. It took place without incident; except for here and there a few bursts of machine-gun fire obviously intended as an incentive for any stragglers, or to probe the undergrowth and dark recesses.

There were still a few elderly, some sick and some disabled, who came hobbling along. There was even one man on crutches, carefully dangling his leg which was bandaged up to resemble a huge sausage.

Greven had already pointed out this wounded man, with a wink: 'Got that wound in the resistance. We can get *him* to confess to that.'

The colonel just shook his head, mumbling: 'What difference would that make?

Torture horrified him and he knew that Greven was even more horrified by it than he was, except that Greven confronted this horror head on, in the same way that he confronted and savagely repressed all his natural impulses.

He did not need to feign indifference. From a little way off, these laggards who hobbled out of the alleyways resembled agitated insects. Once, in the midst of a line of ants, he happened to spot one that was crippled and lame. That had made him smile, like he was smiling now. Such an attitude could not have suited him better.

As he passed close to a group of men he heard laughter, which he did not like. Certainly, he was not expecting such a rabble to be capable of understanding the scale of an event which put them for a moment in touch with the protagonists of History. But decency demanded at least some clear signs of fear from them. Their role was to wait, trembling and sweating with anxiety, for the decree by which their Masters would decide their fate.

Instead, they showed not the slightest hint of terror. They talked calmly about their affairs. There were some who were sending signals to the women's side. Others assumed an air of repose, a look of perfect bliss on their face. Rehm even saw one toss a cigarette to a mate, saying: 'There you go, have this. The condemned man's last cigarette. That way you won't have to endure the pain of paying me back, you old scrounger.'

And they laughed. They laughed without even taking heed of Rehm's approach. They paid no more attention to him than to the sun and the shade.

This lack of concern was insulting. It presupposed a great inner calm which Rehm had not known for years. That time when all he needed to do was to wake up or look around him in order to want to smile at the world, to feel at one with it, coincided with the mysterious golden age of childhood. Thus, these short men with their round heads, these congenital idiots, these insects, allowed themselves to trust in their own destiny, they rested easy in their faith in justice, they were ready certainly to talk about their rights with wide-eyed innocence.

'I'll give you rights! I am the Law here, and I'll make sure you see that.'

The colonel made his way past a shady corner where the women with very young children had gathered. He saw fearful eyes turn towards him. Two little brats with scabby cheeks ran to their mother and buried their face in her skirts.

'Come on, come on! Don't be naughty now. You can see the man doesn't want to hurt you.'

These stupid blandishments suited this old granny with her heavy breasts and dull eyes. She was obviously daft enough to think he was harmless. One of the children was sobbing convulsively.

Rehm was about to move off when his gaze encountered that of a baby who was waving its little hands and blowing out its cheeks.

Rehm was flattered. From the outset he had taken pride in being liked by small children, animals, and women. It seemed to him this was evidence of being in favour with the gods.

If children were taken up young enough and chosen from among the most attractive, it was possible to halt their slide towards degeneracy, regardless of their background... Rehm put out his hand to pat the child on the cheek.

But at the last moment he remembered his insignia and his dignity. Just as well, for at the same time, he realised that the child was neither looking at him nor smiling at him. It was obviously fascinated by something just above Rehm's head; it was the branch of a lime tree bearing a great cluster of leaves where the breeze and sunlight played.

'Certainly not worth me hanging around here just for this event.' But these words did not put an end to his irritation. At

78

such a moment no incident is too small. More than ever, Rehm wanted to exorcise as quickly as possible the image of this hideous race whose children were no longer even real children.

The simplest and most effective approach was obviously to turn on his heels and walk away. Thus, the memories themselves would remain innocuous...

Then he looked at the mother. From that moment, indifference was no longer an option.

He had noticed this particular woman as she went past. He had simply told himself that she was blonde, pretty and better dressed than the others. Now he could not take his eyes off her. He felt gripped by bewilderment.

She had an intense fear of him. He had not been able to maintain his mask of impassivity and she had certainly seen the pale glow of hatred cross his face. It was too late for him to hide it. How he regretted not having hidden it!

What surprised him most was his inability to consider this face an enemy face. This woman had got dizzyingly close to him. No. He could not see her either as a French woman, nor as a peasant woman from this accursed village. Trembling, her eyes wide open, pale as a clear flame, like a call left hanging in the air, she presented him with an image of his own personal defeat.

As a result of some dark spell, this beautiful face became even more beautiful in his memory, when he no longer saw it. The terror and the call of imminent death infused it with a mysterious light. And Rehm called to mind the face of his own youth, of his season of hope. He knew that this secret face, so often lost and so often found, would recede into the distance for good this time. In its place, a vision of this other face would lodge in his memory, and the strange light of panic in a woman's gaze left his pride intact.

CHAPTER 6

Ernst von Greven presented himself and made a suggestion: 'There's a very quick and simple way of finding out whether the denunciation we've got concerning the Maire has any substance to it.'

'How?'

'It's the Maire's daughter, one Mlle Juliette Ducros. I got some information about her, and I've seen her. She's the type of woman we won't need to be brutal with. She'll talk straight-away.'

'What type do you mean?'

Ernst smiled scornfully.

'Let's just say she's the… the 'sentimental' type. That's the word that's always used in these cases.'

'Where is she?'

'Come with me. You'll understand what I mean as soon as you see her… her father put himself forward as a hostage, so now we can claim we've taken him at his word. This tender creature will be putty in our hands. We'll give her our word that we'll spare her father's life on condition that she tells us where the weapons cache is, and she'll spill the beans.'

Rehm shook his head: 'Hmm! Our reputation's well-established. We can make her believe we'll shoot her father, for sure. But not that we're ready to spare his life.'

'You say that because you haven't seen her yet... look. She's over there. The young brunette, very slim, who's looking at somebody on the other side of the square. Probably her boyfriend.'

Rehm looked and slowly his sceptical frown disappeared.

Indeed, this Ducros girl seemed so lightly attached to the earth that a breath of wind would have carried her off.

She was clearly unaware of any danger. Perhaps she herself had not felt the wind that had just uprooted the inhabitants of Verrièges from their homes, including the elderly hobbling along, whom nobody had seen out of their houses in years.

She had the shortish profile of a pre-Raphaelite Madonna. Her hair, very black, fell in braids to her slim and graceful neck, curved like a dove's. Rehm found her beautiful. Beautiful, but weak. Beautiful because she was weak.

He avoided looking towards where the men were gathered. He had no desire to find out who the beneficiary was of the rapturous looks from this picture of beauty, this goddess of fondant flesh, this sweet imbecile. The overly-feminine woman, all love, all-for-love – right here was the very essence of French decadence.

'I think you're right,' he said with a friendly half-smile. 'After all, we should try to get something out of it.'

CHAPTER 7

If Rehm had followed the direction of the look which had awakened such cruelty in him to its intended target, he could have studied on a man's face another extreme emotion pushed to its highest level of purity: hatred.

Francis Bricaud had indeed noticed the sudden interest that the two German officers were taking in Juliette. Now it was them he was watching.

He was watching them and it took all his self-control not to rush upon them instantly. He had already picked out a jagged rock which he'd use first to smash the head of the shorter one – a blond, very distinguished Aryan, by God! Of course, he would be cut down by machine-gun fire at once. But calculating accurately how many strides he needed, he'd have a good chance of first reducing the precious dolichocephalic skull of this Lord-and-Master to pulp.

He had to rein himself in though. He even had to set an example of perfect calm, because of the well-known instability of megalomaniacs and paranoiacs. The people who had them at their mercy and who were getting twitchy in such a strange way were obviously in the grip of delirium. A murmur to the left or the right and the whole thing could turn nasty. As it was probably just a simple charade, Francis wanted to be still there to laugh about it afterwards...

In the meantime, he had no desire to laugh. Never had he hated anybody like he hated these two Germans, apparently so much more civilised than the average among their peers.

In fact, up to this point he had not hated anybody. He had simply railed against entities, symbols, imaginary representations. For the first time, in the presence of human beings he felt himself shaking as if charred from the inside, his eyes unusually dry.

He came to understand that what he hated in these two men was the impression they created of reflection, deliberation, decision-making. They had a future, whereas he, and with him all the inhabitants of Verrièges, at a given signal, could come up against the unacceptable limit; caught up in, and simple captives of, the imperative of things.

And suddenly he remembered that one evening he himself had been the subject of a look of hatred. This memory seemed totally inappropriate, for sure. But it was there. Ineluctable. A man had hated him from the bottom of his heart, even though he was not even the guilty party. The guilty man was big fat Geoffrin, an engineer and colleague. Geoffrin had taken him to the house of one of his workers. 'An extraordinary bloke, you'll see. He does calculations on his own. The level he can arrive at with just rough measures is sensational. I'm a big fan, as you know. So, I'm interested to see what somebody can do who hasn't had any of the basics. An autodidact, you know.' Of course, Geoffrin could not avoid taking on a patronising tone, adding phrases like 'If you were up-to-date with...' or

'If you could learn more about...' Meanwhile, the autodidact – his name was Berton – a thin, pale man, at least fifteen years older than Geoffrin, was staring intently at his two visitors. His books and bundles of notes were piled on a corner of the kitchen table next to a stack of dirty dishes. The apartment smelt of mould and the window opened onto a dark courtyard. Finally, Geoffrin had understood that things 'were not going very well' here. After a long silence, the aforementioned Berton cleared his throat a couple of times, before stating slowly, looking down: 'Obviously *you* have a future. As for me, I don't. I do this because I like fiddling around like this... anyway. That's all!'

So here was one of the sources of that strong, dark emotion which, until he was almost thirty years old, Francis had had the great good fortune to be ignorant of: to doubt your own future and to be confronted with those whose futures casts a shadow over your own. In other words, to feel already touched by death and to know that your enemy is going to survive you.

Francis was struggling to keep under tight control an emotion which created the illusion of him being as hard as nails. Nevertheless, he forced himself to maintain his customary attitude – friendly, but when necessary, armed with an ironic smile.

He had refused to join in with a group of happy jokers who were passing their time teasing poor Mami, trying to get him to repeat for the hundredth time the story of an extraordinary journey to visit his aunt in Albi.

At the cost of some considerable effort, Francis had also got away from his nephew, Gaston, who with all the naivety of a sixteen-year-old was making no attempt to hide his anxiety and was insisting that Francis reassure him.

He would certainly not let himself give in to the early stages of panic. Panic was an aspect of hatred. The already-conquered wanted to rush forward, to strike very hard and very fast while there was still time. There was deep and lasting humiliation in being among the already-conquered. But what could he do, pinned down in this square, the very place where calves destined for the butcher were usually paraded?

He saw the tall, thin German – the interpreter – go up to Juliette, have a brief word with her, then lead her towards the two officers. Juliette showed no signs of fear; she simply glanced quickly in Francis' direction without risking a smile.

Their secret... what a girl! She was still trying hard to conceal what everybody already knew.

The two Germans led Juliette to the mairie. In an over-ceremonious fashion, they stood aside to let her enter first, like the poor showmen they were. They had already taken several people aside to interrogate them in this way. Francis tried to persuade himself that there was nothing to worry about. That Juliette knew how to look after herself, he had no doubt. However, indignation made him shake more and more. So, these men were taking the liberty of interrogating Juliette right in front of him. Perhaps they would try and frighten her; torture her, even. That was scarcely likely, surely. But it was possible. How could you live in a world where such a possibility existed? What huge, unforgiveable oversight had prevented him from noticing this sooner?

Gaston came up to him again.

'You realise,' he said. 'It's nearly three. I can just see the expression on father's face. And the old folks, well... things must be looking really great at home.'

On this occasion, Francis was willing to listen to Gaston. He was even prepared to help him a little.

'It's a good job your father's on the other side,' he said gently. 'At least he can try and do something. I'm not quite sure what, but even seeing what can be done while he's still at large, that's a big deal.'

CHAPTER 8

Jean was searching around.

He had given up running after his father. There was no hurry: the old man would never get to Verrièges. He'd lie down by the side of the road when he got too tired (he was like this every time he had a notion to go wandering off) and he'd wait until the coolness of the evening before shuffling back.

Jean wandered about the house. He could not eat, nor could he attend to the animals. Just going up to the gate to shut it was more than he could manage. As soon as he made a move to begin the smallest task, he felt certain he was wasting time, that he was letting slip a chance at saving them, the only chance…

'If Francis was here, he'd work out what to do.'

He went up to his brother's bedroom. The table – an oversized table he insisted on setting up there where it took up half the room – was covered in a strange jumble of books, brochures, large sheets of paper covered with pencil marks. These sheets had always held a fascination for Jean. Some were crumpled up, as a result of large nervous gestures. There were scribblings, erasures heavy enough to break the pencil and tear the paper. Others, meticulous, contained diagrams, beautiful drawings, superhuman in their delicacy (Francis sometimes looked at them through a magnifying glass). He knew for certain that he couldn't understand a great deal. And moreover he was not even going to make a start on understanding even a little, since he knew that he lacked the ability to see it through.

He preferred to leave it all up to Francis. Francis could interpret these mysterious signs in a meaningful way. In his place, Francis, as he bent over the table that had been fashioned from an oak in the valley where he liked to daydream, deciphered the secret, wonderful language of the urban world on behalf of his brother and all the other ignoramuses. It was reassuring and went without saying that Francis would not have chosen this world if its sole aim had been the humiliation and annihilation of man; something that it was all too easy to believe at times.

Unless… unless Francis himself had been taken in, fallen victim to it. No. That wasn't possible. Francis had always, everywhere, turned out to be a winner. And Francis wasn't capable of betrayal.

Come on! Everything is capable of betrayal. The sun, the calm air, even this sweetness, this coolness which hung about the large-leafed walnut tree in front of the window – all were capable of treachery.

Suddenly panic gripped Jean by the throat. His eyesight became cloudy. He didn't know how to look for a way out. He wouldn't find one. Nor would his brother. At this point his brother was as helpless as all the others. An animal in a pen waiting for the fatal blow. Perhaps he was even prepared to resign himself to it. That was the start of a dubious complicity with the others.

After all, Francis belonged to the Town now. He had converted, defected to their 'civilisation'. And a fine civilisation it was too: under a commander who ruled by divine right just like kings of old, men in uniform, men with weapons, arrived one day and began looting, locking people up, demanding ransoms, killing. And these men had the audacity to claim that they were behaving like this to safeguard their security.

'It makes sense. They're safeguarding the security of their fighting men.' The new solicitor at Fûtiers had the gall to say as much. He had joined the French paramilitary police at the first opportunity and was nicknamed the 'Brat'.

So the murderers complain loudly that they might get killed in their turn, the arsonists that their skin might get scorched by the fires they have set. And all that 'made sense' to the Brat, with his very white hands, as much petrol in his car as he wanted, and who never bothered to hide his contempt for the peasant riff-raff.

'It makes sense... makes sense... makes sense.' Jean mechanically repeated these words that were taking on a diabolical meaning.

He noticed that his forehead was now resting on Francis' papers and he was drenching them in sweat. He leapt to his feet and went looking for some blotting paper to deal with the damage. Was he really that hot, from doing nothing? He clearly had a temperature. He must have broken something, in his shoulder...

Well, too bad, given that everything else was broken... Jean felt as lonely and ferocious as a stray dog. In taking care of his brother's papers however, he regained something of his composure.

He brought to mind the face of Francis aged five, at a time when he used to take him to school sitting on the crossbar of his bike. He was the much older brother who was going up before the draft board. It was a really unforgettable face, one which evoked the rising sun, with such chubby cheeks that from the side his nose almost disappeared. 'Inflatable cheeks' said the schoolmistress laughing. Yes. Lovely cheeks, not too red, but glowing with health, full to bursting. Of course, the other pupils puffed out their cheeks every time they passed him. But Francis was happy to sail by with irrepressible dignity. One day, however, he was the hero of a terrible fight. It was on the road leading out of the village. Francis was waiting for his big brother who, as with every afternoon, was delayed by chatting with his old teacher. Martinaud, a big lump of twelve years old but who looked fifteen, claimed that the teacher was still giving Jean lessons. 'Your brother'll be at school all his life, he's so stupid.' Francis faced up to him: 'Say that again, that my brother's stupid.' Astonished Martinaud just smiled. At the same moment he was hit in the chest by a large stone that Francis had chosen from a pile left by the road mender. To spring, grab the stone and hurl it had all been done so quickly that nobody had time to think of intervening. His speed of action had frozen the others to the spot. Deterred, they felt like a soft, shapeless mass. When finally, with Martinaud at their head, they advanced on the furious little kid with reddening cheeks to overpower him, the bombardment was unleashed.

So much so that when Jean arrived on the scene, alerted by the shouts of the gang of brats in full retreat, there was nothing left of the pile of rocks except for two large round stones that Francis was brandishing in his hands like cudgels. No schoolboy was visible within a radius of fifty metres at least. With his hair all over the place and his cheeks aflame, Francis looked like nothing so much as a lion child. He was truly fearsome... nevertheless, Jean did not hesitate to pat his fat cheeks, at which he broke down in tears and told the whole sorry tale.

The memory of that scene was a great comfort to Jean. Suddenly his eyes welled up with tears, but he felt much better. He had regained confidence in his brother, confidence in himself, in mankind.

Gone was his belief in the existence of those who killed as a vocation. There must have been some mistake, a misunderstanding somewhere.

Previously when Francis, now promoted to the level of child genius by his enthusiastic teacher, was working on his problems – 'superior' problems as others referred to them in hushed tones – he would sit at his table thus: at a slight angle, running his left hand through his black hair, staring at the plaster on the wall. At times like this you could fire a gun in the courtyard and he wouldn't hear it.

He would shut his door and turn his back on reality, but, as he himself explained, this was in order to outflank it, the better to triumph over it. You could have confidence in him.

By forcing himself to concentrate, Jean gradually felt that this attitude would transmit magical power to him. An idea, an idea would come to him... no, not exactly an idea yet. But he remembered that Francis had told him about his projects with his friend Valade the teacher, and with the new priest, abbé Niollon. They were both attached to the Secret Army and

Francis had said... wait! What had he said?

The burning, pounding in his wounded shoulder returned, more painful than ever. Jean could no longer remember anything clearly. All he wanted to do was run back to Verrièges. He put his head on the table once more, on the light-coloured wood. With his eyes closed and breathing slowly, he tried to restore calm.

CHAPTER 9

Francis could never put up with Gaston's company for very long. He was far too young to be an uncle to this strapping lad, much better built than himself. He had sent him off to his mates who were still capable of bursting out laughing, protected by their providential lack of imagination. In what they said, they were more prone to panic, no doubt. But it was still a game. Deep down, their incredulity remained intact: 'Sure, the worst could happen, but to everyone else; not to me. Certainly not to me.'

Francis had made some gestures of reassurance towards his mother. And also to Annie, Jean's wife. The two women did not really need them: his mother, unshakable in her conviction that men were good, was waiting peacefully for it to all turn out fine. Annie, for her part, had never held an opinion on anything in her life; without Jean there, who usually did her thinking for her, she let herself be guided by Jean's mother. Suzanne Lambert was presenting her magnificent, tragic pallor to the sun. But there was no great cause for concern. Everywhere, around every corner of her daily life, she encountered catastrophe. It was a law of nature... she was certainly looking out for her husband among the crowd, although he was not there. Perhaps she resented him for having managed to slip through the holes in the net. It must have been a matter of sheer good luck. Francis knew Philippe too well to imagine him playing cowboys-and-indians through the undergrowth. He would have simply picked a road where he came across nobody and set off whistling, as if nothing had happened. Either you're a poet or you're not. He was a poet and would be 'til the end of his days.

The insistent voice of Félix Mazaud the young innkeeper, made Francis jump. He'd never managed to get used to that tone, like an outraged parrot. Mazaud was having a heart-to-heart with Paul Arlaud as usual. One problem the inhabitants of Verrèges often struggled with was to know who Mazaud preferred: Paul or Paul's wife, Suzy. It was common knowledge that big Félix slept with Suzy from time to time, but even better known was the fact that he couldn't do without Paul's company for more than a day at a time. 'I love everyone, me' was his motto, and he'd be the first to admit it in front of witnesses, for a laugh.

At that moment, indeed this love of humanity was spilling out all over the place. Félix would have liked to speak to every one of the two hundred odd inhabitants of Verrièges gathered there. The words spouted from his little round mouth like a string of bubbles, his belly jumped up and down, his olive-coloured cheeks wobbled, the way he waved his stubby arms around was painful to see. Put yourself in his place: you'd feel incarcerated in fat and at the same time spun around helplessly in a whirlwind of pointless words, half-formed ideas, barely sketched-out lies, excessively fine sentiments which were neither totally sincere nor totally false. This big fat bloke was so human that just looking at him would turn you into a misanthrope.

Francis had given him a hard time since he arrived in Verrièges because of his inexplicable opposition to the amorous intentions of Gaston and his daughter, Ginette (sixteen, a superb filly, as slim and discreet as her father was flabby and unrestrained). The previous day even, Francis had both appalled and totally baffled Félix by referring to him as a pot-bellied Shylock.

But Félix's usual fear, a universal and ongoing fear which kept him in a constant sweat, had now increased tenfold. He was becoming even more outgoing. Whereas normally he would have waited a fortnight before demanding an apology for an insult he might have received, he accosted Francis with an outburst of irrepressible effusiveness.

'So, old mate, what've you got to say for yourself, eh? You poor bloke. Trying to be a smart-arse didn't do you much good this time. Eh? Eh? Don't look like that. You gave me a bit of a bollocking last night. Now what? Given where we are, what the hell does it matter? I don't give a shit. Nor do you, eh? Eh?'

The worst of it was that he was sincere. Hand on heart. You couldn't even hate him. Francis took a moment to stare closely at him. The spectacle was worth it. Here was an image of fear in its purest form.

Moreover, the shift from the latent state to critical state had not been achieved without some damage to the mask – that of 'good-looking bloke of the village' – that big Félix wore. People said of him: 'He's a fine figure of a man' out of habit and simply because he was fat. Old Etienne even added: 'He's a tough corpse of a man' without any apparent malice, but also not without that slight twitch of his moustaches which had given him a reputation for genuine subtlety. Think about it. A metre sixty-five tall and enough width, thickness, roundness, etc... to register a hundred and ten kilos on the butcher's scales: that's as much meat as a fattened pig in its prime... and the women, conjuring up God knows what coupling, suffocation and crushing, said of him: 'he's a powerful man,' or 'he's a proud lad.'

Francis was making an effort to observe this 'pride' and was surprised to find no trace of it. All he saw were fat cheeks made pudgy by his pale complexion, and an alert, thin, joker's nose, a housemaid's nose, altogether out of place. As for his beady, bulging eyes (generally thought of as mischievous), their lively inquisitiveness was as unnerving as the cramped gestures of his shortened arms. No, no. Handsome Felix was not handsome. Not so much a Don Juan, more a wobbly-man that had turned out sinister in the hands of an inept toymaker.

This flabby doll, this woeful plaything, excited as much acrimony in Francis as it did eloquence. At the same time, he exerted a sort of fascination over him. His excessive fear placed a malevolent halo around his corpulence, like a rubber ring. Francis thought of M. Doom and he seemed to be witnessing in concrete form a weirdly supernatural mix of ancient horrors and the all-too-real terror that weighed on everyone.

So, Francis was getting ready to explain to his old school mate just how repugnant he found him. (They had sat at the same bench for several months, because Félix, whether out of friendship, jealousy or rivalry, did not want to leave him and clung on to the number two spot in the class thereby confusing everyone.) But the words dried up on his lips and he remained rooted to the spot in front of Félix with a silly, almost friendly, smile on his face.

So, it was contagious. Now he too wanted to hug everybody to him, exactly like this great big clown. Reflecting on his past, with his arms outstretched and a tear in his eye... it was appalling. Francis quickly straightened up.

'No. No. No,' he said patting Félix's plump shoulder. 'It's not your fault I had a go at you. Relax. I'm even ready to start over at the first available opportunity. You see, we're not nasty in our family.'

Félix frowned and wrinkled his nose. He shot a look of hatred in the direction of young Gaston and an instant later he appeared to be a man again: 'Your family, your family... let's not talk about misfortune just now. You can see, as things are they're not great.'

'You reckon! We've not seen anything yet. Just you wait till those at Verrièges-la-Montagne get the guys from the forest together. Then we'll see something!'

He had said this simply to frighten Félix, and succeeded way beyond expectation. The big innkeeper jumped like he had sat on a snake and let out such a sudden, sharp cry that all eyes turned on him. Even the German machine gunners reacted. They pulled their neck in under their helmets and gripped their weapons.

'Ah yes! Yes!' Félix yelped. 'So that's what you've found. You're so sneaky. Well, you dog, that's quite a discovery. But unfortunately, our only chance is if the *maquis* keeps out of it. Just as well we've had nothing to do with them here. If we'd had a tenth of what they've got up at la Montagne, we'd be buggered. Well and truly buggered, I tell you.'

Francis was not listening. He did not need to listen to anyone. He was the one who had uttered the words which were enough to make it clear, to clarify the situation…

He pretended to be looking for something in his pockets in order to hide his sudden pallor, and he looked about him with astonishment. How come all those people couldn't see what was staring them in the face? It was there, in front of them, written on the Michelin signpost: Verrièges-la-Plaine. Since there was a Verrièges-la-Plaine, another one must exist. The other one was called Verrièges-la-Montagne and the *maquis* were frequent visitors there. He had said it himself, and in loud, resounding words that he would have liked to take back.

And yet, nobody had taken it on board.

It was unbelievable, staggering. At any moment, somebody German or French, could just glance up at the sign.

What a joke!… everything was still farcical. In the middle of this terror, the clicking of weapons, amid the sobs and sighs, it was clear that everybody was playing a very simple game of Blind Man's Buff. All they had or needed to do was turn their back on the evidence.

But then, if men hadn't clung above all to their game of Blind Man's Buff, there wouldn't have been any murder, robbery, war, nor…

Francis took a deep breath. He was still struggling to recover. No logical argument came to his aid.

Without worrying further about Félix who was still squawking into the void, he hurried over to his friend, Valade. The young teacher had just detached himself from a group of important persons and was wandering through the crowd responding gently to the witticisms hurled a little too loudly at him, like at a meal where the wine has already addled a few brains.

Except, if the wine of fear was loosening a few tongues, it was also whitening a few faces…

'Listen for a moment, Charlot,' Francis said in a low voice.

'Yes.'

'Are you sure there are weapons stashed at Verrièges-la-Montagne?'

'Fairly sure, yes, but I don't see how…'

At that moment Valade understood. His fine, round face went ashen. With both hands, he grabbed Francis forcefully and convulsively by the arm. He held him close, as if to support him and at the same time, to prop himself up. 'Oh God,' he muttered over and over. 'Ah! Oh God almighty.'

The two young men were both equally struggling for breath. Like Francis just now, Charles Valade looked around him warily, with the look of a thief who's afraid he hasn't hidden his loot well enough.

'What can we do? he asked.

He blinked; he struggled against panic – unsuccessfully.

'Not a lot, I'm afraid!' said Francis. 'If there are weapons at la Montagne, this isn't the time to send the SS there. They should be warned.'

'Warned? Yes, obviously, if we can… but how? Who'll do it?'

They surveyed the scene around them. The sun was at its height, baking hot, and the breeze barely agitated the leaves.

The German soldiers, motionless and heavy like barbarian effigies, were waiting for their superiors to return.

'It's not possible,' said Francis. 'It's not possible that we're stuck here powerless to do anything.'

Valade continued to look around at the gloomy crowd. He was covered in sweat.

'God almighty, man!' he repeated, breathing more and more heavily. 'How do we get out of here? Or rather who can get us out of here?'

Francis, straining every muscle, was concentrating with such effort he had a pain in the back of his neck and his temples. But what could his strength and emotion achieve, here, under the little black gaze of the machine guns?

CHAPTER 10

No. There was nothing Francis could do; immobilised as he was, overwhelmed by the anxiety that descended like an increasingly thick mist on the hundreds of men and women corralled into the town square.

And yet, his old worktable, with his books and his papers, saturated in his presence, still retained some power.

Jean had taken up exactly the same position his brother adopted at work. He had picked up his pencil mechanically. He was writing down names; beginning with his mother who never believed in misfortune. Very slowly he traced the name of the old man, his papa. His father had always known what to say to him to get out of trouble; but that day the burden was too heavy for his ninety-year-old shoulders. Then Annie's name, his wife. Annie couldn't do much, but she needed everyone to such an extent that nobody bore her any ill-will. And Gaston? Already complicated! Not yet eighteen and already he was all 'eaten up', as he said, by heartache. He could be heard, lying on his bed, sighing, moaning and talking to himself. He was thinking of Régine; that Régine, whose father, moon-faced Mazaud, was reserving her for a townie who wouldn't make her work. Living like a pig in clover – that's what he was after, that one!

And then there was Francis. Francis had really made Jean laugh that day when, along with a few bottles of cider, he had spent more than an hour in discussion with abbé Niollon and that big joker Baroutaud, who was the young boss of the sawmill and whose father had been killed by lightning at the age of forty-five.

Baroutaud was just trying to shock the abbé by using some ripe language. 'Ah, you bollocky little priest, away with you…' he shouted. 'You poor excuse for a man, I don't give a shit about your God, any more than you do about your first holy water. But you, you, my little pal, look here, I love *you* as much as I do my hunting dog. More even. First, you're as stupid as him. You both go off on a scent in the same way: always the same noise, always on the same track, the only difference is you never see the game.'

The others were doubled up with laughter.

Abbé Niollon was enjoying himself as much as the next man, and moreover he was not slow in emptying his glass. Francis meanwhile had an idea in mind. He wanted to get the little priest to admit that he had no liking for the Legionnaire of the region even though he was one of his most regular church-goers. Abbé Niollon finally came out with it. However, Francis could not get him to admit that he was in the Secret Army (just to imitate the teacher, Valade, as some malicious parishioners pointed out) and that he was getting ready to join the *maquis* at any moment. The abbé was on his guard and had not said yes. But he had not said no either. And he was very careful to point out that he had not said no. Francis kept coming back to Verrièges-la-Montagne, his bike rides to Verrièges-la-Montagne, despite the brutal six kilometre upward climb, and in all weathers.

On a scrap of paper, Jean had written out in capitals: VERRIÈGES-LA-MONTAGNE. He brought to mind the thin, but less and less pale, face of abbé Niollon: riding up steep slopes was good exercise for him.

All at once, Jean found himself shivering oddly and feeling daunted. In a choked voice, he muttered: 'Why was the abbé going to Verrièges-la-Montagne so often?' like a schoolboy rehearsing a difficult passage.

And before he had even got to the end of the sentence, the penny had dropped. Jean crumpled up the paper and tossed away the pencil.

Once on his feet, he stood motionless for a moment, stunned. He wanted to be there already. He wanted it so badly, it was so unbearable to be still standing on the spot, that this sudden tension seemed enough to make him explode.

Finally, he set off running. He leapt on his bike, wobbled a bit left and right, then pedalled for all he was worth towards the checkpoint where he had been stopped the first time.

CHAPTER 11

Greven had taken it upon himself to interrogate Juliette Ducros.

His French was nothing like as good as Rehm's and it irked him that in front of him he felt a bit like a candidate in front of an examiner. However he was sure that the moment the colonel opened his mouth he would jeopardise any chance of success. He had to strike fear into her from the outset. And the ability to strike fear did not depend on the force of the tools employed, nor even the method. It was a question of an art in which talent was everything. And Greven had shown on a number of occasions that he was talented .

He offered Juliette a seat. She refused it.

'Mademoiselle,' he said, endeavouring to adopt a neutral tone of voice. 'We need some information that you can give us.'

The girl simply raised her eyes and looked at him with curiosity but without the slightest fear. Greven was a little disconcerted by the lack of hostility in her eyes. 'She's even more stupid than I thought...' But a sneer would not clarify anything. Juliette was embarrassing him. Until he managed to uncover the secret of this extraordinary detachment, there was a danger of him just talking into the void.

This was the first time he had experienced an impression like this. He was much more at ease when he encountered hatred and disgust – which was most often the case. Emotions such as those were active and liable to ferment, almost incompatible with logic and lucidity. But this girl with velvety eyes – this gentle little female, so soft to the touch that Greven's palms tingled each time he looked at the curve of her neck and the double swelling of her breasts – she seemed impervious to any feeling of hostility. She was absolutely serene because in her eyes Greven counted for nothing. She remained absent. Or rather, she was quite simply oblivious.

Oblivious! At a time like this!…

Greven looked out of the window and his scorn intensified. This rabble, this miserable infestation of larvae which had nothing human about it except outward appearance. Second-rate human matter, unusable, from which you could expect nothing but disorder. Such inferior beings had an existence which didn't deserve the name of 'life'. They let themselves slowly descend into death, while clinging on to the slope with incomprehensible obstinacy. Sickening.

And yet we still need to find reasons for exterminating such a rabble, and even collect 'incriminating evidence'. As if they hadn't condemned themselves by their own hand.

So here he was, him, Ernst von Greven, whose triumphs had been lauded at the Academy, here he was, wondering what was going on in the head of this little doll.

This time he did not hold back a smile. On the contrary, he prolonged it with pleasure, with quiet confidence.

He did not even turn round to face Juliette. What she

thought of him did not matter. But he noticed that Wolfgang Rehm raise his eyebrows with a bored look. Good. Good. If he wanted to play at 'wise old men', fine, but it wouldn't be for long... he settled himself into an armchair which sat on a dais, and without even bothering to speak French correctly any more, exaggerating the heaviness of his diction and statements, he continued: 'Mademoiselle, we have no choice but to execute your father. And yet we're offering you a chance to save him.'

'Me?' Juliette exclaimed.

Her astonishment was sincere. She had not been able to hold back this cry.

'You', said Greven heavily. 'It's very simple: just tell us where the weapons are hidden. We give you our word that your father won't be executed.'

He had spoken slowly and it was not in order to make himself better understood. It was because he knew that the meaning of his words was ineffectual. He was relying solely on his tone of voice to intimidate the girl.

Juliette said nothing, but the colour drained from her face and her eyes which suddenly locked onto Greven's, shone with an intense, almost supernatural brilliance.

Greven shrugged his shoulders and returned to the window.

This was going nowhere. He recognised his mistake at once. The girl wouldn't talk. Perhaps she didn't even know anything.

He heard Rehm approach her and wanted to warn him. Bah! That's his funeral. It was no skin off his nose if he made himself look ridiculous.

Of course, the colonel had the informer's letter in his hand. And he was already speaking, in an unabashed, syrupy tone.

'Mademoiselle, please understand that we have proof. This letter from a Frenchman makes clear that the mayor has personally taken charge of the weapons. His guilt's not in question as far as we're concerned. But we aren't here as the instruments of justice. We are simply trying to protect our troops. The important thing first of all is to destroy the stock of weapons. If you help us to find it, we will treat your father as a prisoner. Otherwise, we'll not only blow up the arms cache, we'll destroy the entire village. Your father will be the first victim, but there will be an awful lot more... think about your responsibility.'

Greven held back a laugh. But he could not stop his fingers from drumming out a jolly gallop against his boot. 'Poor Wolfgang, you really do need her to spit in your face.'

Juliette did not seem minded to make the smallest gesture. She looked back and forth between the two Germans. The same light which emerged from her expression gave a strange brilliance to her pallor. Even then her face expressed no hatred, but rather, an immense surprise and a sort of incredulity. She never dreamt of asking questions, still less of defending herself. The distance between her and them was too great. She didn't understand. She couldn't accept that there were such beings as far removed from her as these two men. Faced with this sudden discovery of absolute baseness and ugliness, she was gripped, devoid of feeling. She might have shown the same dismay if, on lifting an inoffensive-looking flat stone, she had found a writhing swarm of vermin underneath.

In fact, the colonel himself understood that there was no point insisting. He avoided looking directly at Greven and addressed him dryly in German: 'Take her away, please. My orders are as follows: the women and children are to be taken to the church, the men will be broken up into groups in barns, garages and other premises with large capacity.'

Greven saluted and asked, very calmly: 'And afterwards?'

Rehm shot him a quick, hostile glance.

'I'm going to the radio lorry. I'll communicate my decision from there.'

Greven repressed a desire to swear. It was like Rehm was trying hard to waste their time.

He took Juliette back to the group of women. There he caught that great brute Sergeant Strauss, that gorilla with the heart of a shop girl, red-handed in an act of humanitarian sentimentality.

CHAPTER 12

Strauss meanwhile, was grimacing horribly. His tanned face, armed with a solid, pointed nose and with skin so thick that he could be thought of as a human rhinoceros, was thrust forward as if he was going to bite the two women who were dogging his footsteps, talking, whining and gesticulating.

First of all there was Mme Ducros, the mayor's wife, a matronly, fleshy woman, as soft as an overripe plum. She was attempting to lay out some facts in a clear manner, as well as moderate the temper of her companion, a solid lass in nurse's uniform who was waving a medical bag under the sergeant's nose.

'This poor girl is about to give birth... give birth, to have a little child.' She interwove her fingers on the belly as a way of depicting enormous roundness. 'She cannot give birth on her own. All her family are here. You cannot leave her like that. Giving birth... giving birth... having a little baby... like this, baby, fat cheeks.'

Strauss wrinkled his formidable nose, showed his teeth and growled: 'Silence. Be quiet. Wait for interpreter.'

Mme Ducros settled for glancing round to find the

interpreter. But the other woman had no fear of the rhinoceros-sergeant.

'Interpreter be damned! It's me Melanie needs. Not him. Me, the midwife... I'm the midwife. Here. Look at my card. Madame Brousse, midwife. That's me. Me, midwife... giving birth to baby... immediately.'

Two soldiers pushed her back with the butt of their machine guns. She yielded to the pressure of steel but did not move one step further back.

'Yes, yes, sweeties. You've already made your point. But this is not how we do things.'

As soon as Greven appeared, she addressed him: 'I'm the midwife. I'm in the middle of a birth. They pushed me outside with a machine gun in my ribs. They turfed everybody out – mother, father, younger sister, the kid brother and the old man who can't stand up. She's on her own. Completely on her own. We cannot allow such a thing. I am going to her. I'm not afraid of them shooting me. Just don't push me around like that...'

She moved the barrels of the machine guns aside and advanced. The soldiers had to grab hold of her roughly in order to push her back. She opened her bag wide, clanked around among her instruments, finally took out a speculum and brandished it under the nose of one of the SS who did not know whether to laugh or get very angry.

'You see I am a midwife. This here is not a weapon. It's not for killing – quite the contrary...'

Greven came up and said in the iciest of tones: 'We will deal with this woman and have her taken away.'

Mme Brousse, not in the least intimidated, shouted even louder: 'Taken away... go and see for yourself just how mobile she is. It would be murder. Are you murderers?'

It was obviously not a word to be uttered so loudly. Even Mme Brousse realised this and fell silent.

The faces of the motionless men became visibly paler and their eyes blazed. Once such words were out in the open, anything could happen.

As Mme Brousse made to head off in the direction of the rue du Village, Greven approached and stared at her, a hand on the handle of his revolver. This time Mme Brousse said nothing and took her place again amongst the other women.

'We'll do whatever's necessary,' Greven said briefly to Mme Ducros.

He passed on the Colonel's orders to Strauss. Then turning to one of the SS soldiers who had escorted Mme Brousse, asked to be taken to the woman having the child.

He had time to overhear Mme Brousse explain in a different, strangely altered, voice.

'That one, I could see he was different. I could see he'd have enjoyed killing me. Yes. I saw it, I tell you. Good God, what sort of men are these?'

Nobody replied. A profound silence now reigned over the men as well as the women.

And in the silence the midwife said again: 'With me waiting here, I won't be with Melanie to help her. Poor girl…'

CHAPTER 13

Mélanie Labaille too was beginning to discover that it was good to complain.

What was that lot up to, when they should be here looking after her?

And yet, up until then she'd never thought she could pass for a 'poor girl'. She managed very well when it came to clothes. As she moved nearly three times faster than her mother, she was left with quite a lot of time to strut through the village. The old crones, who hated her, tried to persuade their sons that the swaying of her hips was leading her inexorably to the gates of hell. But the old biddies were wasting their time. They would never make Mélanie into the slut that they took such intense pleasure in imagining her to be. Mélanie loved Robert – sweet Robert, so delicate, and who seemed so well-behaved – and that was the end of the matter.

'Let's face it, they shouldn't have left me like this… here I go again!… Maman! Maman!… you can't leave me all on my own. Listen maman, you *know* Robert's going to marry me.'

No. It was certainly not her mother who had decided to abandon her like this. Of course, her mother called her a slut.

She also told her she was up to her ears in vice and bemoaned the fact that she had ruined her future by letting her lead too easy a life. This is what she had found comforting. But deep down, these were just words.

It was her father who had driven everybody out of the house and left it empty, even though it was said of him that in his time he'd screwed every woman in the region. 'Randy as old Labaille' was a phrase she sometimes heard. And when he heard it, he was happy to laugh at it. So what?

That didn't stop him walking straight past her when her belly was large, raising his eyes to heaven as if she didn't exist. Made no sense. And the last time he spoke to her it might have been better if he had kept his mouth shut. 'I'll feed you and your bastard,' he growled. 'Yes, I'll *feed* you, but I'm not speaking to you.' When she reminded him that Robert would marry her on the day he chose, he said with gentle menace, 'As for him, make sure he never shows his face in my presence.' And he carried on as if she had never interrupted him. 'I'll feed the two of you, but only because I've got no choice. The sooner you're out of here, the better. That's how things are and that's how they have to be.'

Old fool! Bloody old fool!

It did her good to swear out loud like that, except that her voice immediately broke into a series of rapid hiccups.

The pain came in waves now, tall waves that picked her up and dropped her all at once. Or rather, no, not her. Her body itself did not move. It continued to lie miserably on the pallet her father had made for her in the storage room. The only reason he didn't make her lie outside was because he didn't dare. He was afraid of what people would say. Bastard! He'd

114

always been a brute and a bastard, with his self-righteous airs.

Oh… Oh… Oh… she was off again. She rose, she was on the crest of the wave. Then came the crash, heavy and bruising, as if she had been thrown onto the paving stones in the street. Go on, then, since you enjoy it. Don't worry about me. Throw me on the ground. Tread all over me. Do what you like, only don't leave me on my own. You don't dare say it, do you, that you want to throw me onto the paving stones. Oh… Oh… Oh… that wave again. Brutal, but it couldn't carry her very far. It dumped her almost immediately. Her belly seemed about to split open. No, it wouldn't split. Not yet. It was only the aftershocks of distant underground explosions which welled up from terrifying depths. Something inside her was about to rip open, widening a black and purple tear. And she thought of her father. More and more she thought of him, and him alone. Old Labaille's square face drew near, with its thick moustache which brushed her face. His Auvergne-style moustache which he was so proud of. He boasted about it. He was always boasting about something; especially when he talked about his time as a pit sawman, before setting himself up as a joiner. At that time he knew where to find girls who were willing… he talked about them with contempt; he held an eternal grudge against them for having given him a moment of pleasure. Bastard! Filthy Auvergnat brute! Mélanie knew full well that she held him in the same contempt that he had always felt for the girls who in his youth had given themselves to him. When she was still little and obeyed him like a slave, he used to hate her as much as he loved her.

Oh… Oh… Oh… I can't stand it any more. I don't want to go on. Throw me down hard onto the paving stones and get it over with. I'm not afraid of you. I'm not afraid of anything. You thought I'd be a good girl when you made me tremble, opening your grey eyes a bit wider, during a thunderstorm… no. She was no longer afraid of him, or anything else. And this was something new. An hour earlier, she still felt a sense of dread when sensing the light of those icy, grey eyes upon her. In the midst of this incomprehensible collapse into hiccups and drool, she felt a huge relief, a truly miraculous relief. She was tearing herself away, leaving for good, not coming back. Anything was preferable to going back to the time of fear. She wanted to suffer, really suffer, suffer unto death. With all the strength of her muscles, she tried to increase the violence of the storm. And her father was there, close by, black and moustachioed like a Moor in a picture book. So serious, so grotesquely serious! Ready to tell her off, to remind her of his sound advice, his warnings. It was enough to make you die of laughter.

She was not laughing. She was too busy gritting her teeth in order not to cry out. Old mother Brousse had said to her: 'Shout out, my dear. It'll give you the courage to push.' Not true. Mélanie found that she pushed much better if she gritted her teeth. She wasn't one of those weaklings who needs to shout to reduce the fear. All the same, she would have felt better if old Brousse was there. No doubt it was her father who'd kicked her out. Ah well, too bad! So much the better! She'd do without Mme Brousse in the same way she'd do without her father. It was much better like this. When she went off to meet Robert Leboutet in secret (Robert, the miller's son, was certainly far too well-off for her to be accepted by his family) down there amid the broom bushes, she felt her heart give a great leap of joy at the thought that she was getting away from her father. She was so happy about this that she could not stop herself saying as much. And Robert objected: 'So, you don't come because you love me, but mainly because it pisses off your father.'

Poor Robert! Poor little Robert, who wasn't there either. He was terrified of her father's moustache, was little Robert. He daren't come near. He must be snivelling in some corner somewhere... she really wanted to be there to comfort him: that was what she liked most about him: when he was acting like a kid, a sort of doll. He for one would never have a big moustache. He'd never say: 'That's how things are and that's how they have to be.'

She loved him, her little Robert. She had never loved anybody else.

'Ohhhh!' This time she had gritted her teeth too late and had cried out. And she had felt better for it. Mme Brousse was right. It was a relief to cry out. It helped to let it all out. After all, they were sure to hear her. Her father would be saying: 'She's being punished, the little tart. She's up there whining now.' But... no... that's not what Mélanie wanted. He mustn't think I'm complaining. He mustn't think I'm sorry about something. I'm not sorry about anything. And I want him to know it. I'm going to laugh and laugh and laugh. I'll laugh as hard as I can, until my belly splits.

As she was getting her breath back, she heard the grains of wheat scattered about the floor cracking under the weight of footsteps, and then she saw a face bent over her. At once she thought of her father, but it wasn't her father. For a moment she even thought it wasn't a man's face. It was too thin, with

117

sharp well-defined features. But it was a man. His expression left no doubt in that regard. It was a hard, imperious, gloomy expression. And cruel. More cruel even than old man Labaille's. Obviously, this man was one of those who say: "That's how things have to be."

Mélanie started laughing in pain again, this time even louder. She tried to lift her mouth, full of froth and laughter, towards the enemy face. The face backed away quickly and took on an expression of horror which did not hide an intense curiosity. So Mélanie took hold of her blankets in both hands and threw them on the floor. If he wanted to see, he'd see everything – this nasty farm boy, this evil snot-nose who thinks he's so frightening.

Her laughter caused her such pain that now she could not help but grimace and howl like an animal. She had the satisfaction of seeing panic appear on the thin face which disappeared smartly. He got a fright at least, the little brat.

But this did nothing to reduce her suffering. Nor her fear. If they didn't come, she'd die of fear.

CHAPTER 14

Ernst von Greven bolted down the steep stairs. Once outside he took deep breaths. He had felt totally suffocated in that dust-swirled garret. He congratulated himself on have sent away the soldier who had led him there. That imbecile would have started smirking, for sure. And at the first sign of a smirk, Greven would have given him a beating. Even alone he was shaking with exasperation, and he walked around stamping, as if crushing a repulsive reptile.

Horrendous, horrendous. Everything here was horrendous. In this jumble of houses, life had a rotten stink about it, unbearably thick. And he had to see that woman's belly, flesh in the raw, screaming, monstrous. Their flesh... their fecundity... their life... ugh!

A soldier came to notify him that, according to Strauss, their searches had turned up absolutely nothing. Greven just manage to suppress a shout of anger. He simply asked: 'Did he ask you to inform the colonel as well?'

'Yes, lieutenant.'

'Good. I'll tell him myself.'

At the thought that Rehm might yield to his scruples,

his old maid scruples, he felt his rage increase. But we're not having it. If necessary he would go over his C.O.'s head.

'Move. Quickly. Quicker!' he shouted and gestured to the SS soldiers who were leading their little flocks of men.

Greven, who had always shown such impatience, barely managed to stop himself stamping his foot. It was unhealthy. A childhood sickness perhaps. But then, a sickness which he preferred, which he made no attempt to cure himself of. Quite the opposite. His mother had always indulged his smallest demands. She considered them like sacred laws. She organised her life and the whole household timetable around his desires.

And yet Greven felt neither tenderness nor gratitude towards her. If he had been able, he would have erased her from his memory. Not just at that particular moment, but once and for all. 'Go away, disappear forever. I won't remember you, I swear. Yes, I swear it.' If he had been able to get rid of that obsessive presence with a gunshot, he would have pulled the trigger with sheer delight. But mother remained, inexorably. She was there, angelic, just as he had always seen her: so thin and pale, almost immaterial. Her eyes were transparent and the same colour as his. He would have liked to tear those eyes out of her head: they were not made to see what they saw. 'My mother is a saintly woman.' Each time she appeared, she was accompanied by these words, by this immutable judgement, written once and for all across the heavens.

It was while he was leaning over the pallet of the woman in labour, in the loft pierced by rays of sunlight, that his mother had intruded. As usual he seemed to feel the pressure of her long, fine hand on his arm, with gestures always so gentle that he had to pay careful attention to prevent them disappearing unnoticed. And, as usual, Greven felt himself harden, become a block of pure hatred, ready to kill, intent on killing. For him this was a duty, the most overriding and compelling of all duties. He had to destroy this ignoble world that a holy woman like his mother could not see, and yet which she saw through her son's eyes, which were still her eyes.

The horror! The horror! The evidence was there. His mother had undergone the unimaginable indignity. She had given birth. She, even she, may have whimpered.

His mother was also present in the flesh: she herself had been flesh, similarly tortured and torn... no! I know that this happened, but I disavow it. I repudiate what I know. I repudiate it, I'll rip out any knowledge I may have of it. I repudiate everything which could know it, or even suggest it. I hate the man in me, just as I hate all men. Don't worry, mother, I will avenge you. I will kill relentlessly. I will kill myself in others a hundred, a thousand times, until the others kill me.

He went down to the river. On his way, he cast a few brief glances in the direction of the stores, sheds, barns and wine cellars, all the large spaces in the village where the men were being led in small groups. He had the satisfaction of noting that the taste for humour seemed to have dried up completely. The silence that began when with just one look he had defeated that vulgar, braying midwife, lasted still. It was up to him to make it last forever.

Perhaps these jokers, good-natured lads, lovers of life, those who were too full of life were beginning to understand. Now was the time. The machine guns had been set up in pairs at the entrance to the last barns he saw, ready to create a crossfire. At last, order and truth were casting their shadow over the village.

Near the radio-truck, at the bottom of the slope, on the bridge nestling among greenery, close to a watermill whose wheel churned up foam with a gurgle like a laugh rising from a woman's throat, Colonel Rehm was pacing back and forth. As soon as he saw Greven he strode forward and asked: 'Well?'

'Well, nothing. We arrived too late. All we found were traces…'

'Traces of what?'

'Traces of weapons destroyed just before we arrived.'

Rehm observed him closely for a moment. Greven was contemplating the countryside with an air of nonchalance.

'Nobody said anything to me about these traces,' said Rehm. 'Come on. Show me the ones you've uncovered. I want to see them right now.'

He was already heading in the direction of the village. His colour was up. He was getting his strength back. Greven, rooted to the spot, waited until he retraced his steps.

'Well,' said Rhem. 'What are you waiting for?' Let's go and examine these traces together.'

Greven pronounced slowly in an icy tone of voice: 'There aren't any yet. But I promise there will be tomorrow. We've got everything we need in the lorries.'

Rehm hung his head, no doubt to hide a less than friendly response.

Greven continued: 'One truth I took away from your conversation at the mairie is this: we aren't here to punish the guilty, but to ensure the safety of our own. So, it doesn't matter whether the inhabitants are guilty or innocent. We don't even have to ask the question. Moreover, the orders we've received aren't open to doubt. And you know as well as I do that General B… rarely goes back on his decisions.'

The colonel straightened up so quickly that Greven had the absurd notion that he was thrusting his jaw out in order to bite him.

'I can only repeat this,' Rehm said dryly. 'I reserve the right to decide the moment when the order to open fire is given… if it is given.'

Greven opened his mouth to protest, but Rehm had already saluted stiffly and turned his back on him. With an anxious look, he scanned the empty road beyond the lorry.

The lieutenant went pale. He imagined his hand moving upwards to his revolver. He even imagined a whole argument in order to convince high command that he had to act quickly in order to prevent a delay which would have been fatal to the whole unit. But he remained rooted to the spot, unable to either move forward or back.

All at once, Colonel Rehm rushed off to meet a large, thin, livid peasant who had just got off his bicycle and was weaving towards him.

CHAPTER 15

At the first roadblock Jean had come across only gloomy, arrogant soldiers who refused to give him the slightest scrap of information, who had not even listened to him. So, he had gone by way of the bridge.

As soon as he got there, he recognised the officer to whom he had already shown his papers.

He noticed at once that the German was watching the road, in expectation of something; something more worthy of his attention than Jean for sure, because it took a long time for him to turn his gaze in that direction. His tormented face carried signs of high emotion. He seemed to be looking beyond Jean among the thick depths of the forest to conjure up an adversary worthy of the name, a true enemy, neatly defined, well-armed, measuring up to his heroic aspirations. His eyes shone with a fanatical flame. He was surely waiting for a sign from heaven, and he had it in him to believe that at the right moment he had received one.

Jean had stopped. He took a few more hesitant steps trying not to stumble too much.

The guard called out: 'Halte,' in a voice that was not brutal nor even imperious, but more like that of a conscientious functionary.

Jean looked at the broad-faced guard, his patches of freckles, his blue eyes, small and very mobile, which expressed nothing but lazy curiosity. He also looked at his helmet, his heavy, dusty boots, and again at his little eyes where indifference was already settling back in.

Then, a little further off, Jean examined the other officer for a while, the very young one. Up until then he had only noticed his stiff, motionless silhouette. But this stiffness and immobility were much more expressive than the mechanical blinking of the soldier, or the beautiful tragic mask of the senior officer. That one there had come to kill, and he would kill.

Despite the sweat that drenched his face and which dripped off his chin, Jean began to feel cold again. He would have liked to be even colder. He wished he could shrivel up until he disappeared. What was he doing there?

These three men, obviously mad, stood in front of him like some sinister allegory. There was the one who powered the machine of death, the one who seemed to be driving it and finally, the one who crushed with the mindless precision of a forge hammer.

The colonel's face, full of pathos, was the worst of decoys. Because of their outwardly human appearance, Jean believed insanely that he could address these beings like he would any other man. Besides, they were no more than slaves, instruments of destruction, as incapable of acting freely as the jaws of a trap are capable of stopping the springs which snap them shut.

The oldest of them was looking him directly in the eyes now. And Jean saw clearly what was expected of him. It was not a means of knowing the truth, but simply a justification – one more weapon. This look was not hateful, nor even malevolent. Worse than that, it was a cunning look. One animal spied another which was going to be its prey, or was going to lead it to its prey.

So, he had to struggle. Despite the fatigue, despite the fever, despite the despair… the bastard! He was expecting me. I'm the one he was waiting for. He suspected something was going to happen, he did. He was on the lookout for the clumsy oaf who'd betray himself and would set him off on the right track. One word too many and I'd be useful to him. Yes, I was coming to his aid. Diving in head first. I was on the bastards' side, now and forever…

There probably were munitions, at Verrièges-la-Montagne. There everything would have been easy.

Jean was appalled by the idea that at any moment in his state, he could become delirious and blurt something out. He felt a desire to flee tingling in his legs. The shrewd gaze of the officer was not letting him go. He had to get away from that gaze.

'I thought I'd be able to get through by now,' he said.

He was already turning away.

'Come on,' the officer said dryly. 'Talk. I can see you've got something to say.'

'No. Only what I just said.'

He had not managed to adopt a natural tone of voice; too tired, too impatient to get away. Already he saw himself heading at top speed to Verrièges-la-Montagne. Why hadn't he thought of this solution straightaway? It was the only solution. He had wasted precious minutes.

'I'm arresting you,' said the colonel. 'And we will make you talk all right.'

Jean nearly set off running. It seemed to him that the German's eyes, those pale eyes which at first had appeared compassionate, could read his thoughts… it was just an effect of his weakened state. Well! Got to come up with something, quickly.

'Very well,' he said, leaving his bike and striding towards the village. 'All I ask is to join the others.'

The two officers exchanged looks. The younger one shook his head and Jean noticed that his hands opened and clenched as if he was struggling to overcome a sense of impatience pushed to its very limit. Finally, the other one waved him away and walked slowly towards the village.

PART 3

CHAPTER 1

The departure of the women and children got underway.

The silence then became so complete that even the Germans themselves could not bear it. And as they dared not talk to the women brutally, they contented themselves with uttering confused mumblings which were now like encouragements, now like fatherly grumbles. Certain ones allowed themselves to pat the odd shoulder or the curls on the back of a neck. But the looks they received, emerging from bottomless black depths, soon made them remove their hand.

The interpreters and those soldiers who spoke a little French tried to construct a facade of goodwill by piling explanation on explanation which nobody asked them for.

'We're taking you to the church. Keep calm.'

'It's for your own safety. If the *maquis* appear... you never know.'

'It's too hot in the square. The sun will give you a headache.'

'The priest wants you all to pray together.'

Some children took advantage of this unwise remark to launch into a friendly rumpus.

'There's the priest. Over there,' one of them said. 'He must come with us.'

All at once a chorus of shouts arose from the line of schoolchildren. 'Come with us, Father.' 'Good old father.' 'Well done, Father.' Shouts of 'father' were being thrown around with such abandon that the SS started mouthing off in a very unfatherly way. One of them even stopped and turned towards the priest with a perplexed look...

The latter dived into the thick of the crowd of men as fast as he could.

'Hey up, Father,' called big Baroutaud. 'I reckon the little 'uns are taking the piss. You might even say they frighten you.'

'It's not them I'm frightened of,' said the priest eying up the hesitant German NCO.

'Don't you worry,' said Baroutaud. 'He'll leave you here with us lot. He's seen you're a bloke, even with your skirts. Do the kiddies always take the piss out of you at catechism lessons like that?'

'Not always, no. Sometimes. It's better like that. They wouldn't dare make fun of me if they didn't like me a little bit.'

Baroutaud puffed up his cheeks before bursting out laughing noisily.

'Ha, Father Bollocks!' he brayed in a heavy and affected *patois*. 'Good moment to talk about love. If you want to teach us to turn the other cheek, you'd better get a move on. Now's the time.'

Lavaud, the solicitor, who was universally disliked and

took the town's coldness towards him as a sign of his natural distinction, risked a wink of connivance in the direction of the abbé Niollon. The priest pretended not to see and pointedly made his way towards the back of the square where, apart from big Baroutaud, there were Francis and Gaston Bricaud, old Labaille, Charles Valade, Mami the idiot, the innkeeper Mazaud, Gindreau the butcher, Paul Arlaud and several others whose company the distinguished M. Lavaud prided himself on not keeping.

An initial group of men had already left. They had not gone far. They were taken into the main room of Mazaud's café, the one where in peace time there was a dance every Sunday. Through the glass doors of the front room with both its shutters open, the SS could be seen setting up two machine guns.

'Hey! Nobody asked my permission to set up their stuff in my place,' Félix remarked in a none-too-certain voice. 'These gentlemen so renowned for their good manners! What are they cooking up?'

'Don't worry,' said Gindreau. 'Filling your place with so many of us is a sign they're not going to burn it down.'

'What! Burn the house down!' cried Félix, going pale. 'Couldn't you have talked about something else?'

Just then, Francis saw Charles Valade moving towards the other side of the square, to the end where the Germans were dividing the men up into small groups.

'Stay with us, Charlot,' he said.

'I'm coming back… I'm coming back… just need a word with the mayor.'

M. Ducros, fittingly, was almost at the front of the group.

Francis was afraid Charlot might tell him too much and wanted to go with him.

He had barely taken three steps when Mami put a tough, blackened paw on his arm. Francis was one of the few in Verrièges who occasionally took the time to listen to him, and he dared not brush him off.

'Let me go, Mami. I'm coming straight back.'

'Yes,' said Mami, bowing his head solemnly. 'I'll let you go, but not before you've shaken my hand.'

To get it over with, Francis held out his hand. Mami took it and kept hold of it firmly. He began to shake it up and down very slowly, fully and solemnly. Francis wanted to pull away, but he could not have done it without some force.

Mami looked him straight in the eye. He wore a gloomy expression. His exaggerated arm movements made the whole ironmonger's shop he carried around in his enormous multicoloured pockets jingle. Pliers, spanners, screwdrivers, knives, files, even small hammers filled these pockets which he had got one of the women he occasionally worked for to add to his blue dungarees. He boasted that he carried a garage mechanic's workshop around with him. 'For when I get a car,' he confided in a whisper and a wink.

He suddenly sped up the piston movement of his arm and said very affectionately: 'Poor Francis, you see... things have turned out for you like for all of us. You're clever though. Oh yes, you're clever. But you have to go through with it, like everybody else.'

Then he made a sudden turn and went to grab the hand of Fr. Labaille who made no objection. His attention was elsewhere, his forehead furrowed from the effort of thinking.

'What's up with him, then?' Francis asked Grindeau.

'Bah! Events like this, and with the sun as well... it's tipped him over the edge. At first, when he'd seen only the women, and a lot of them were in white dresses, he thought it was a wedding and he went around congratulating everyone. Now he thinks it's a funeral. Brain's turned to mush!'

Jules Grindeau, still as fair and rosy-red at thirty as the day Marie, his mother, accompanied him to school for the first time along with a thousand words of warning, tapped his forehead with an expression of pity.

Francis looked at him, then at Mami. The contrast between these two faces was disconcerting. Whereas Grindeau, the prosperous businessman, seemed vacuous and completely helpless, the tanned and weather-beaten face of the congenital idiot spoke of virility, energy and strength. When Mami was in one of his silent moods, his features even took on a sort of concentrated wildness and nobility which made strangers turn and look at him as he passed. It was a bit of a laugh and an easy trick to get the tourists to take a photo of him to add to their collection of 'regional types'. Francis was not keen on this game. There was nothing particularly funny about the fact that from the moment of his birth, this jester had been given a tragic mask. In fact, he presented a sort of negative version of the human condition, for no stock of tomfoolery and clowning around had ever protected anybody right up to the end. It always had to end in tragedy.

Having now become as superstitious as he was in the first ten years of his life, Francis could not help but see a sinister omen in Mami's unpredictable behaviour and double error.

Meanwhile, the departures continued. Francis suddenly

noticed that he had let his mother and Juliette leave after an absent-minded glance, as if he had all eternity to talk to and smile at them again. An unbearable anxiety stopped his breath. If this occasion proved to be the last, those few distracted seconds had just ruined his life.

CHAPTER 2

Inside the church, fear had really begun to take hold when the interpreter with the long clownish face was unwise enough to reply to a question from a schoolchild: 'You've been brought here because there are some men who want to defend themselves. There may be some shooting.'

This immediately gave rise to twenty or so questions which melded into a confused braying. The interpreter stopped his ears and beat a hasty retreat.

Then the children quietened down. Those who were with their mothers re-joined them and snuggled up to them. The little refugees gathered together in a side aisle of the nave and remained there, motionless and pale, their eyes fixed on the door.

At first, numerous women knelt down to pray. But the central nave was soon so crowded that they got to their feet again.

First Holy Communion had taken place a few days before and the Virgin wore a crown of white flowers. The scent of lilies still floated in the rich light of the stained-glass windows.

For as long as the silence held, everybody was calm.

Some three-or four-year olds were already starting to chase each other in and out of the pews. Expressions of reassurance were being swapped.

'This will all be over very soon, you'll see.'

'Of course. We've not done anything wrong.'

'They've got nothing to gain from setting everybody against them at this stage.'

Suddenly bursts of machine-gun fire rang out. Then a number of babies in prams who had been put in the chapel under the protection of St Anne started bawling.

At the same time, as if responding to a signal, the slightly older ones, who had been unworried up until that point, rushed to their mothers uttering piercing screams.

The tiny ones were cradled, and those who had learnt to talk were told fibs. The din subsided a little.

But it was not possible to bring calm and reassurance to all. The children over seven wore such a grave expression that certain of them resembled a dream-like version of their absent fathers and brothers. Looking at them, their mothers could not hold back the tears.

From time to time, above the low rumble of murmurs and oppressed breathing, there rose a flood of questions like bubbles to the surface of a lake, sudden and irresistible.

'Why isn't the priest here if it's true they want us to hear mass?'

'Maman, tell me. Are you sure Pierre didn't try and hide? They're firing at the people hiding, aren't they?

'Where's papa? Tell me where papa is. They don't want to kill him, not my papa?

'When's mass going to start?'

'Why can't we go outside, since it's so miserable in here?'

A little refugee from Clichy called Mimile Bréchat had a knack for finding a form of words which quickly fomented worry and fear to an unbearable degree.

He seemed scarcely more than five years old and was a classic little runt of the suburbs where desolation was widespread: a yellowish complexion, sticky-out ears, over-large knees and spindly wrists. His gaze, intelligent and gentle, latched on to that of the women with such trust that not one of them would have dared silence him. Furthermore, he had an extraordinary voice, neither serious nor loud, but so full, so resonant under the high vault, that it seemed amplified by the anxiety of the whole crowd.

From the outset he had asked: 'Is it so that we don't see the men being shot that they've hidden us in here?'

'Goodness, no! You keep quiet now, little Mimile.' His old Aunt Fanny gently chided him as she leaned over him.

Fanny was one of the few paupers in the village. Her workday consisted of scrubbing floors, digging gardens, rinsing the washing, carrying out all the tasks which more fortunate housewives found too hard. She was a great gossip and never let anyone forget that her sister's husband, a labourer from Clichy, was a first-rate man despite being a bit of a drunkard and a brute and working in the black market in Normandy where he expected to make a killing very soon. Unfortunately, he often forgot to send money to his wife, so much so that Mimile had to be entrusted to his aunt. 'If it wasn't for me,' Fanny explained. 'The poor mite would be in the rubbish bin by now, what with a mother who'd picked up her husband's habit of getting pissed.' Naturally everybody was nice to Mimile. Besides, they had seen his mother and had decided she was all right because she relentlessly recounted the story of her life which was a wretched one. The villagers felt very superior when they listened to her enumerating so many misfortunes, none of which would ever threaten them: the country struck a blow against the town.

Mimile's plain speaking had gained him free entry to every house in Verrièges.

'What a stroke of luck!' said his mother. '...thinking of sending him here. I've never had any luck, all my life. But this little one who's often first in his class, has brought me some. Now he'll never go hungry. He'll be a man.'

Mimile certainly wanted to be a man. He listened attentively to the advice his aunt gave him and expressed his approval with slow nods of the head. It even took him several minutes before it all flew out of his head.

Then his hollow, powerful voice was raised again: 'They're not firing with rifles.'

'No. Machine guns.'

'So, it's not with rifles. That's good... but, tell me, what are they shooting at?'

Fanny Bréchat went 'Ssshhhh' and leaned towards him muttering some lengthy suggestions. Two or three more minutes of respite, then the giant voice again rang out: 'That big skinny joker said they were only firing at men who resist. But anybody with any guts will resist. My papa – he'd resist.'

Fanny told him to keep quiet. But another voice rose out of the darkness, a voice full of impatience and surprise.

'Maman, tell me, please: they haven't killed papa have they?'

Immediately several women burst out sobbing, and the children in their cradles, as if on a signal, once again started up.

With her face bathed in tears and her grey hair in disarray, Fanny Bréchat held Mimile tightly in her arms as if hoping to stifle the voice of anxiety within him.

Suzanne Lambert was ashamed to be one of those who had not been able to hold back her tears.

But still! Not being able to smile at her husband or her son in the market square, that was too much to bear! The bitter taste of recrimination suddenly filled her mouth. Typical of him! When the country was mobilising, he had slipped through her fingers. It would have been easy enough for him to get a special posting, but he preferred to leave. He wanted to see for himself. He wanted to know... she flew into a rage, and it was quite a rage, which made her believe that everything could endure, that life went on.

Fortunately, her own baby, little Daniel, was not one of those who had screamed. He had not even woken up. His mouth was open in a half smile, his pink chubby cheeks, stroked by the reflections from the stained-glass window, shone with an ineffably reassuring serenity. Suzanne brushed the illuminated cheek with a light kiss. The little poppet let out a big laugh and without waking at all, made as if he was trying to catch a fly.

'He's as lovely as the baby Jesus,' old Julie Bricaud said very softly. 'Don't worry. Nobody would dare hurt him.'

Juliette Ducros, who was not far away from her friend Suzanne, heard these words and felt like throwing herself into the arms of this sweet woman, Francis' mother. But she did not dare. Her love had to remain secret.

Just as the sobs and sighs of a hundred breasts had produced a dull vibration throughout the nave of the church, even Juliette, for the first time, had trembled.

Fear was taking hold of the village. It had the universal enormity of the wind. For a while, it was irresistible.

Juliette felt her strength desert her. What if it were true after all! What if the brutality and stupidity of the men in boots had the upper hand? What if life itself wore the face of those devious, obstinate officers with nervous hands...?

But this woman, Francis' mother, couldn't be wrong. A man remains a man despite his moments of delirium. They would back off in the face of all these children, all this hope, all this life.

Juliette had knelt down in an attitude of prayer. But all she could bring to mind was the face of Francis. You, Francis, you're the only one I can talk to. No. This is not the time for prayer. I have to talk to you. I will talk to you, regardless of the distance, regardless of prisons if necessary, regardless of the whole world. I know you'll be able to hear me.

CHAPTER 3

Francis was walking along in his group towards the end of the village.

The Café de la Poste had taken in one of these groups, then the storeroom belonging to Poutet the Lime and Cement Merchants, also the Breton dairy farmer's barn, and the Laplagne beer warehouse, then a hotel, a wine cellar and a former shed for carriage horses.

Francis found himself at the tail-end of an interminable line, and he already knew that he was going to be herded into the barn belonging to Blaise Blanchard who had quite close links to the Bricauds. In front of this barn, Francis, fork in his hand, had often thrown sheaves into the thresher, inebriated on glistening sweat, laughter and resounding shouts, intoxicated by summer and youth.

But he turned his back on these memories to repeat his self-accusation: 'You let them leave without so much as a glance. You squander everything, out of habit. Now you have to look at them through the eyes of memory. Look at them, with all your strength.' He did not need to force himself. On the contrary, he was worried about the overwhelming flood of memories. Huh! All that meant simply was that he was afraid. Like everybody else.

His mother's face was always a comfort: laughing, or at least smiling, lit up with pride, with enthusiasm, with approval and hope. Wonderful maman. An endless source of courage. Yet, there had been one painful moment between the two of them. Just one. The day he was taking his final exam, to get into the École. Fed up with relentless cramming, he had secretly decided to flunk out, to escape this 'infernal machine' for good. His mother had guessed as much. As she had said goodbye to him, she could not hold back the tears. This had made him angry. 'Don't cry. I want you to stop crying immediately. I'll get in, okay! In the top ten. Is that all right with you?' The smile returned at once to eyes still full of tears; fresh and shining like a March morning. And Francis had kept his word in full. What a comfort it was now to have been able to keep his word like that. There you go! Your young son, the youngest, the one who was never there often enough, who could never please you as often as the other... your son who arrived late, the simpleton who was all fingers and thumbs, who was not a bad son though, at least not a disloyal son.

As for Juliette, he seemed not to have given her a second thought. No time. They had only been lovers for a few weeks. Not his first adventure, for sure! But certainly his first love. A surprise. A big surprise, in fact.

He had invited her to dance at this party in the barn on a farm lost in the middle of the forest. It was organised with the aim of distracting young men from joining the *maquis*. And he had felt from the first moment that he had no control over the event.

At the end of the dance, however, Francis had tried to get away. Stunned, incredulous, not daring to risk conversation, certain that all he could do would be to stammer, he bowed and took a step back. But Juliette had taken a step forward and they were still touching. As if she were alone with him, oblivious to the murmur of voices and laughter, she had let her gaze immerse itself in his without a hint of shame. She had slowly lifted her arm, and her little hand had gripped onto his arm with unexpected force: A veritable claw. A little later they had left side by side to lose themselves in the paths bordered with darkness and moss.

Ever since that night she had been present within him. He did not have to utter her name, nor recall the words they had exchanged. They spoke so little...! She was an unavoidable presence. With her he had quite gently and to his surprise entered an enchanted world where he no longer had the option of thinking, nor of remembering even.

CHAPTER 4

Looking at his watch, Francis realised with a shudder that it was only two hours ago that all this had started.

His nerves were frayed as if he had been tortured for days on end.

He had to struggle, to talk, refuse to accept this slippage of time. Francis looked around him for support. Then he noticed that his companions had already set about fighting back against the invisible walls of silence.

They were talking, joking, laughing. As a final group was separated off from the column, those around Francis continued to call out to those who were moving away.

'Hey, see you soon. Don't use this as an excuse to get out of paying for your round.'

'If it goes on too long, have a game of cards.'

'Don't worry, we'll keep busy: Jules just got his tobacco ration. There's enough for half a man, and we're going to be two smoking like four. Everything'll be just dandy.'

Francis saw the German colonel walk past and realised that he was listening in. He was on his own. He walked quickly and noiselessly, like an intruder, like a phantom. His face was remarkably pale.

'Looks like a ghost, don't you think?' said Gaston who had rejoined him.

Francis nudged him gently with his elbow. The German might have heard him. He had turned his head in their direction and was observing them. His attention was alerted by their shouts. He seemed scandalised, incredulous even. Not a trace of compassion, just wounded self-pride. On the whole, this 'leader' cut a poor figure.

And for his part, Francis had an overwhelming urge to shout out, to show this sorry bastard, this Wagnerian butcher, that he despised him. Anger boiled up inside him and stopped him from finding the right words. Then he started laughing – thunderous laughter which went on and on.

Several others laughed as well, in solidarity. Francis stopped as soon as the German had gone off. He was a little surprised that nobody had asked him why he was laughing. Then he noticed that everyone in the group was talking without listening to anybody. They spoke for the sheer sound of the words and the brief intoxication that they brought.

So! That's what courage was in such circumstances: Keeping the storm of words swirling and above all don't let your neighbour realise that your throat is tight and your mouth dry. Overcome your fear so as to avoid increasing it in others; overcome it or, better still, deny it.

Even so, there were those who sometimes cast their eyes about with the furtive glance of strangers. It was obvious that these men had, like Francis, just made an internal inventory of their most precious possessions and had tried to prepare themselves for the worst.

During moments of distraction when they forgot to perform their role, their gaze seemed to come from afar. It was already the ambiguous gaze of an old photograph; it comes to life at the very moment when a person is pronounced dead. The insolence of youth is lost in the misty fading of features, such that it is the fixed image which, in its humble way, accompanies the being whom time also gradually effaces.

Perhaps these men living under threat were struggling very humbly and timidly to resemble the memory of themselves they wished to leave behind, if there was anybody left to remember them…

'If I'm one of the hostages, how many years, or how many days would Juliette allow me to survive?' The question immediately seemed to him the most futile of games. It mattered little what Juliette would do if he was not there to endure it or enjoy it. All he wished for her was to live as fully and as happily as possible. And above all to stay eternally beautiful, just as she was for him.

All around him, imperceptibly, each man was giving himself up to silence. There was a real danger in this. The silence raised a towering solitude around each and every one. It was a chasm with terrifying but fragile walls. At all costs they must not be given the time to solidify.

Quickly, then. Let's shout. Let's laugh! But Francis wanted to call for help instead. It was Charles Valade, stuck in the *Café de la Poste* with one of the first groups, whom he was missing badly.

CHAPTER 5

Jean realised that he would not make it up to Verrièges-la-Montagne that day. He could not cycle up any more slopes. Passing the meadow he had mown in the morning, he had come off his bike, and that had barely been a slope at all.

His feet refused to push down on the pedals; rather they were expecting the pedals to push them up. The bike had lost its speed and Jean had almost ended up in a ditch. He had lain down by the side of the road looking at his meadow. He shut his eyes; his mouth uttered some gentle words. 'That's proper dry, that hay. Good moment to bring it in.' And at the same time he thought that he was wasting the most supremely important moments of his life. He was just an animal, a poor simple animal who lies down on the ground when its strength gives out.

He was in the grip of the worst nightmare. He had to keep going to save his life, and not just his own, but he could not put one foot in front of the other. His eyes began to mist over. He did not know if he was crying or if he was about to faint. He needed to take a rest for a minute and he could only rest if he stopped remembering.

Then he mumbled again, vaguely and gently: 'The hay's dry. Perfectly dry.'

His hay was indeed dry, and the day had been beautiful. As at the end of so many beautiful days, the sun was beginning to set with its usual majestic slowness on fleecy hills, heavy dark green in colour. Just next to his face, the cool shadow of the trees lengthened, one blade of grass at a time, stirring up swarms of teeming, buzzing insects. Down there, on the plain, in the hollows filled with heather, the rustling and shifting was speeding up with measured regularity. And at the edge of woods and orchards, breezy exhalations alternated with sudden shudders of freakish summer winds. The hay in Jean's field and in all surrounding fields was so deeply imbued with light and heat that it hardly seemed to be lying on the ground. It was woven together lightly with the burning air in one and the same ecstatic vibration.

Verrièges was there, in front of him, to all appearances as calm as any other evening. The houses with their roofs of mossy tiles sat amongst the foliage as naturally as in the countryside where the granite rocks sit among the broom, the dry grasses and the heather. This harmony had always protected them; such dwellings seemed indestructible.

Jean refused to give in to despair. The earth had always been welcoming to men who were tenacious and calm. Justice existed because this harmony between men and the earth existed. Jean's tenacity and goodwill were limitless. At any hour of the day or night he had always been ready to give his time and effort, even to the point where his strength was exhausted. His life cannot have been in vain.

The huge, monstrous mix-up was going to disappear,

leaving nothing but a memory as fleeting as that of a nightmare. Perhaps it was just a matter of waiting…

For Verrièges, time had already stood still. When it was set going again, everything would be back in order. Jean's efforts, his fever, his rasping breath, his hot sweats and icy sweats, all of that was part and parcel of the mix-up. All he had to do was to give up on his gruelling, pointless attempt to leap beyond the bounds of possibility, beyond his own limits and ahead of himself.

From the outset he had been wrong. He had been mistaken to believe in the possibility that cruelty and chaos would win out. Goodwill was invincible. Thus, in direct contact with the earth, Jean recovered a little of his confidence. He seemed to hear M. Boiget's voice again, that voice which was incapable of falsehood. M. Boiget explained clearly that the Good was the ultimate aim of humanity, such that even the steps of Evil marked a movement upwards toward a supreme Good which would be revealed in due course, inevitably.

Suddenly, in the midst of a silence of which Jean had not yet measured the depth, the clock struck the half hour.

As if in response to a signal, he got to his feet with barely a stumble. He had to set off.

He could not get up to Verrièges-la-Montagne by bike, but he would find another way. Mme Leboutet the Miller's wife had a gas-driven car. She would surely lend it to him. It was all downhill to the river; It was easy.

CHAPTER 6

The voice of bronze that sounded the half hour made Rehm shudder.

He took up position in the radio lorry, some distance from the loudspeaker. The short sentence that he had to utter was ready. He had spent a long time weighing up each syllable.

Of course, it would be a fine thing for the order to ring out, like a clap of thunder from a subject sky, just after the striking of the bell. True tragedy often owed such fateful and grandiose punctuation to chance.

The loudspeaker, muted and pointing in the right direction, quivered in readiness. Behind him, a little way off from the lorry, Greven was watching; he had no doubt. He felt his gaze like an insistent and secretly furious nudge. It was a most unpleasant sensation. It was even more unpleasant to him to notice at the same time that his hands were shaking and he was sweating profusely. It was streaming down his forehead and neck, his shirt was soaked under his armpits and was sticking to his skin.

He swung round and shot a look of defiance in Greven's direction. The look missed its target: Greven was engaged in giving orders to an NCO. The two of them, with their noses to a map, were in animated discussion.

So Greven had understood, long before he had, that all he needed to do was adopt an attitude. Greven was quick on the uptake, for sure; not so quick that he missed the essential, unfortunately.

Rehm knew that he, rather than this little fanatic, was the man to be entrusted with the great missions: him, Aryan Man, impervious to pity or remorse or any other slavish sentiment. He had been just such a man for years, and he still was, provided at least that he ignored the stifling heat, the stinking lorry, the dust, the sweat, the stupid and perhaps disapproving looks of those helmeted clods.

He was not retreating. He knew the necessary words. He seemed to have uttered them before. Not here, but in a world where they had their place, in a world worthy of them. There they resounded long in the crystalline air which carried their echo across the whole face of the earth.

The Heroic Man accepted in other men only two sentiments: absolute and sacred admiration, or an equally absolute, sacred terror

However, here nothing went according to the heroic law. Here he sweated like a pig, his hand trembled suspiciously, his heart beat too quickly and too heavily. Here, those whose destiny it was to admire him, seemed formed from the same no less opaque and dumb stuff as those who should have been trembling and prostrating themselves as he passed.

The villagers continually disconcerted him. As they were being led to torture they laughed, they joked, some of them even sang. He hated them and this hatred felt like a defeat. He should have been holding them in serene contempt. But for that to happen, he would have had to stop seeing and hearing them. And he could not help but lend an ear to the tone of a voice filled with tenderness nor let himself be fascinated by the look on the face of a child where the reflections of leaves were playing, nor even to be moved by the stunning beauty of a woman who was going to die.

As for the men, who were generally short of stature, inelegant, with nothing going for them physically, bizarrely lively and often ridiculous, these men were not as strange as he had first declared. Moreover, there was not one among them who seemed ready to play the role he assigned them. They slipped away from him, and their evasiveness was wholly unexpected: they refused to answer hatred and scorn with a corresponding hatred and scorn. One moment they were too far away from him, the next they were too close: never the correct distance.

At one point, Rehm thought he recognised among the group the voice of Karl, the family chauffeur. During his childhood, this Karl had one day taken on an importance which was both sudden and disproportionate. It was a day of great despair. Little Wolfgang decided he was no longer fit to live because he had been lying to his parents: a real lie, sustained over several months. It had all come to light and Wolfgang expected to die of shame. Karl tried to console him: 'It's not so bad. A father, at the end of the day is not a God. He's only ever a father. Look a bit further off. You'll see there's nothing to lose your head over. Just live well.' But when the child tried to look further, all he could see was himself lost in an icy death-like wasteland. Then he thought that Karl was in fact one of the dead who was still making the gestures of the living. He was terribly frightened of him and at the same time, he took pleasure in his company: an unworthy, degrading pleasure. In confusion and shame, he had completely lost his footing.

Yes. It was unthinkable, intolerable that the men in this village just as Karl had done previously, should presume to observe him, to come to an opinion on him, to judge him.

In his eyes, this was the supreme Evil. Moreover, his resolution had been weakened and his hand had trembled briefly; he needed no greater proof.

CHAPTER 7

In the dark depths of the barns, cellars and garages, amid the festive dancing dust, in the thick smell of sweat from heat and anxiety, the men had begun talking again.

They spoke to their friends when they found them nearby. They also spoke to the uninterested and even to those they did not know. They spoke in order to hear their own voice and to have that voice heard again. They did not expect a reply and scarcely listened to what others were saying. All they sought was proof that they were among the living, that they could still raise concerns. When they got to talking about the future, using words like 'soon' or 'tomorrow', they repeated them with tireless prodigality. In this way they renewed their insurance against unnameable, inconceivable absence. 'Tomorrow' was their magic word, their formula for exorcism. Tomorrow they were going to do more work, they were going to repair all the things they'd neglected. Tomorrow they'd be good, they'd be fair, they'd become attentive sons, considerate husbands, fathers who were both firm and indulgent at the same time. Tomorrow would be the day of redemption, the first day of truth, the most beautiful day in the world.

They had gathered close to one another, squeezed together to form tight blocks such that around them there were large areas of emptiness where the mad winds of terror whirled.

From one moment to the next, despite the stifling heat, they piled up against each other still more, as far as possible from the gleaming metal of the machine guns.

However, they could not always suppress a shudder as they found on each face the same strained seriousness, the same clenching of the jaw. There was also this dangerous glow in their expression: an unknown fire, more vivid and yet more pale than that of a fever, almost transparent. This friend, this parent, this brother, was he about to go under, slip out of reach? Was he going to drift away? At the very moment when you might grab him and hold on to him, was he going to turn on the spot into an elusive stranger? This had to be prevented at all costs. You had to smile at him, talk to him about familiar things which kept him attached, which fixed him for all time to this place on earth, to this moment before the catastrophe befell. This unappreciable moment when they knew clearly what 'yesterday' meant, or when they uttered 'tomorrow' with such sweet and reassuring indifference.

Gaston had been talking to Francis like this for a long time, providing him with very irritating details about the hay, how it would be ruined if his father didn't manage to get it in by himself. His friend Jef Juéry, a lanky eighteen-year-old with a mane of black hair, as dry as a beanpole, and usually so touchy that the townsfolk would cross the road to avoid talking to him, even Jef was becoming chatty. Yes, the dark, romantic Jef, nicknamed 'the mute', was in full flow. He spoke to Francis as if he was a twin brother, a companion in his escapades and a confidant of his anxieties. 'It's stupid,' he explained. 'That I didn't join the *maquis*. The guys in the forest often suggested it when they came to get supplies, and it upset me having to say no to them. But it's the same old story. There's work to be done in the fields, and that same day my old man had to run around all over the place on business, and then my mother's always tied up, what with her little grocery store: it's not like she gets a lot of customers even when the weather's good, but it only takes one person passing through to find the door shut and they kick up a stink for three days and there's four regulars lost. So... so you tell yourself I'll go when I've fenced the orchard. Then it's when the grass is cut. And then you end up stuck. If I'd killed just one of those bastards, I wouldn't be feeling the same.'

Baroutaud and Mazaud protested. They were of one mind in this: Jef was a poor, brainless kid.

As for Mazaud, above all he loved life and did not hide it. He was happy with his bistro, situated just at the entrance to the town: he was happy with all of his little family: he was happy with Paul Arlaud. So, he turned away in horror from this Jef in order to get still closer to Paul. He wanted to press him to his heart. He couldn't help but touch his arm, sniff him. Beyond the odour of tobacco, beyond the dull whiff of mouldy flour given off by the miller's hard-wearing, twill jacket, his sense of smell easily detected Suzy Arlaud's perfume. Ah Paul! This excellent, comforting Paul who was always out walking the rocky country byways where the crack of his whip would set up the rustling partridges, how gladly he would have kissed him! 'People understand nothing,' he kept repeating. 'Not a bloody thing. They don't even try to come to an understanding.

They spend their time mouthing off at the drop of a hat. They don't know what this is all about. It's simply a question of living well while you're alive. That's all!' And Paul Arlaud, as usual, approved of this wholeheartedly.

CHAPTER 8

Valade the teacher was being kept in the Poutet cement store near the entrance to the village. He was getting to the end of his last cigarette. The two packets of 'Decade' had been distributed left and right. His mouth dry, his eyes bulging, Valade felt abominably tired. It seemed to him that over the last few minutes he had just been repeating the essence of what he had been saying in the classroom for the last eleven years in the job.

He did not utter the same words to everybody of course, but he wanted to offer the same comfort to all; to communicate to them the same firmness, the same contempt for the enemy, and above all, the same trust. Yes, trust and hope. Not that he was counting on the *maquis*. He had not told Francis, but he knew that the available forces were too widely dispersed to intervene in time. Ah well! This was not the moment to disavow himself. He had always been an optimist and he intended to remain one even in a hail of machine-gun bullets. If they took hostages, he would be among them – no doubt about that. Very well. He was ready to die whenever, even if his death seemed pointless. If it occurred today, then it would not be pointless. Sure, he would have preferred to die in the heat of battle, considered to be a finer death. Huh! It was absurd to talk about a fine death. Hideous whatever the circumstance, death had to be overcome. This was possible provided you did not succumb to memory. Horror of death arises as soon as you begin to remember; in other words, the moment you build illusory bridges towards impossible survival. That was a slippery slope; terribly slippery.

'Come on, you human skeleton, move aside. No point insisting. I'm not going to deal with you. Go and see him, over there. He needs you. He lost it some time ago.'

Mami, white as a Pierrot (he had rolled around in lime plaster as soon as he arrived) only stopped him for a moment.

'No, no, Mami. I don't have any cigarettes, not even a butt. I can't help you.'

Even poor Mami realised that something decidedly unfunny was happening. Nobody had the time to comfort him.

As he had exhausted the supply of cigarettes from his friends, he spoke to one of the two SS mounting guards. He repeated 'Cigarette… cigarette…' He had even traced with his index finger the imaginary curls of smoke which he then observed, wide-eyed, for a long time. The Germans just watched him closely and studiously which cut Mami to the quick.

'What's with that arsehole, looking at me like that, with his zebra costume and his piece of scrap metal? Something's wrong when a bloke won't give me a cigarette. I tell you. And no need for you to look at me like that neither.'

This was aimed at Labaille, the carpenter. In fact, Melanie's father was staring at him as if seeing him for the first time.

In this half-light, the 'simpleton's' thick, mop of curly hair covered in plaster, formed a halo around his hard face with its gleaming cheekbones. Labaille all at once thought he was in the presence of one of those saints in the church which ever since he was a child he could not look at without shuddering. He almost fell to his knees. He hastily turned his back on Mami, saying: 'Bloody nutcase. Talking bollocks, as usual.' But nothing was as usual. The carpenter felt all his certainties crumble. He wanted to run to Melanie's side. He'd been wrong. Perhaps he'd acted badly in putting her on that old pallet in the little attic. Who knows? Perhaps he'd been wrong all his life. He examined his hands; opened them: closed them. He knew them, these hands. Hmm. Not that well, all the same. It was the first time he saw them obey him so precisely. Open, close... open, close... they were there to do something; ceaselessly; one thing after another; that was the only way to live. The tireless motion of his hands calmed him. No. He hadn't been wrong. He had acted like he should have acted. 'It's for your own good, little Nini. For your own good, that's all.' He loved her a lot, his little girl. He wanted nothing more than to stroke her mane of black hair, to hold her in his arms. He would say to her: 'See, I love you. And I'm holding you tight. You're not going away this time, right? You're not going to walk out again. You don't have to go out in the evenings when I can no longer recognise you in dark corners. I'll hold you and keep you safe, my little one. It's for your own good... for your own good.'

Melanie had stopped badmouthing her father. She had completely given up fighting back. Now, she was losing it.

She no longer knew if she was laughing or if she was shouting or if she was sobbing, nor even if there were sounds coming out of her mouth. Bathed in sweat, limp as a rag, it seemed like she was turning to water, like her body was melting and becoming one with an element of great undulating movements which could only be the sea. Indeed, she'd heard that only the sea had this great rocking motion. Perhaps death did too. Everything was becoming viscous, and vaguely grey, like the most profound fatigue.

She could no longer move. She needed someone strong to help her. So, she called out: 'Papa… Papa…' He wouldn't come straightaway, of course. He had his pride. He was a hard man. But he would come, finally, because she needed him. She carried on calling him, simply, in a calm voice. He would come since she would not tire of repeating his name.

CHAPTER 9

What Francis really could not bear was the fact that around him all he saw was an attitude of humiliation. Even in those like Paul Arlaud, or Baroutaud, or Mazaud who were keeping up a certain verbal aggression, he recognised the bent back and the evasive glance of those who have been punished since the day they were born.

Baroutaud, who was a bit more sensitive than the others, was talking about his childhood. Tears were welling up. He said: 'D'you remember when we learnt *The Soldiers* in Year 2? *And they watched them marching, proud barefoot boys, marching on a startled world.* Ah, no kidding. I so wanted to be a proud, barefoot boy. But when they stuck me in hobnail boots weighing a kilo each it was no joke. And now, look at them, that lot, how they keep us in line.' Poor Baroutaud! So ready to play the soldier that he never fully lost respect for a uniform.

Deep down, Baroutaud felt he was to blame and spoke to exonerate himself. Mazaud too, and so many others… let's be logical: if there's no crime, then there's no punishment. That sort of trust in the order of the world was pitiful. Francis wanted to scream. Except he didn't scream. And for that, he too felt blameworthy.

And he was. He always had been, ever since war was declared. Guilty of fighting half-heartedly, of not putting all his energy, all his passion into persuading those around him to grit their teeth and hit hard. Once war was declared, every minute that he had not dedicated to fighting the murderers of peace discredited him and condemned him. These insubstantial minutes constituted the time of servitude defrauding the time of liberty.

From the outset however he had understood – how could he not? – that the life of a free man was no longer allowed. Even so, he made an effort to sleep a little longer. To sleep in order to dream that life would continue, that liberty would defend its place in the sun by itself, by the very radiance of its light. And when sleep eluded him, he faked it. Thus, meekly, the ghosts of past dreams accompanied this phantom sleep. There is nothing more docile than dreams, and nothing more debilitating.

At the same time, despite his anxiety, his torpor continued. He remained curled up in the hollow of a vague hope, and his mind made little attempt to rid itself of the dreams of a future which swaddled him. There, in front of the little black mouths of the machine guns, he still believed in his future. If he was chosen as a hostage, at the very instant he was engulfed by flame or his guts were shredded by burning steel, he would still believe in it. He would still think of getting out of it… this was an unworthy, and incurable, evil. And yet, several times he had risked his life, without hesitation, without shaking any more than the next man.

No. He was not particularly cowardly, in peace or war, but that did not stop him feeling ashamed. His inertia had slowly undermined him; he had already lost many of the reflexes of a free man. At that moment he should have got to his feet, shouted to the others to lift their heads and not let the hideous beast assume that they were resigned to their fate.

The hideous beast took on such disconcerting forms! One of the SS guards near the doors to the barn could have been posing as the archetype of a coarse brute: a low forehead, shifty little eyes and hair which called to mind, appropriately enough, the yellowish bristles of a huge pig ready to rush off to the acorn patch. But the other one... the other one was tall, slim, dark-haired with a strenuous expression on his face and the pinched lips of an accountant eager to do better: the sort of accountant whose boss would not hesitate in trusting with the cash box. Certainly, before the war he took part in leisure activities in an exemplary fashion. Whether he was playing a team game or having a family picnic in Nature with a capital N, *der Natur*.

Beyond the two Germans, on the stable wall above the door, Francis could make out several dozen, blue-painted, oval or rectangular plaques which commemorated the triumphs of various bulls, heifers and milk cows in agricultural contests. And there you have it! Due to the all-powerful machine-gun animal, a prize-winning pig and accountant could reduce all those he was talking to, whom he knew, whom he called by name, to a heap of corpses in a matter of seconds: Fernand and Paul, Gaston and Jef, Pierre, Jean, Antoine, all those young boys intoxicated by a secret passion, all those 'serious' men responsible for numerous projects, those patient old men who knew to whom they would pass on their wisdom, and perhaps, their hidden gold.

It would have been better to talk more, because reflection was the worst of enemies. It painted this experience now in the colours of farce, now in the colours of melodrama. Laugh! He should have been laughing…

Sadly, he was no longer laughing. The time for laughter had passed forever in this little corner of the world. Neither he, nor any of the villagers, were under any illusion about that. Even the stones – dark, impenetrable and yet shot through with a spasmodic vibration in the leaden, storm-filled heat – these very stones felt the breath of the oncoming tragedy.

Nobody could help but feel it. Not even Mami. Not even the most lumpen peasant with hands the colour of soil. Not even 'handsome Alphonse', the pâtissière's pampered son who strangely resembled one of those beautiful saint-honoré cakes on display every Sunday in the family shop window, a man who had never had any occupation other than to attend mass regularly, to flirt in secret with his sister's friends, and to pick out startling ties.

In truth, this was what was heart-breaking: to think of just how untragic these people were. They killed rarely, and even then, without pleasure or violence, such that living in their eyes, was a very simple affair. Their vices, their virtues, their passions and their faults most often remained hidden even to themselves and ran little risk of bringing down the Wrath of God and Men on their heads. Life flowed for them as it did for the trees in their forests – dense, slow and muted. Lulled for centuries by the murmur of the icy waters of their rushing streams and by the song of the wind in the thickets and across the plains, they struggled to lift their gaze to the horizon. Even when one of them moved away, it took years and years to wake from this vegetable torpor, from this blessed state which could be taken for strength, but which almost always remained a simple brutishness. Happy brutes. Precious brutes, bearers of the patience of the world. Good brutes. My equals, my friends, my brothers, wake up! Open your eyes for a moment. The world is watching you, you who have never looked on it. Yes, yes. I know. Why would you look on it? From time to time this world sent you a discreet call: little printed sheets, leaflets in neutral colours rained down on this village. Without drums or fanfares, the sons, brothers and fathers – the best, as it happens – took the tram and then the train… what's more, some returned, more or less crippled, one-armed, wheezing or doddering. As for the others it was said that they represented the tribute that the village owed to 'civilisation'. Why not? The living never cease paying their tribute to death – the self-righteous say to 'nature' – That's the law. Since you've always accepted this law, why then – my fine brutes, hearty brutes, innocent brutes, my brothers – since by tradition you accept throwing into these scales everything which was precious to you, everything that was a source of smiles, laughter and tears, that gave taste to your fruit and a meaning to frost and storm, a language for when dawn and twilight return, well! my dear friends, my only friends, why then, today, are you astonished that the world has herded you here, in tight little bundles, like sheep, or pigs, or cows? Well then, you bumpkins, sons of the soil, yokels, ugly bastards! A lot of you thought they were well protected when you said: 'They're not going to eat us.' I, yes me, Francis, I don't see why they would stand on ceremony.

Face the facts a little: they can absolutely eat you, and even crush you, or boil you, or distil you or smash you to pieces. They'll do what they want with you, since you've said; 'Life above all else' and therefore recognised that you are the last of the earth. It's astonishing, yes astonishing, that they haven't already done more.

Increasingly exasperated, Francis withdrew a little from the group among which the drone of all too familiar voices could be heard. He noticed that the SS guard with the conscientious furrows was watching him out of the corner of his eye and that his finger was mechanically stroking the trigger of his machine gun. Thus, the almost perfect human brute gained reassurance from contact with the perfect mechanical brute.

Francis was sorely tempted to move a few steps closer. He eyed the two SS men in turn with a smile of impartial curiosity. He saw with no little satisfaction their fingers stiffen into the regulation position. Poor blokes! It did him good to hold them in such calm contempt. He shrugged his shoulders and regained his place against the wall near Gaston who was pale and tense, and Jef who was still talking nineteen to the dozen as if he wanted to make up for a ten-year backlog.

Francis did not listen to him. He did not have a second to waste. An intense dread rose from the pit of his stomach and spread throughout his body. He gave himself instructions with febrile haste: don't waste my time looking for attitudes, don't waste a minute, not an instant, live with all my strength, live fully while I still can, while Juliette is still alive.

Almost immediately he reached a sort of state of serenity. Since he had arrived at a summit, since he could never live a more intense life, he no longer wished for anything. Time was no longer a useless torture to him. He didn't need to be constantly constructing a future. He no longer believed in a future.

CHAPTER 10

Stifled whispers from the mouths of children still looking for comfort made the silence of the church even more desolate. It was the silence of the primeval forest, muffled by undergrowth and haunted by the groaning wind among the invisible canopy. The children were not sleeping. Their gleaming eyes were searching all around for the answer to a huge, inarticulate question. Why us? Why? They did not understand but they felt the need to hold their breath, so that the wild beasts did not notice them.

Juliette had never really felt fear, but she could not escape the contagious anxiety. She drew tight to Suzanne, her best friend, her elder. Shoulder to shoulder, they listened to the calming voice of Julie Bricaud.

'Of course not,' said this ancient and very gentle voice. 'They won't harm us. Why would they harm us?'

That was that – the truth. Nobody could harm those who had nothing more in their hearts than enormous love. Juliette had understood this from the outset, and it was only due to simple physical weakness that she had let herself be intimidated for an instant.

Now she would not let herself be diverted from the truth. She shut her eyes firmly. She would also have liked to shut her ears to all the noise, to all the fear-filled outbursts. As in the legends of the pious, her love would be a magical suit of armour. She was eighteen, she was in love, she was loved. It was simple. Nothing could prevent her from setting out along the dazzling pathways of summer. Those paths which she had followed blindly before, she now had to discover with her eyes wide open, in the arms of Francis. They would leave together, go to the little house by the sea, bought just before the war and which her father had only been able to take her to once. She could see herself on the threshold, turning the key in the lock, opening the door and pushing Francis inside in front of her. 'Go on. What are you waiting for? Get in. You've already got several weeks to catch up on – each week longer than a century.'

Suzanne was watching old Julie comforting Annie, her daughter-in-law. Annie was concentrating on nothing except her gestures and the sound of her voice. It was better that way. No words existed to equal the soothing power of that maternal voice. But Suzanne heard Annie Bricaud repeat tirelessly: 'All the same, if Jean was here…'

Poor Annie. To everybody, including herself, she was just Jean's wife. She had never been able to exist in her own right; before being Jean's wife, she was her mother's daughter. And here she was without either of them. She was finding it hard to breathe. Her hesitant, little voice sometimes floated up from the shadows, like that of a lost child. Without Jean here she was nothing.

He was the one who decided for her if she should be happy

or sad. The day she learnt of her mother's death, she had run out to the fields to find Jean; only when he had also heard the news was she able to cry.

The silence became deeper still. Outside, the sound of footsteps could be made out. Scarcely a noise at all: rather a memory of ghostly footsteps. Shining eyes sought to make contact with other eyes. There were no shouts, just a few brief sobs.

And this time, Suzanne did not tremble. If she had to make that fearful crossing at least she would make it in a calm and collected manner without dropping the burden which gave life all its value.

Her hands on her forehead, leaning forward, like those who were praying, she felt increasingly flooded with an indecisive light where reflections of dream and daybreak mingled. Time swelled within her like a slow sea-surge. It seemed to her that she was losing her usual contours. She was disintegrating. She was floating. She had returned to that morning when she discovered absolute tenderness. She was at her parents'. The wind was quivering in the large poplar which shaded the window. That October morning, filtered through foliage, the sun caused flakes of gold to dance on little David's bed. He had just been very ill. During three weeks of vigil and hidden tears, Suzanne had felt an entire life die away within her and a new life being born. It was on that morning that this second birth took place. Henceforth she would no longer see the world with her own eyes. The eyes that mattered most were those of the child in whom a trace of fever still flickered; those enlarged eyes which fixed on her with such trust that she struggled to hold back the tears. She had renounced her own childhood and her own youth, and she gave herself up body and soul to a happy defeat.

'Thank you,' she murmured. 'Thank you, you've given me this peace.' She looked at old Julie's eyes; a little grey, a little blue, sometimes green, always so unclouded that you forgot at once that they were the eyes of an old woman; the joy and youthfulness that shone in them came from an inexhaustible source. Of course, she was a *paysanne* like so many others. But if Suzanne had not had her by her side, her courage would have failed long ago. The bravery of an old woman like Julie pushed back the boundaries of hope indefinitely.

Old Julie lived more than others. She walked everywhere, and at a pace which only slackened when she reached the very frontiers of exhaustion or death. And naturally, this was a daily occurrence.

She had so much to do. There was always somebody to help, to console. When all those in the household had been provided for, she had to rush off to some neighbour who was sick, or bored, or overworked. And why not invite some unfortunate passer-by in for a glass of cider, a piece of bread.

By now, Annie was on her knees, her face in her hands. Old Julie also prayed, then remained kneeling, looking straight in front of her. She was gathering her strength. It would be necessary to fight back against the assault by terror, to protect those who were doubtful, those who were losing their grip, those who were panicking. She was there to be fearless when others were fearful. I've always been there to do what others couldn't, and what they didn't want to do. I clean up what they make dirty, I cut their bread, I sew their buttons back on, I listen to their stories pretending to believe them. Everything must be done noiselessly, it's best if nobody notices me passing through. More often than not, they don't even see me, and in this way, I surprise them in their moments of happiness. They are there, on this earth, without burdens or cares, the joy of living carries them along in an invisible stream. My gift to them is the infinite indulgence of the world. So, without knowing it, they welcome God. I know it though and I'm happier than they are. Neither tiredness nor sickness can do anything to change that.

After you get to seventy, you're always sick, more or less. I've never been a big woman, nor a strong one. I certainly have to stop for a day or two sometimes to get my strength back. And throw a fever into the mix and that stops me getting out of bed even. Then I sing. It's a good moment for singing. You have time to remember the old songs, songs from back when there was no pain or tiredness. Songs raise a wind which carries off the smell of sickness. Those who come near me, those who push open the door of my little bedroom, hear the trembling of the fever in my voice before they smell the fever. They know I sing to drive the fever away and I can see in their eyes they already feel slightly relieved. 'If she's singing, she's fighting. And if she's fighting, she'll pull through.' When I feel the approach of death, I'll put all my remaining strength into a song. Even if I only sing two or three words, I know they'll be happy. 'She was brave right up to the end.' And they won't be wrong. I'm not afraid of what I'll find on the other side of my death. It's the death of others – my father, my mother, my sister – which terrified me because I couldn't do anything for them. I was abandoning them. But it's not time for me to die yet, not by a long chalk. I can still be helpful. I help them all.

They often need me, whoever they are. Him, the Old Man, the Father, he who controls all things and who's foreseen all things, he's lost without me; he's never known where the bread is, or where he put his knife down, or where he threw his dirty shirt, or where a clean one comes from. It's not because he's so old: he's always been like that. And Jean's just like him. Gaston's no more of a child than those two. Sometimes he's even ashamed of it. He's not yet used to my ways…

I can't abandon them. I won't abandon them. My little animals need me even more than my men. I'm the only one who never forgets to feed them. I'll go even when it takes me ages to walk to their pen. I'll go every day. When my back's too stiff to bend down, they'll be up on their hind legs, they'll put their smooth, shiny head in my hands. My pretty little ones… I'll always be doing something. We women can always find something to do.

Around her, there were many expressions like hers, both humble and proud.

There were so many that she smiled a smile of confidence at Suzanne and Juliette, at those two faces, so young they seemed immortal.

CHAPTER 11

'I've never known a population of such rustics,' said Greven at that moment. 'The women especially. They behave like simple animals. I've never seen one of them show the slightest feeling. No gestures of farewell. No sense of pathos. Just brutes, that's all. Brutes who deserve less consideration than the animals in their stables.'

He spoke with genuine disgust. But his hatred seemed excessive and Rehm knew that at that moment it was aimed at him. He had found a way, he thought, of expressing his hatred of him with impunity.

Never mind. He was beaten. To begin with, he had just broken the silence.

Rehm cast a scornful look down at this terribly young face, one which formerly had seemed so handsome to him.

'I think you're mistaken, Greven,' he said slowly. 'So totally mistaken I find you indecent. I'd have been less ashamed of you if you'd suddenly rolled on the ground, frothing... yes, frothing, making yourself filthy in every possible way.'

He had deliberately made a clear allusion to the scene in the hotel bedroom where he had witnessed the young officer's nervous collapse.

He saw Greven's face tense up and he had an insane wish. "If only he'd raise his hand against me, here, in sight of the two guards" This moment of violence would clear the air. Rehm did not know exactly what he would do, but he was sure that with Greven's first move, the heavens would open, he would breathe easily and he would see clearly again.

Greven reined himself in and in a dry and impersonal voice as if he were reeling off lines he had learned, he said: 'We have our orders. An example has to be made.'

There! It was over. The chance was lost. Rehm felt the sweat trickle down his chest. The leaden sky lowered and was becoming heavier by the minute. Forgetting Greven for a moment, he muttered: 'An example. Of course. But not this time. Not these.'

Greven's dry voice took on a sneer.

'You made the mistake of looking at them, that's all.'

'What about you? Did you have the strength to *not* look at them?'

'I looked at them too. I even looked at them long enough to see the future filth in them; the filth that's their true being.'

Rehm made a gesture of weariness. The nonsense the young party members came out with was beyond remedy.

'Far be it from me to instruct you…' Greven replied with feigned deference. '…but any revolutionary action, whatever it might be, is impossible if we begin to question our responsibilities. Responsibility can only be individual. Since our action is collective, we must refuse to take it into consideration.'

To hear such old errors, formulas which had for ages been

mouldy and desiccated, coming from such a youthful mouth was a torment difficult to bear.

There, before Rehm's very eyes, error and the proof of error met and became confused in a brief, sharp and dazzling conflagration. Moreover, Greven could not see it. He and his like would never see anything. If the future of the world belonged to them, there was no hope.

In effect, there was nothing else to do but obey. Obey!... obey!...

As Rehm turned away, he saw a silhouette moving towards the village on one of the stony paths which were being patrolled by motorcyclists. He thought he was the victim of a hallucination.

This man was a carbon copy of that thin, dark peasant called Jean who had had already been here. This was Jean aged beyond imagination, a Jean from another era. It was the way he walked that gave the impression that he had risen from the depths of some prehistoric time. It was not broken, nor tottering, nor even painful. The old man moved with a disconcerting lightness. You would guess he had always walked like this, that he could walk no other way; he walked lightly or not at all... his youth was simultaneously present and absent – that's what was really hard to conceive of. What's more, the old bloke stopped after a few paces with a little stamp of the feet as if he was losing his balance, and he remained there, breathing heavily, his head thrust forward a little like a runner waiting for the starting gun. He was not waiting for a signal. He was simply waiting for the ghost of his youth, the bounding youth of a man born to hunt and fight, to come to his aid once more.

Rehm adjusted his binoculars to observe him more closely. His skin was the colour of old rope; the unkempt hair of his moustache and his ill-shaven beard were not white and would never go white. They looked more like strange iron-grey lichen. Dressed in an old hunting jacket and blue cotton trousers, his body floated in such a way that you would think that all that remained of him was a minimum of tendons, skin and withered muscle. A genuinely wild abstinence and fierceness was turning him into a living mummy, day by day, year by year.

In surprisingly clear detail, Rehm remembered a French book in which there was a portrait of an old man just like this. Softened by this connection to such an opportune memory, he wanted to turn to Greven and say: 'See how mistaken you are. That one's not destined to rot. He'd burn without giving off any stink.'

But already Greven was observing coldly: 'I wonder which imbecile let him through.'

He cast an ironic look towards his commander but added, in a conciliatory tone: 'If he doesn't live in the village, we can order one of the men to send him off in the right direction.'

He made a move towards one of the guards. Rehm stopped him.

'No. I think that man is one of the last who's been able to live their life as they wish. We'll leave it up to him to choose how he dies.'

His gaze followed the tall silhouette which stumbled now and then. When the old man had disappeared round the corner, Rehm reckoned it would take him a good half an hour to get to the centre of the village. He would give him this half an hour.

And thus, he gave himself a supreme deadline, time enough to cast a final eye over the world of living men.

CHAPTER 12

During the course of his walk, old Etienne had not really understood what was happening. Indeed, he had not made any effort to understand. The moment he joined the 2nd Engineering Corps in Africa at the end of the last century, his adjutant had told him that a soldier does not try to understand. Ever since, he had always found it best, in the presence of all the adjutants of the world, to observe this fundamental precept of adjutant wisdom.

The man who had stopped him first, at the same time indicating the huge, odd sort of pistol he carried across his chest, certainly had the face of an adjutant. A big red face drenched in sweat. Old Etienne was also sweating because as usual he had forgotten to follow his doctor's advice – walk with short steps; short, measured steps.

Huh! Etienne dismissed short steps. He devoured distance with great strides until he felt himself gasping for breath. He then got his breath back and set off again. To begin with he covered a hundred metres. This decreased very quickly – fifty metres, thirty metres... until that humiliating moment when he could only progress in bursts of eight to ten steps.

This fat blockhead (who didn't even think of wearing a lightweight uniform in this heat) must be getting bored. He had observed Etienne's approach with some sort of amusement and had only planted himself in front of him in the middle of the road at the last moment.

'I'm going to Verrièges,' Etienne had said, pointing out the bell tower. 'It's not too far. I can get there under my own steam, thank you.'

'No,' the German stated, without raising his voice. 'Forbidden.'

Old Etienne had had the time to get his breath back. With the agility of a young man, he had taken a step to one side and outflanked the astonished German.

'Not forbidden for me. I'm ninety-three and in a hurry. Too much of a hurry to bother about your stuff.'

And he went on his way, heedless of the cry of 'Halte!' from the German who had swung round.

Etienne could take two more steps before catching his breath. When he looked back, the German had lowered his machine gun and his face bore signs of great embarrassment. Then old Etienne winked and burst out laughing. The German seemed bemused, then hugely relieved and he too started laughing. He did not wink, but his expression took on a mischievous glow. For a moment he was on old Etienne's side. He wanted to get up to no good with him; the two of them would play a merry prank on the powers-that-be...

So, in spite of his increasing fatigue, Etienne continued towards the village by way of the back lanes. When he noticed any Germans, he looked in the opposite direction and tried to appear even older than he was. The most irritating thing was that the more breathlessness overtook him, the more his sight, which was usually good enough, began to blur; when he stumbled on large pebbles, he tottered and fell to his knees. He did not hurt himself badly, but what a business getting to his feet! It required as much effort from him as walking thirty metres.

At one point, an edgy burst of machine-gun fire not far away made him respond with a reflex which dated back forty years: he threw himself forward onto the ground. He puffed and panted so much getting to his feet that he swore he would not do that again, even if every machine-gun bullet in hell whistled about his ears.

A few steps further on he fell again, however.

This time it was not a stone he tripped over, but the hand of man lying face down. At first this detail left him indifferent. All he thought about was the effort it would take to get to his feet. Although he was only kneeling, he felt totally exhausted. He groaned at the very thought of setting about pulling himself up, his right hand on the handle of his stick, his left on his knee.

He took his time to catch his breath. When his vision cleared, he recognised the man lying prostrate across the lane. It was M. Lambert, the businessman, father of young David. Etienne did not need to see his face to know who it was. He had often seen him come and go in the company of Francis. The two of them spent hours talking together... 'Philippe. It's Philippe,' Francis would shout and would run to meet him. Sometimes, old Etienne would join them in conversation for a while, but it soon tired him out. Once he was tired, he just listened to the sound of their voices. He knew well the supreme happiness that two men find in discussing every thought that passes through their heads. At such moments, you feel impervious to attack and master of the world, twice over. Old Etienne could recognise those men who always carried a world around in their heads, a world they could offer to their friends. He did not forget their features, nor the way they moved, nor how they stared off into the distance. M. Lambert was one such man, no doubt about it. He seemed destined to live forever...

'But there he is, sprawled in the dust. My Francis' friend, young David's papa; little David who climbed up to fetch the best plums for me at the end of the branch. It's not possible.' With strength he did not think he had had for at least twenty years, Etienne turned M. Lambert over. Yes. It was him. It was his face which was lying in this reddy-brown puddle. The blood which oozed from his nose formed a muddy lump. The area around his kidneys had been shattered where the bloody holes were concentrated. And yet, there was still a smile on the dead man's lips.

Here was the horror. This known smile, this former smile which had survived, this smile was still there, at the same time as this *thing*.

This new thing, unknown, inhuman, unnameable, un-acceptable... Philippe now looked like he had abandoned himself, put himself in the hands of just anybody. Not that he cared what became of him, since he was no longer there. Looking at him closer, old Etienne found in that very smile something totally new, a sort of haughty scorn, contemptuous even. Not only was Philippe no longer there, he looked like *he had never been there*. This was more distressing than the blood, the blackened mud, the shredded guts.

Etienne could not catch his breath, for real this time. He could not manage to swallow his saliva – a thick liquid flowed down his throat. He told himself it was tears, but he could not help feeling it was thick and black, like coagulated blood. He no longer knew where he was. Here, in the open air, in the dry, in the light of a summer sun, he was drowning.

'NO!'

He was saying no to everything. He did not want to drown like this. He did not want to stay on his knees, crushed by a weight heavier than all the burdens he had carried in his long life. He did not want to recognise this man. He did not want to have known him, to have talked with him. He did not want this death. Death which he knew was inevitable and doubtless not far off – the death of his father, his mother, his brother, the very recent death – last year – of his younger sister's husband (that poor Paul who was always laughing, who was laughing when he was waxy and stiff in the light of the mortuary candles, who was still laughing in his memory) – such familiar death was a great sadness, for sure. He disapproved of it as a weakness. It's wrong to just give in to it. But he did not greatly fear it. He too would die since it was not something you had any choice about. He had made up his mind. He had said: 'We'll see later.' which was his way of indicating that he was at ease with it. Yesterday, or even this morning, he was ready. But now? No! It was over. He did not want to be left lying there in the stones. And ever since he had seen this face, even the softest bed would not be worthwhile.

Who knows, maybe he too would have that treacherous smile, that smile of absence. The new one, the unknown being, said: 'It's not true. You haven't seen me, haven't heard me. I've never been alive with you. The proof is in front of you. Take a close look. And dry your eyes. You should be laughing at this.' Perhaps Etienne was crying. He didn't know any more. But he was sure that he was not crying either for those he loved or for himself. He was crying without sorrow and for no reason, just as if he was about to drown in no water. The absence was just beginning, an inhuman absence, unexplained, unwanted, unimagined.

He was wondering whether to get to his feet when he heard the clock in the bell tower strike once. At the same moment, a dull, powerful explosion resounded, followed by a massive din of gunfire, furious screams, cries of agony and the roar of revving engines.

A hell of a shudder ran up old Etienne's spine. Was this it, the call to the Last Judgement?

A response was needed. Fine. Here I am. With a single movement he was on his feet and, swept along with a greater lightness than he had known in his youth, he stumbled at speed towards his village church. He did not want to die alone, stretched out across this road.

CHAPTER 13

It had taken Jean a long time to get Mme Leboutet's gas-fuelled car going, despite the frantic exhortations of the poor woman who kept repeating that her son and husband had been in town since morning. It had also taken him a long time to get to Verrièges-la-Montagne. He could scarcely drive this crazy mechanism which suddenly started grinding and jerking, the engine coughing and choking. In his haste he took the bends too sharply. In the middle of a wood he had to struggle for an hour to get a wheel out of the ditch. His shoulder was not hurting so much, but he had no strength on that side. It was as if the joints had been transformed into a large ball of burning oakum. Furthermore, with his fever he must have been running a temperature close to 104. It certainly felt like it.

When he reached Verrièges-la-Montagne, he did not have to explain anything. Two stocky lads took him at once to a little room in the café and introduced him to the headmaster of the secondary school, M. Labarre, with the words: 'This is Commandant Raphael.'

M. Labarre, in shirt sleeves and wearing solid army boots. seemed much bigger, much more forceful, than the deferential man that Jean had seen before. He had already been briefed. Talking to the six or eight grave and silent men around him, he quickly explained he had just found out that Verrièges-la-Plaine was totally surrounded and under guard.

'I also wanted to say…' Jean stammered. 'I thought the *maquis* were here. I didn't say anything, down there, I wanted to warn you first.'

M. Labarre simply put a hand on his shoulder. Instead of replying, he got angry that nobody had poured him a drink yet.

The pharmacist arrived and apologised for failing to find the doctor. He felt Jean's shoulder for quite a while. By way of explanation, he talked about torn ligaments and a hairline fracture at the top of the humerus. Jean was not listening to him and insisted again that they had to attack the Germans immediately.

'Yes, yes. It's first class, what you've done,' repeated M. Labarre, like he was congratulating a child. 'Obviously it would have been better if you'd come here immediately, rather than waiting several hours. Of course, you weren't to know that. Anybody would have…'

Jean stopped hearing him. His vision suddenly became blurred and he felt himself slipping into a deep sleep.

When his hearing returned, he kept his eyes shut for a moment.

'There's nothing more we can do,' M. Labarre was telling his men. 'Even if it wasn't too late, we don't have enough weapons, nor enough available personnel.'

Jean got to his feet and protested vehemently. He tried to shout, to get angry. In his head, the words speedily lined up, but it seemed to him that very few emerged from his lips.

186

M. Labarre's expression, so compassionate, so full of deep sadness, weighed on him. He hated this man, this M. Labarre, for his calmness. Above all, he wondered why he was repeating more and more slowly what he had already said, like some machine out of control and without moving his lips: 'There's nothing more we can do.'

'But you're not going to leave Verrièges-la-Plaine in German hands. You've got to… got to…'

Again, there was nothing but a black hole.

M. Labarre lifted his spirits, reassured him and told him he would do the impossible. His slow, warm voice was comforting. He forced Jean to take two aspirins. He gave him a revolver and sat him down carefully in the seat next to him, in a proper car this time, not a piece of junk like Mme. Leboutet's old Celta.

Come to think of it, who's taking care of the Celta? M. Labarre assured him that one of his men who knew Leboutet was following some way behind with the gas-car.

In the time it took to close his eyes and open them again, Jean found himself back home in the farmyard. This was not at all what he had in mind. He wanted to take part in the fighting, help liberate the village. M. Labarre's voice became even more persuasive.

'Come on, old chap. You've got a fever. You can scarcely stand up. When I said there was nothing to be done, I was talking about you. In your state there's nothing more you can do. We need to keep you calm, while you wait for a doctor. I'll send one as soon as possible. You heard the pharmacist: a fracture to the top of your humerus. No doubt about it. You can't mess around with that. Come on. Be reasonable.'

Jean agreed to get out of the car, but he refused to go to bed. Was M. Labarre mad, worrying about his little scratch when the others, down there, were in agony?

M. Labarre pushed him the other side of the gate which he shut carefully behind him. Then Jean realised, unsurprisingly, that he could no longer walk straight. He had difficulty steering a stumbling course towards a pile of straw mattresses next to a barn, onto which he collapsed.

PART 4

CHAPTER 1

Operation annihilation. It was a question of being methodical. Method. Method, above all else. First and foremost, immobilise every living, moving being, riddle them with bullets, pin them to the ground, walk over them, make a mess of them.

The first explosion, so violent that the ground shook, had not killed anyone. It was just a signal; the signal which at last announced permission to murder. More than permission – duty. Stunned by the heat, semi-paralysed by a long period of indecision, by the old routine of 'correction', the killers had to react very fast, with unbridled frenzy. Everywhere and at once, rifles cracked, hand grenades boomed, machine guns crackled. Bullets ripped through thickets and foliage, tore the bark off trees, split the stones on the road, smashed the plaster on the front of houses, shattered the granite of porches, scattered lumps of slate and tile across the roofs. From here on, it was no longer a question of checking identity papers, of making sure that this old man, this woman, this youth had a legal and authentic right to the status of martyr. All that was human was there to die. Lorry drivers who were stopped at the first roadblock and who had no idea what was going on, having come from a distant town in the south, were summarily machine gunned then meticulously finished off with a bullet to the back of the neck. A tram had stopped at the entrance to the town and the employees were insisting on being allowed in. When the signal came, the Germans interrupted the discussion by taking out their revolvers and firing at point blank range. Then the machine gunners smashed the windows of the tram. The ferocious howls of the murderers drowned the terrified cries of the passengers who tried to flee or take cover under the seats. The mopping up was done with a hand grenade and finally the vehicle was set on fire.

Certain farmworkers had carried on working, thinking this would affirm their blameless innocence, and also believing vaguely that they could ward off the evil eye or intimidate the murderous Beast. Those who were well within range were killed immediately. Others were hunted down by armoured vehicles or motorcyclists and fell here and there, among the furrows, in the deep lanes, across the fences and green hedges. A hundred metres from Verrièges, some builders continued to raise the roof timber of a house. It was fun for these warriors, who had once seen themselves as liberators, to pick them off like pigeons. The wounded who were still moaning were reduced to silence by two grenades which turned the future home into a huge blaze.

Those inhabitants of Verrièges – elderly invalids, the sick, the wounded who could not drag themselves to the assembly point – were still in their houses. There were also some recalcitrant individuals hidden in attics, secret spots, cellars. The mopping up teams swarmed up the staircases, fired on anything that moved, and anyone which the bullets had spared were beaten to death with rifle butts or kicked to death. Certain SS, maddened by the carnage, plunged their knives into anything that gave any semblance of life – the wounded, animals or corpses. Blood spurted everywhere, trickling down the stone staircases, spattering the walls and doors.

All necessary steps had to be taken. The order was to annihilate, to leave no witnesses. Kill everything that could speak, that could see. A glimpse would be enough to constitute a witness perhaps. Who knows if the gaze of an animal might not retain the reflection of a previously unknown, unimaginable horror which would in itself be an accusation?

The sight of blood sent the SS into a panic. The blood of defenceless victims is not the same as the blood of enemies. It smells of shame and of the irredeemable which obliterates a man's clarity of thought quicker than the most powerful alcohol. These killers were no longer men. They had started out as soldiers; now they were carrying on as executioners.

After the actions they had just carried out, they understood they would never encounter any mercy, or pity, or friendship, or any human feeling. So they forbade themselves any feeling of pity; they knew that the only possible aftermath of murder is another murder, then another, and so on to infinity.

They killed everywhere, forcing themselves to be methodical, since that was the order. But none could resist for long the vertigo of blood.

These small-scale operations were just a prelude to the wholesale carnage which had been prepared for in the barns and garages. The doors had been shut; this part of the trap was working without a hitch. The victims gathered in there could wait a bit longer. But it was important not to give any runaways the slightest chance.

CHAPTER 2

Robert Leboutet did not want to leave Melanie in her attic, alone and in labour. He had managed to sneak as far as old man Labaille's house. It was a large building where three families rented a floor each. Robert lurked in the cellar.

When the noise of footsteps and numerous voices in the street had died away, he emerged from his hiding place and risked taking the stairs. Immediately he heard Mélanie's screams, which both terrified and reassured him. 'If it's already started, that means they won't take her away at least.'

The creaking of boots on the stairs, on several occasions, forced him to hide again. All the doors were still open. At the first sign of danger, Robert went into the kitchen and slipped under a chest. Outside the only sound he heard were two or three motorbikes going back and forth between the various exits from the village. When everything was calm in the house, he crept carefully back upstairs. Mélanie's cries had reached an alarming crescendo. Unfortunately, they could be heard in the street. Each time, one of the Germans who were patrolling the streets sprinted up the stairs to find out what was going on. Often, he did not hang around, but sometimes he did.

Still, Robert managed to reach the attic. At that moment, Mélanie was not crying out so loudly. She was groaning from deep in her throat, her head lolling back and forth. The look she gave Robert seemed to him heart-wrenchingly gentle.

'It's over,' she said. 'You see. It's over. I'm hardly in pain any more.'

'But,' Robert cried frantically. 'We have to take the child, wash it… I don't know. We've got to do something.'

'Yes,' a pale, sweet voice replied. 'Yes, dear little Robert. But I… I don't have the strength,'

Robert lifted the bed cover and recoiled, daunted. That blood, all that blood… what should we do, Lord, what should we do? This little lump of flesh wasn't moving… perhaps the child was dead. Robert took hold of it, lifted it up and placed it quickly on the sheet.

He was not afraid. Actually, he wanted to laugh. Only, something had to be done… what had he been told? The cord… yes, there was a cord that had to be cut and tied off. But where was this cord? Where was it to be cut? How? And what with…?

He asked Mélanie if she had any scissors. She smiled at him, a smile full of tenderness, and took his hand.

'Have you seen it? It's ours. Our little one.'

At that moment, the noise of boots resounded on the stairs again. A heavy noise this time. There must have been at least four or five *krauts*.

'It's them,' he said. 'I have to hide. I'll be back when they've gone.'

In a glance he saw that neither Mélanie's cramped refuge nor the adjacent attic offered him anywhere to hide. He went down a floor and hid as before in a corner obscured by a large yellow wardrobe.

From the racket that the men in boots were making, he realised that this time they were beginning to ransack the place. Upended furniture fell apart with a crash, doors flew off in pieces, whole piles of crockery smashed. Bastards! They're taking the silverware and valuables and destroying the rest for the pleasure of it. But, hang on… the area round this wardrobe was going to get very dangerous. Robert remembered on the floor below in a lumber room there was a load of broken old furniture. Maybe they wouldn't want to rummage around in there. He quickly made his way down. If one of the Germans had looked up, Robert would have been caught. In the lumber room he hesitated between a wardrobe that only had one door and the empty casing of a tall country grandfather clock. He decided on the clock. It was rickety and fell backwards as soon as he touched it. He caught it before it hit the floor, placed it gently down and slipped inside.

The Germans came in. Not content with kicking the wardrobes and chests to smithereens, they fired off several bursts of machine-gun fire into the room. They didn't bother with the grandfather clock. Robert had made a lucky choice.

Face down on the floor, his nose in the dust which smelt of ratty mould, he had plenty of time to congratulate himself on his good fortune. After all, he was still alive. He was alive and he had a child. The essential thing was safe. The Germans could pillage and ransack the houses, they wouldn't dream of hurting a new-born baby.

One of the Germans was climbing the stairs talking loudly. With his nostrils twitching, Robert was fighting a terrible urge to sneeze.

On the floor above – where Mélanie was – the machine guns crackled again. Robert took advantage of this to let out a sneeze, and relieved, he wondered what those imbeciles could be blasting away at through the skylights. Then he heard two shots, on their own, sharp; two shots from a revolver for sure.

Two shots?… Robert threw off the clock casing with no regard for the noise and rushed for the door. He tripped over an overturned bench and fell. The door to the lumber room had been shut and it was due to this that he did not get killed: by the time he got it open and reached the stairs, the Germans were on their way out, crashing around on the floor below. Robert rushed up to the attic.

He did not have the strength to cry out. He fell to his knees in the middle of the narrow attic space, among the grains of milled wheat, among the drops of blood which had spattered the whole room. He dared not look on what had been his wife and child. He put his fists to his eyes to stop them seeing, to bury them in his head, to crush the very memory of the horrific vision.

Was such a thing possible? He had loved and he had had a child. One moment he had known a father's pride, so innocent and so stupid he wanted to laugh. And now…

No! There were no monsters, not in this day and age. He had been told that, many times. He wasn't going to start believing in ogres, not at his age. Don't open your eyes. Not that. If he opened them, he'd go mad. There. That's it. The truth of it: he was mad. Him, not the world. The whole world couldn't go mad. If he was mad, nothing had any importance. He opened his eyes and the proof was there, in front of him.

Robert felt that he was about to howl. But a thick smoke enveloped him and made him cough, stopping up the howl in his throat.

The house was burning. Robert guessed this rather than understood it. He did not want to understand anything, and he no longer clung on to life. With indifference, and also with composure, the sleepwalker's composure, he took the necessary steps to escape.

He left the attic without regret. On the contrary. With relief. Because he did not believe, he could not believe, that the only glorious moment of his youth, this great shaft of light that had passed through him, could have ended like this. Rushing down the stairs where the fire was already beginning to roar, he was moving beyond the only Mélanie he knew – that of his memory; laughing, passionate, a great mane of hair and defiance in her eyes. With one hand over his mouth, he got to the first floor, sticking close to the wall, dodging the tongues of flame that the half-destroyed banister shot towards him. The cage of the staircase below him glowed red and roared like the mouth of an oven. But calm and detached, Robert felt invulnerable. He crossed the kitchen where he had taken refuge at the outset and opened the window. Standing on the ledge he put his heels together, moved forward deliberately, like in a gymnastics lesson, and jumped into a freshly dug bed.

Unscathed, he bounced like a ball and in three strides reached the neglected fence where he disappeared among the tall growth of nettles, thistles and large-leafed burdock.

CHAPTER 3

The Germans were searching everywhere: in the cellars, the sheds, the bushes, the hedges. When they found nothing, they fired off a burst from their machine guns at random. However there were some nooks and crannies which escaped their attention, and these hid human beings, cowering, hunted like murderers, like wild beasts.

Armand Graetz, cousin of young Daniel whom Jean Bricaud had met on his first attempt to get into Verrièges, had managed, despite a leg in plaster – he had broken it the previous Sunday falling out of a tree – to heave himself up on top of a wide wall covered with a thick growth of ivy which hid him.

His cousin, Daniel, had managed to persuade Dr Joly's three sons who lived in the big house next to his, to disobey the order to assemble. Their parents were away: the doctor having been called out to an emergency – a difficult birth, twenty-five kilometres off – and their mother was visiting her family. The youngest, Pierre, decided to copy Daniel and get the hell out. The other two Joly brothers found it easier to hide at the back of a storeroom stuffed with a considerable jumble of old furniture, rusted washing tubs and other clutter.

A German found the brothers and they were gunned down against the wall where Armand Graetz was hiding. He saw them collapse, with blood running from their nose and their fists clenched. The two of them were the best of comrades and the older one had won an honourable mention for a Greek translation in the *Concours Général*.

Several times, young David Lambert had heard the bullets shredding the leaves above his head. But he had also known how to take advantage of the movement of the soldiers

He got through hedges by crawling on his belly, not trying to break through them. His face and hands were scratched and he left torn strips of shirt everywhere, but he got through. Just as he got to the houses on the outskirts of the village – here he was separated from the woods by a stretch of thick meadows which bordered the stream – he met Albert Mazérat, the young garage owner, and his old mechanic, Pierre Duprat. The two men had gone to ground in a patch of maize which had been heavily machine gunned. Albert had emerged unscathed. Old Duprat had a bullet in his thigh. He was bleeding profusely and never stopped moaning; his leg was getting heavier and heavier, and he was feeling very weak.

David helped Albert support him, or rather drag him, because while they slipped from garden to garden, along the walls, or across the raised beds of beans, cabbages and peas, they rarely risked moving other than on all fours.

When they got to the meadows of tall, uncut grass that ran alongside the river, Albert realised that they could not carry on dragging the wounded man. They would be too visible on all fours. They had to crawl along the ground, and Pierre was in no fit state.

'Leave me,' said the old man. 'It's no more risky for me here than anywhere else. I don't want to go on.'

He turned and lay on his back. His eyes, very blue and surprisingly childlike in a face which was lined and tanned like an old sea dog, were fixed on the sky. His beard covered most of his face with flecks of white as he had not shaved since the day before yesterday, Sunday. The pain and loss of blood had sapped all his inner resources. He was moaning without realising it. He was slipping away.

'Don't talk shit, Pierre,' Albert growled. 'You know very well; I'm not leaving you here like this. Nobody can be seen from this side. Too bad if we can't cross the meadows. We'll go by the sunken road, keeping well down.'

The glow had totally disappeared from old Duprat's eyes.

'You're talking nonsense,' he murmured. 'You won't get away with it, dragging me. We'll be spotted and gunned down ten times. Go on. I'm the one who got you here. I don't want anything to happen to you on my account.'

'Shut up!' he said. 'Let me sort it out. I saw a wheelbarrow in front of Grangeaud's barn when we went past. We'll put you in it and I'll push you to the woods in no time.'

Old Duprat shook his head, but Albert had already gone.

David helped him load the old man in; in this quiet corner, everything seemed easy to the point of being vaguely unreal. He was ready to follow the wheelbarrow along the lane. Albert grabbed his shoulder and shook him hard.

'Hey you! Don't be crazy, kid. It's enough that I'm taking the risk. Off you go, quick. Slip through the grass like an Indian. Know what I mean, eh?'

He gave a wink. Before, David had been suspicious of Albert with his shifty little eyes and the way he seemed to be underhand. Now he felt great tenderness towards him, and he even found his round, freckly face very handsome.

He wanted to go through the meadows, for sure, but to begin with he kept the other side of the sunken lane to accompany his great hero, Albert the Mechanic, at least as far as the stream. The thickish alder hedge blocked his view of the barrow which he followed just by the squeaking of its rusty wheel. He went ahead to position himself at a gap he knew, one which was no doubt used by game and by hunting dogs.

And there, just as he put his face to the opening, David saw the back of the kraut...

He ought to have called out to Albert to warn him, but he had no time.

The German had already left his hiding place and was firing. The squeaking of the wheel stopped amid a chaos of gasps and a clatter of splintered wood.

David did not want to see any more. He tried to turn away, but he could not. The wheelbarrow in one last surge had come up against the hedge. It had not even tipped over. It stood upright, well-behaved, its two smooth handles held out to whoever might wish to take hold of them. And on top, chest to chest, but their arms spread wide and hanging outside the barrow, lay Albert and old Duprat. Albert's round, jovial face was in profile, his cheekbone still raised in a smile. He seemed as jolly as before. It made no sense. It was horrible. How could he be happy, while poor old Duprat was directing that accusing gaze to the heavens – that justly indignant gaze in his deep blue eyes? It seemed impossible that these very eyes, gentle to

201

the point of weakness not five minutes ago, were now there, staring and bulging, filled with such powerful denunciation and curse. The old man's mouth amid the whitened stubble of his beard offered up words that were too terrible for human ears, but which certainly echoed throughout the heavens and would carry on echoing to the end of time. To the End of Time…

David had heard that you had to close the eyes of the dead, but the very idea of touching that oddly visionary face made him shudder. What did he see, this old man who was usually so placid, to have transformed so quickly and so completely into another?

David, who felt no emotion when he had heard the burst of machine-gun fire and the hateful whine of the bullets, now felt fear: fear of the pain that wounds would cause, fear of bleeding, fear of being maimed, fear of everything.

Turning back, he crawled along by the stream. Gunfire clattered at the top of the lane, up where they had loaded the old man into the wheelbarrow, and it seemed to David that he was the target. He moved as quickly as possible all the time flat to the ground. His back tingled. In all the places he feared being hit, he felt pain in advance.

When shooting broke out from the edge of the wood, David slid into the stream by the stump of an alder, with just his nose and mouth above the water to breathe. He only emerged from the water when he had found a deep, dried out gully which allowed him to make it into the wood without being seen.

No sooner was he under cover than he began trembling so violently that his teeth were chattering. At the same time his sight became blurred, and he had to lie on the ground. Although he understood that he was more or less out of danger, he remained overcome by the certainty that he had just experienced a total and irremediable disaster.

He did not want to go on living. He no longer wanted to see the light of day. He buried his face ferociously in the moss which crackled like thick velvet. No, he no longer wanted to be in a world which had killed his father, which had killed Fernand, which had killed Albert and the old man with the sky-blue eyes. He would not move, he would await his end here, in the innocence of the leaves that rustled in the breeze.

Jean:

It's true. I must've had one hell of a fever.

I can't even go with Commandant Raphael. He doesn't trust me, not surprisingly.

'You're not well. You've got a fever. We'll take you home, you can lie down and wait for the doctor.'

So, I stood up and for a while, I kept going enough that he gave me a pistol. I put it in my pocket. It's still there. It's a piece of work. It wouldn't take long for it to break through the lining. I don't know if it's English or German written on it, but the mechanism is simple. And then in the car, when old Lasserre said: 'Understood, Commandant Raphael.' I couldn't help myself. I started laughing my arse off.

I knew M. Labarre, the head of the secondary school too well to think that anybody could call him 'commandant'. And on top of that – Raphael? Raphael's the painter who was keen on angels and Madonnas. And there's the other Raphael – the messenger, the driver...

Maybe my explanations bored them. I can't even remember what they were saying. I don't even know how I got here, next to a pile of straw mattresses. I've missed something. Maybe I fell asleep.

I've got a fever.

They were right. I'd have been useless. I can hardly stand up. I'm not steady on my feet, but it's better when I walk. I can even walk quite well. Ma's right: if you're feeling a bit under the weather, just have a walk. That'll sort it out.

Run! I should run. I can't leave my mother there, nor my father, or my wife. They're all there. All of them. From the oldest to the youngest. What have I done to deserve this? Who picked me out to be punished like this?

In the car, I asked: 'You don't think anything serious is going to happen to them, Monsieur Labarre?'

'How should I know. There's no obvious reason to do them any harm, since the search won't turn up anything'.

There was no mistaking the expression he'd taken on: he was trying to prepare me. It's the same expression people take on at a funeral. They told me stories with exactly the same look on their face that those false witnesses had the day my grandmother died. I was only eleven, but it's young enough to die; I felt myself die with my grandmother on a night filled with the howling of dogs, and I've never fully come back to life. And again, in the same way, when poor Marcellin, my schoolmate, my only friend, died from meningitis.

There's nothing more we can do.

No. He didn't mean that. He just wore that expression because of the others, to give himself authority. It's not possible.

They're men after all, those others, the Boches. They can't take it out on the innocent.

I don't know what I'm saying. I've got a raging fever. It's massive. There's nothing else. It's the fever that makes me hear this bang... bang... banging. Echoing in my head, hollow like an old barrel. Or else they've set off on a march, with drums beating, crashing down on us, on the colour of the sky, on the light of day. Everything's undermined. Everything'll sink. But no. It's bombs falling and exploding. No. I'm sure they're not bombing Verrièges. They can't be. They wouldn't dare.

There's nothing more we can do... not enough weapons.

But yes, there is. There's always something that can be done, Monsieur Labarre, even if you're not an angel, or a commandant. If there's nothing to be done, I wouldn't be here any more. I'd be dead. Dead, yes, quite dead. Already dead twice, a long time ago. Dead five times again today. Ah! You ask why 'five'? The number surprises you. Ah, well, so let me make this clear... you suppose I'm just babbling. The delirium, the fever, no? Fever, yes. As for that, I have a fever. But I'm not delirious. I've never seen things so clearly. All the things I usually see, and more besides. Follow me closely, Monsieur Labarre, and don't take yourself too much for an angel – your cheeks are too flat and you've forgotten to shave. Follow me closely. I'm counting on my fingers. At Verrièges they have shut in my mother. That makes one. Secondly, there's also my boy, Gaston, who followed your night manoeuvres all last year, Monsieur Labarre. My wife, Annie. That makes three. And my father. Yes. Him. Old Etienne, ninety-three-years-old, who had to go and see as well, and they rounded him up with the rest. That makes a good round four. And the fifth, he's the one you know best: my brother Francis who studied in Paris, like you.

If I'd said that to him maybe he'd have taken me along, not dumped me here like a parcel.

The old barn's there in front of me, under its roof gnawed at by honey-coloured moss. The straw sleeps, sheltered, next to Dollé, the old threshing machine. An incredible confidence breathes between these clay and granite walls. This is the land of confident stones; stones have become accustomed to lending their impassive support to the comings and goings of generations of humans. They grow grey peacefully along the roadside, among the stretches of heather and gorse, in the walls of the low, solid houses. The stones of this land can't believe that things collapse.

Nothing to be done... not a thing

I can't shake off this fever. I don't even want to try. I threw the packet of aspirin in the dirt. I drank some water. I drank three big glasses, I would've drunk more, I'm thirsty, it feels like I've got a mouth full of sand. Sand and ash.

Not a thing

Hey! I recognise that rhythm: tee-tum... tee-tum... tee-tum... it's the train. The train's carrying me off. I've just landed face down in the dust of the road, left two teeth there. I imagine my teeth, crushed into the road, with blood on them, and the train carrying me off: tee-tum… tee-tum… tee-tum…

'It's a nasty accident. We need to take him to a doctor. Can we use your car, Monsieur?'

'No, you can see, here, the wheel's completely bent. He rode straight into me. These motorcyclists are an absolute menace. Come on, you have a train in half an hour. Get a move on.'

Tee-tum… tee-tum… not a thing… not a thing…

They pissed me off, down there, with the way they squeezed my shoulder. It hurt so much I could've howled. But I didn't have time to howl, I didn't let myself.

'That's a bit of a bugger, you know, the thing with your shoulder. There's some blood loss somewhere. Your whole arm is going purplish.'

He was the new pharmacist, this one. He's quite young but he has the look of a squashed rat. I've never seen a squashed rat's face. I don't know what I'm talking about any more. The fever… "You've got a temperature" They bug me with their fever. Me, I've got plenty of time now to deal with my fever.

No!

I threw his aspirin in the dirt. I don't want to take care of my fever. I don't want to sleep. Certainly not sleep. I'll never sleep never again, I swear. I'll croak, with my eyes wide open, defying sleep. I won't sleep dead: five times dead.

My dogs run away when I go past. Just now one of them was howling. What do the dogs understand? Do they see further than me? They can certainly hear a hunting whistle when I hear nothing at all. What if they could also see into the future, know what's going to happen. I'll go. I'll go and ask them… Ah! Poor creatures, they wouldn't reply. I've already given them a good beating, just now, like a madman. They spoke to me in their own way, however, and I couldn't understand them.

Nothing to be done... nothing more to be done...

Ah well, too bad! I'm going there anyway. I'm going to talk to my dogs. It's mad. But I really want to be mad. It's easier to be mad than to bear all this. There! I'm mad. I want to talk to my dogs. I can talk like the dogs, with all my strength, like this, for a long time.

'Oooooooooooh...!'

Enough. I mustn't cry out. I need to hold it together. But that kept going all on its own, as if I had snapped the brake cable... I stop, but with a lot of effort. If I just let myself go, I'd howl endlessly 'til I was blue in the face. It's the only natural way of saying what I feel. It's my way of being true. The more I howl the more frightened I become. It's the horror, the bottomless pit of darkness.

It's good to howl when there's nothing else to say. But I mustn't. I feel too much like a dog. I'm getting close to the abyss. I could become a dog for good. And that, that's proof it has to stop. Germans or no Germans, men are still men. They won't allow that.

CHAPTER 4

For the crowd of men shut in, the torture of waiting did not let up.

The doors to the barns, sheds and garages had been shut, then opened again. When they were re-opened many pretended to believe they were being released. "There you go. It's over. I told you; there was no danger since we haven't done anything." And yet, not one of them moved. They had understood. Ever since they had noticed the way the two officers directing operations looked at them – one with a troubled expression, the other with an all-too clear expression – *they knew*.

A dark foreboding, a tradition of misfortune, counteracted any optimistic reasoning. They were on the side of the victim, on the side where catastrophes exist, but not miracles. This was obvious above all to the old and the not-so-young who were already satisfied that there was only one promise that the world kept with absolute certainty: that of death.

As for the very young, it was enough that they had picked up the rumours currently circulating in the world. Every day, without paying a great deal of attention, they could hear bombs drop, walls crumble, bullets bury themselves in chests, or the sound of a shell burst on paving stones. The music was the same from one end of the world to the other: it was explained to them that war was not the only thing that killed – there were criminals, thunder, the clumsy, floods, madmen, illness, wild animals, not to mention the usual games of time and chance. An accident was always on the cards. Always and everywhere. Oh yes! For sure. But that in no way lessened the rage at suddenly finding themselves in a rat trap. "I'm the one caught in this trap", growled a furious voice inside Gaston Bricaud. "Me, a seventeen-year-old. Me, out of everyone, here and now. Me, who's never done anything, never been for anyone or against them. Me who, ladies and gentlemen, would run to the ends of the earth to avoid getting caught up in the squabbling of old fools. Me who, in my little corner, would very much like to be treated like the last man on earth – yes, yes, I know you're not happy about that: well, too bad! To hell with you and your morals. All I ask is to be forgotten, to have no part in your huge, imbecilic and macabre farce, in your mad dogfight, in your game for arseholes!"

An unusually thick sweat flowed down his forehead and trickled along his nose. He could not take his eyes off one of the Germans who was guarding the door, the one with little piggy eyes.

'It'd be so quick,' he had said to his friend Jef. 'To stick my thumbnails in his eyes. I bet I've got time to blind him before the other big sack of lard shot me.'

Jef had grabbed him by one arm and Francis grabbed his other. 'If you get the chance…'

Imbeciles, the pair of them! He couldn't put up with them any longer. He stared down at the earth floor of the barn. Like that, at least, he could no longer see the eyes of the others, eyes filled with anxiety and tenderness, their feverish eyes, their unbearably over-affectionate eyes, loved too much, regretted too much.

Jef's voice, however, was still buzzing in his ears. And then there was Jef's father, old François – dark-skinned, dark-haired, usually so sombre and taciturn – who was getting all emotional evoking the days when Jef and Gaston were first equal at school – Jef was top in maths and Gaston in French. Get lost, old man! A disgust close to hatred twisted Gaston's mouth. How he now resented the importance he himself had attached to the congratulations he received from Father Valade, and to his report cards full of praise. He could not help but see that image of his father Jean's tanned face glowing as he read these reports, as if he had caught the sun from inside. He resented having had this long childhood from which he had still not properly detached himself. But at least he refused to get emotional. Nothing was worth that. Not even the memory of kisses from Régine Mazaud who had gone to a lot of trouble to escape the prying eyes of her father. (Him, old potbelly, dirty sod. He used to say; everything for me and nothing for anybody else…) Gaston had kissed Régine so hard the previous day that her upper lip, which she would bite, had swollen up and was painful. Régine! He made fun of her little mannerisms. To begin with she was never what he expected her to be. And then, she was daft to let herself be called Gigi. Another of her father's doings. Gigi! What a stupid idea… no. Régine didn't count for much. She still hadn't said yes enough.

Everything had happened *before* the beginning, before *his* beginning. The chaos before the creation. The beginning had remained an eternal tomorrow. He would have got there, for sure, but he hadn't yet. To die today was to die dispossessed, stripped of everything, closing his eyes on the void, on eternal solitude. Tomorrow! He demanded a tomorrow, hope, the sun rising again, again and again, and so on to infinity.

Faced with the void, he was exasperated listening to the others, the old men, listing their rights and enumerating their goods. And those who, like Francis, focused silently on their riches, seemed to him the most distant, the most foreign… in the end his excessive fury and rejection formed a red mist in front of his eyes which acted as a form of protection.

CHAPTER 5

There were increasing numbers of those who, having reached the very final stage, were entering into silent dialogue. They were conversing with distraught vehemence. The imaginary words came with the speed of lightning and had the beneficial power of exhausting body and soul, the horrors of memory and the horror of the present moment all at the same time. In this way, the condemned innocents attempted to soar beyond nothingness and to exorcise it.

Everywhere, deep inside the barns, through the dust long grown cold which irritated the nostrils, drifted the ghosts of dead summers. In the garages stinking of petrol and sludgy grease, among the mist of lime powder and the bitter stench from the bottom of barrels, a shadow was born and began to thicken, becoming more and more solemn.

There were some who, to reassure themselves, said: 'Well, the sun's gone in. We'll have a storm before long.' But this explanation failed to provide any satisfaction. They knew that this universal darkening was no more natural than the dull explosion heard just now, which could have been just a clap of thunder, but which had unleashed the shooting in the village.

This ferocious crackle, the rasping of metal, these rumbles were the announcement of their fate.

The haunted shadow of a faint and eerie buzzing of flies made foreheads glisten with sweat and made expressions strangely vivid – vivid like flames beleaguered by wind and night.

The weight of life, our life, my life can still be felt in my muscles, still felt on my forehead, still felt in the world. It can't suddenly stop. It can't disappear. It's an over-thick tangle of chords and vibrations. A limitless, possibly endless tangle. I've still got so many things on the go. Me, I've got two hectares to clear… me, I've got planting to finish off… the wing of a building under construction… my loan is due next month… my son should be coming back from the *maquis*… the October session of the *baccalauréat*… the tyres that were promised for the car… grandpa's teeth that need seeing to… the material at the dressmaker's… tiles for the attic… corrugated iron for the barn…

Everyone had unfinished business.

There was the man who, with no intention of making himself heard, was talking in a rusty, whistling voice which rolled the words in reddish gravel, and kept repeating to himself that his son had to know that he hadn't kicked him out because he didn't love him, but because he loved him as he should love him, for his own good. 'It can't be that I won't get to tell him one day, straight to his face so that he doesn't forget it. It's not possible. I don't want him thinking I was angry with him for real, for always. But this can't be done.'

There was the man who was having second thoughts about being a police sergeant, and who hadn't been able to grab hold of that kid the other evening who called him an arse-kisser and a sell-out. He wouldn't feel at ease until he held him at arm's length and looked him straight in the eye: 'I'll tell him, to his face. That little mongrel thinks I want to give him a beating. But it's not that, not at all. He has to understand. I won't let him go until he says, "Ok, Louis. It's sorted now. I get it." I was saying again to my old lady this morning when I got up: If I re-enlisted at that time, it's because I had no choice. That's all there is to it. And once I'd set off, I couldn't turn back. As for being an arse-kisser, not on your life! And once my pension turns up, I'm coming back here. As I promised my old lady. My word is my bond. I said it, and it's true. With me, it's straightforward.'

Then there was Tabaret who after forty years, whenever he went out, still wore his father's best suit. However, Old man Tabaret, aka 'Beardy', on his death bed had expressly asked to be buried in it. Tabaret junior, or *Fine-tête* as he was known, had promised him this, shedding real tears. Then, no sooner had the old man's eyes been closed by his own trembling hands, than he started quibbling. 'He can't see me any more, as sure as I'm standing here. He's not to know how he's dressed. He'll never know. Besides, before he kicked the bucket, before he'd gone back to his second childhood, repeating himself, and seeing things, he'd given it to me, he'd given me his wedding suit. And that's the voice of reason. If he's somewhere, with all his faculties and his beard well groomed, he'll tell me, like he used to tell me when he walked upright: "*Fine-tête*, I really like your head, let them say what they like. You did what you had to." That very day, he had put on the hard-wearing serge suit to go and pick up his ration book and monthly margarine.'

But the discomfort which had always unsettled him, did so a little more than usual, he was sure. He said to himself: It's this stifling heat. Only, the heat would not have given him this strange tingling down his spine… so he justified himself, remembering all his acts of generosity: the hot wine he brought up to the old man, and the onion soup, and the four doctor's visits (each as useless at the next). Besides, he fed his summer workers well; he'd be ruined if he carried on like that. Meat or salt beef several times a week, not to mention omelettes, sometimes even ham; and not least of all, bread, as much as they wanted, good bread, as good as you get in town.

Then there was the miller who maintained that he shouldn't be feeling bad about having refused – that very morning, after so many other mornings – half a bushel of wheat to the old woman with the veil who could no longer survive on the income from her devalued annuities. I give to the ones I know. I can't give to everybody. The farmers are so suspicious these days: everything has to be weighed and weighed again. Of course, I have to skimp a little, otherwise I might as well close the mill down. And there's no way of telling them all, not one of them understands the niceties of the trade. In my soul and in my conscience, I do my best. There. I've said it. In my soul and conscience. Those who don't want me to make my living don't deserve to be provided for. I slice off just the right amount, without skinning them. If I was a bad man, they'd deserve to have some of their skin taken off as well. Also, the more that's taken from them, the nicer I find them. So, it's not all loss on their part.

And there was the mechanic who fixed a car by blowing twice into the fuel jet but produced quite a hefty bill even so.

He didn't do it in a spirit of malevolence, it was just that he had to reckon with his wife and daughter who bought their clothes at a dressmaker in the city. He didn't dare upset either of them because of the three affairs he had allowed himself with guests at the Hotel Farebout. So, with his *patronne* living the high life, he made up for it as best he could. That's life. But he only levied his tribute on those who could afford it, word of honour. In the same way, he only urged his song of seduction on those women who really enjoyed the singing. After all, it's not my fault if the boss-lady was born with no ear for music. And what's more, she was too well brought up for me to be able to judge her before taking the plunge. And then as his mate the carpenter carefully explained to him, you shouldn't take too literally the precept they taught you in catechism lessons: 'Do unto others as you would have them do unto you.' Without this negative turn of phrase, everything would become much better: act, act first, give pleasure to others and thereby give yourself pleasure. Quite right! He's a 'Master Cabinetmaker', despite his poor eyesight and flat feet. What's the point of concerning yourself with the literal meaning when it was the spirit of the thing that mattered? the priest himself had declared. Attend to the spirit and you'll be fine.

Many would have wanted to protest their innocence. Cry out like children 'I'm not the one'. They hadn't hidden any weapons, they hadn't tried to fire at the Germans, they hadn't wanted the war, they'd stayed as far away as possible from any conceivable combat. The pacifists, the non-violent, the humble, the real sheep... yet, at the same time, anger gripped them and they denied their innocence. 'Ah, the bastards!' said gentle Paul Arlaud who had been repatriated from Germany only a few months previously. 'They'll have got me no matter what. The only consolation I have is that, if I'd had the chance, I wouldn't have missed them either. I pissed them off too. In the *stalag* we were only entitled to two blankets. I had five. And when I was at the farm afterwards, the mother and daughter there certainly got what they were entitled to! But even making cuckolds of them wasn't enough. They should have kept their hands off: scorched earth, before and after them. Not that they should think they frightened us. Not on your life! They're far too stupid for that. There's nothing as stupid as a Nazi, I tell you. And even if they kill me, that won't stop me from being right.' Many shared his opinion. They were the ones who were not too afraid. Even if they were sweating abnormally and every now and then had to go and piss in a corner, this fear was physiological and they knew it was nothing to feel ashamed of.

But there were those whom anxiety pushed much further, into the realms of primordial terror. And they could not, did not want to believe that they were being punished like this, for no reason. Their whole being cried out for confession, they called for absolution. Each action they brought to mind seemed to them impregnated with a mysterious guilt. For too long they had believed it was impossible to live an innocent life. They should have spent a long time examining their conscience, making amends… terror pricked their skin when they thought they felt the burning breath of the demon on them. Hell was already here, on earth, and they had been pitched into it, alive. How could you not believe it was also there on the other side?

CHAPTER 6

This hell was still located in the landscape of the human imagination. But there were those who received no help from other men or from their mythologies; those who did not conjure up death and hell, because they already carried death and hell in the very fibre of their being, because terror had for a long time been woven into their existence. Those men, who on a daily basis nourished death like an animal in a barn, familiar but never completely domesticated, dizzyingly soon forgot the few attitudes that made them participate in the human community. They no longer dared look up for they could not have borne the sight of that insulting serenity on the faces of the chosen ones in this great adventure, that visible transfiguration that could be brought about by the memory of a time when they felt eternal. Faced with such a challenge, they would not have been able to restrain themselves from biting and roaring like wild beasts. They had seen death too often, had known it too often. It was everywhere, as natural to them as breathing or moving off in search of the next prey. On the stony paths or in the shade of thickets, they had tripped over the bodies of animals. Farm animals fell by the roadside, dead from toil. The slaughterman poleaxed bulls, sheep and the knife to the throat finished them off. Vegetable rot often breathed over them more powerfully and more obsessively than all the scents of sap.

These were the ones who were aware of their death, the ones who touched the depths of horror. For them this waiting was the worst of tortures. And yet they did not let themselves go entirely. In a surfeit of energy, they shut their roaring rage in the depths of their chest. They held back from clawing at this world of stone which held them tighter and tighter, which squeezed their chest until it suffocated them, which was going to bury them, make them opaque, more dead than the dead, as dead as objects. From time to time, the stone walls parted, and they saw, they made out, the image which had been the door to their disorientated world, the revelation of death without end. Some of them only recalled crudely coloured engravings in which murder victims directed a short, glassy stare upward. Others remained frozen next to a mortuary chapel at one end of which a death mask only just refrained from sneering in their face. Others screwed their fists into their eyes in order not to see too clearly the remains of their beloved dog or their cat, or their doll lying formless across the path; others vainly tried to blow life into a little pile of feathers lying in the hollow of their hand... and there was one who saw his father, a forty-seven-year-old colossus, lying on his back on a bed, left neglected, his jaw slack and his nostrils pinched like a very old woman's. He was Julien the butcher. His father had been as red in the face as him, and even stronger, so strong that he seemed capable of living forever. Like him, he thoroughly deserved his surname 'Camard', as his nostrils were as wide and deep as caverns. He was an exemplary butcher. He loved killing. He did it with verve, with elegance and technical finesse. He'd got the blacksmith Aubert to make him a slaughtering hammer which was worthy of a patent. And it was absolutely necessary for Julien to see him slumped on his bed. The women – his mother, his sister, his aunt, and others – had demanded it. The shock had been so extraordinary that Julien could not stop sharing this with each of his friends in turn. He would never have believed that somebody who has been so much alive could also appear to be so dead. The strongest man in the area was more dead than a calf or a sheep, or even a stud boar. Julien tried to reason thus; he told himself that if he is so completely dead it was because he had died of his own accord, all on his own in the corner: he had fallen when he was ripe, as a fruit falls from the tree. A pointless argument! Julien was hurting all over and his stomach heaved as if he was trying to tear himself up out of his own entrails. 'It's just that I'm not used to it,' he told himself. 'Stands to reason, nobody's got enough time to get used to seeing his father stretched out like that.' And he stood there, rooted to the spot, fascinated by a small wet gleam nestling in the corner of one of the dead man's half-closed eyes. The worst thing was the way absurd ideas came to him. He wanted to talk at random, very loud, to shout. With great effort he restrained himself from accosting Bernard, his cousin, standing next to him, his beret in his hand and his face frozen with horror. The words he managed to hold back were so clear in his head that he wondered if Bernard could not guess them… today, Bernard was no longer close by, but the words were still in Julien's throat and he had to stop himself from shouting them out loud, loud enough to make

221

up for a delay of fifteen years. 'Bernard, tell me it's not him any more. Quick, Bernard. Tell me it's not my father, that my father's not there any more. You see him, Bernard, you see it's just a lump of dead meat. Deader than other meat because it's not good to eat... not good, you hear me! Not good to eat...' Finally, the Julien of fifteen years ago had rushed towards the door. He had run, his teeth chattering, his whole body trembling, to bury his head in a pile of straw at the back of the stable. He was desperate and the taste of that despair had never totally left him. He now rediscovered it intact. But this time an unexpected tenderness was mixed in with it. So, for the first time Julien wanted to grieve for his father. He grieved soundlessly, holding back the tears just as before he had fiercely held back the howl of delirious horror. He had understood. It was from his own death that he wanted to flee. It was his future, his inevitable corpse that he saw carefully laid out on a bed like the remains of an animal on a market stall. He was the one to be transported, chopped up and quartered. And why not eat him too?... good. He now understood and he knew he understood. And he said to himself, with an infinite sigh: 'So. That's all it is...' Yes, that's all it was, and Julien was no longer afraid to look at the others.

Thus, little by little, expressions lost their wild intensity. They became almost transparent and seemed immense.

PART 5

CHAPTER 1

According to the watch, it took less than a minute for the crossfire from the machine guns to reduce two to three hundred men to a few mounds of bleeding, panting flesh. The killers fired methodically at the average height of the chest. The bodies crumpled quite quickly, but not to a man. Some stayed upright for a long time, in threatening attitudes, as if inhabited by a new, supernatural life in the interminable seconds. Their gaze was fixed on the gaze of the executioners with an unforgettable intensity of menace. Some stretched out an accusing arm, others lifted hands which shook for a moment upwards to the sky, like strange meteors from the beyond, like terrible omens. There were those who, after the breath was stopped in their throat, cried out in a powerful voice which would never be snuffed out. There were others who sneered open-mouthed, who buried the teeth of their unforgettable hatred deep in the void. Some who witnessed it speak of it willingly, others equally against their will. To know such things is to feel shame, to want to stay silent, but which cannot help but be said. There is no freedom of choice where crime is concerned.

And the machine guns were hell-bent on murdering these corpses once more; the bullets sought out chests, shredded limbs, tore apart guts and shattered bones.

When all that remained was a pile of human wreckage, the SS took out their revolvers and went around delivering the *coup de grâce*. They did this out of habit, forcing themselves to be conscientious. Wherever they made out the back of a neck, a temple, an open mouth, they aimed their weapon and fired. With some their hands were vigorous, well-practised and steady. However they acted with a rapidity which hinted at obvious haste, maybe even a tiny amount of urgency and jitters. Ernst Von Greven, still close to the wellspring from which he had long since lapped up the philosophy of the modern hero and superman, had a strong sense of the danger that the long wait presented for the soldiers. It could begin to look like hesitation, and for those retarded minds that were still plagued by the stagnant reek of morality, time for reflection. The killers themselves had spent too much time eying those they were going to kill and could not have stopped themselves thinking: 'These are men, unarmed men, defenceless. I'm not going to kill them in combat, so I'm not acting as a soldier. I'm executing them. And I'm executing them unconvinced that they're guilty, without knowing the judgement that condemns them, nor the judge.' So they hastened to fire on anything that emerged from the pile and which recalled the human beings they had looked at face to face.

Once all that they had before them was a bloody mass,

their task seemed easier. They hurried off towards piles of straw, hay and dry wood – they had already noticed where these were – and covered the bodies with them. They did not seem unhappy with this task. They competed with each other in enthusiasm and speed; they jostled each other uttering guttural cries; they larked around, they bumped into each other, they wanted to be like children. Those who managed to escape the machine guns – three in all, no more – heard them joking around. Some were even laughing… they built large pyres. They were going to set fire not just to the corpses but to the last traces that remained in them of what had resembled honour. Afterwards, they would have wiped the slate clean, they would have broken all the ties, they would no longer be like children. Never again.

They struck matches and set them to the pyres. After the wood and straw, the clothes caught fire, then the flesh which gave off a lot of smoke and a suffocating smell. Then the SS left. Some were stumbling. They said: 'It's the smoke.' But they were feeling intoxicated, a strange, terrible intoxication which would never totally leave them.

CHAPTER 2

In the church, when the women and children first saw the door open wide, they sighed with relief. A few little voices cried: 'At last…!' They had heard the bomb explode and the noise of gunfire almost everywhere. They wondered what terrible battle was taking place beyond the walls of their retreat. But they believed that they themselves were safe. They would finally see the blue sky again, they would know.

Two Germans came in and the door was shut behind them. The children fell silent, and the mumbling of prayers picked up, became more audible. The two helmeted warriors drummed their heels on the echoing flagstones. Their coarse faces were terrifying to the children who drew back and clung tight to the women's legs. At the same time, these men tried to smile and put on a fatherly appearance. In passing, one of them held out his hand to pat the fat cheeks of a little kid who was transfixed with terror. They looked about them and conversed in a low voice and business-like manner, like electricians who had come to sort out an appliance. At first, they put the box they were carrying on the communion table, then changed their minds and moved it, placing it precisely beneath the hanging candelabra. They took out lengths of what looked like white string which they carefully unrolled. The one who created the impression that he liked children – and perhaps he really did, back when he still belonged to the world of men – seemed willing to hand one of these strings to one of the little kids who was watching him with interest, to have as a plaything, no doubt.

He moved back towards the door after having said a few words to his comrade, who, taking out a box of matches, lit each one of the strings. Then he too left. The fuses burnt. The spitting flame climbed quickly towards the box. Some women shouted: 'Cut them off, quickly. Stamp on them.' They wanted to get forward but they were immediately stopped in their tracks, hampered by the stampede of children at floor level, overwhelmed by the weight of a whole crowd uttering piercing cries. The panic had started. Run, get away as quickly as possible from that infernal machine which was surely going to explode…

It did not explode. It burst into flames giving off a bright phosphorescent glare, while billows of increasingly thick, increasingly choking, black smoke rapidly filled the church.

In their frantic reel, the screaming mass, stamping and half-blind, somehow found the doors and pushed them open. Now, the men who had been German soldiers saw emerging along with a cloud of acrid smoke, a flood of women staggering, coughing their guts up, holding a baby to their breast, or half dragging little boys and girls by the hand. And these men opened fire. The bursts of machine-gun fire crackled and the fugitives collapsed piling up higher and higher, so high that those still inside, choking for breath, could not get over them.

Hitler's men then pushed the bullet-riddled corpses back into the church, and closed the doors, waiting for the fire to finish off its destructive work.

They carried out their task with great conscientiousness, although astonished by the determination to survive exhibited by such supposedly weak creatures. The weakest in fact, the most helpless of all. They were even surprised to see at one point the stained-glass windows at a height of several metres shatter into pieces as if some supernatural force had allowed the suffering women to rise into the air. But they were soon reassured: the bodies fell heavily on to the rocky buttresses of the church. There they lay motionless, but just to be sure, the Germans directed a few machine gun salvos at them.

The work had to be very well done... and it required a good deal of application, monstrous application, to be convinced that this was still a question of work.

Jean:

Those high-pitched cries, what's that? And that disgusting smell? Is there a chance they dared to...?

Come on. I must keep calm. I don't know what I'm saying. It's the pigs. That's all. That's why I thought I could smell grilled pork... my pigs heard me and that set them off. That's all.

My poor pigs, it's not fear that makes you squeal, you lot. It's hunger. Nobody's been around to see to you since this morning. Good pigs, sad pigs, shitty pigs. I've still got enough strength to bring you your food, with my left hand. This swill has had time to cool down ten times, but you'll eat it up all the same. Here we are. I'm coming. And I'm not walking so badly.

There they are, all eight of them. That'll make a huge slab of pork hung up on the wall. There's something indecent about their pale pink saddles in the half-light.

No more… no more…

I just can't feed the pigs any more. It's not so bad now. As far as you pigs are concerned, I'm still the almighty. Their pink backs press harder and harder against the flap which is coming apart; two tons of pig rippling, rolling and wobbling, a great wave of fat.

This time, here we go, my head's spinning. I can't stay upright. And why do these animals smell of roast? God, I'm half dreaming. I'm losing it.

Even so, I'm going to feed you, my pigs. Yes, yes, I know, I hear you, I understand. You're very sweet, all lovey, as gentle as cherubs. They have various love songs, they coo, they make entreaties and lamentations to me, they provoke me, they make mischief and sentimental protests, as well as exasperated reproaches. They adore me. They swoon.

Yes, yes. I know. I don't want to keep you waiting. I'm not doing it on purpose, but I can't find that key. Just hang on a minute, Good God, you're deafening me. I'm all over the place.

It's you… you… in your state, who can't…

'Bloody pigs, you already smell of roast. You stink. You bastards, minced meat, roast meat, meat for eating, digesting

229

and shitting out! Shut up! Or I'll let you die of hunger. That's good to see, a pig dying of hunger. Nothing would give me more pleasure, today.'

I say that, and at the same time, here I am spreading out your swill, careful to divide it up equally. I yell at you, but I obey you. I can't stop myself obeying you. I've always obeyed you. I serve the pigs, I indulge them, I feed them, while for the others I can do nothing.

That's all... not enough... not enough weapons...

I could never stand pigs; the only animals I don't like. I prefer to deal with stuff; stones or planks, they're more friendly than these treacherous fatheads. Besides, Francis was right when he said: 'A total bastard always resembles a pig even when he's thin, even when he looks refined and delicate; most of all, when he looks like that. So, it's like his fat has been pushed deep inside, out of reach, unassailable. But it's always visible, in what he says, at the back of his mind, stuffing his face, helping himself first of all...' Francis, my little brother with the red cheeks, who made me laugh so much, who made me believe in so many incredible things, can't you say something to them, you who always find a way of getting out of scrapes. Tell them, explain to them that it's impossible.

These pigs are snorting so much, they're doing my head in. And they still smell of the grill. Bloody hell, it's a bit strong.

'I'll sell you, you shits. Next market, at any price, I'm getting shot of you. I'll stick you in the pig wagon and off we go! Done and dusted. You understand: any price. Huh! The racket's calmed down; so quickly I dropped my bucket. Some of their slops spilled on my espadrille. I ought to wipe it off. Oh, what the hell, I'll leave it. You'd think the pigs understood me, that they're listening to what I'm going to say to them still. It wasn't possible this morning, but now everything's possible. Now, the innocent are punished and the guilty have all the rights. Now, everything's ready for something that's never been seen before, for something that's been unimaginable up 'til now. Whoa! There they go again, starting to scream their heads off. Listen to them, listen to them, listen to your lords and masters calling you to order. 'We're tired of waiting, peasant.' You're at their beck and call. It's not the farmer and his pigs; it's the pigs and their farmer.

I need to get a move on. I'll feed the sheep as well and lead the cows and bulls out to the meadow. Where's that linchpin? I had it in my hand just now. How cack-handed I am with my left hand.

'Hey! You! What d'you want, eh?

He looks at me, straight in the eye. He looks at me, and again, he creates this incredible silence, a silence like that of the calm in a storm at sea, a silence which makes you expect a miracle: the clouds are going to open up on a dome of blue sky, the waves are going to part and a road will extend ahead of us, straight and trustworthy, the mountains of water are no more than a landscape, the nightmare is no more than a memory and a long meadow of calm water stretches before us sown with the reflections of spring flowers and the beautiful eyes of friends. The siege has been lifted. He's the first one to let me know; Gaston turns up on his bike, the others support grandfather who's delaying them. They make a funny old crowd...

Oh! Oh no! I'm still there and that filthy stench has filled my nostrils again.

The commandant said: 'There's nothing more to be done, now…'

And there it is, loud and clear. No miracles for me. Just that dirty animal who's looking me straight in the eye. Why's he looking at me like that? 'Oi! Dirty pig!' He's still doing it. I don't believe it. Gives me cold shivers up and down the spine. If I was still able to feel frightened, I'd be frightened, for sure.

'Hou! Hou! Hou!'

He hasn't flinched in the slightest. He's still looking at me. He's trying to put the evil eye on me. He thought I couldn't stay standing. He's not wrong…

'I'm going to fall over…'

My head tips me forward, over the door. Quick, quick, the key! If I move the flap around, if I give them their swill, they won't attack me. Starving pigs, they're dangerous.

'I'm falling… I'm falling…'

That's it. I'm down. In the middle of the pigs. They're going to rip me to bits with their teeth; Sod it! I don't even want to defend myself. None of that happened. I'm dreaming of pigs, that's all. And to prove it – they're very much alive and the smell of the grill… from the start, it's been just a bit of fever, a little bit of fever.

'They won't dare. Never. Not us, from this house. No-body's done anything. Not to Gaston, especially. Gaston's so young. My little Gaston, my only son… they won't dare.'

CHAPTER 3

In Blancard's barn, Francis, Gaston and Jef all hit the floor at the same time as the others. A little sooner than the others... this half-second advance came to them thanks to the coolness of the youngest, of Gaston who during the long wait had seemed to be on edge to the point of panic. Gaston grabbed Francis and Jef by the arm and dragged them down with him at the very moment the machine guns were about to spit their fire.

All three of them were at the back of the barn not very far from one of the little ventilation doors. When they had moved towards this door they said it was to get a bit of air. In fact, they were behaving like threatened beasts who stand around their hole, ready to spring away.

The mass of dead and wounded ebbed towards them in a slow, heavy movement. They were almost entirely submerged by them. It was hot, sticky, twitching with spasmodic rumbles, filled with horrific gurgling. The machine guns were still firing and the impact of the bullets on dead flesh resounded in the flesh of the living. From all around came the sound of death rattles and sighs. The most awful of these were the cries of those who had not been mortally wounded and whose voices were still recognisable. A long, sharp, desolate cry emerged from the mouth of François Juéry, Jef's father; the wailing of a tortured child as if pain and despair had suddenly shattered his strength and virility. Jef went rigid with horror. He was bathed in icy sweat. He wished he had never been born. A new burst of gunfire put a sudden end to this unbearable lamentation.

The voice of big Mazaud had also been shattered into a pre-human bleat. The dry crack of a revolver shot interrupted him.

The machine guns fell silent. All that remained were the revolver shots which here and there cut off the last human voices. However, the mass of bleeding flesh continued to wail in its own way. It was an organic groan, vague and dull, made up of trickling, sudden collapses, cracks, tearing followed by hissing breath, bubbles bursting from thick liquid, sloppy bursts, rumblings, foul cascades of excrement liberated from open sphincters.

Jef felt the weight of a tangle of limbs, some flabby, some stiffened by sharp contractions. Something wet and slimy covered the back of his neck, the whole left side of his back was bathed in a warm pool. He was suffocating. He could not stand it any longer. He had to get out of there or be driven mad from horror and disgust. With great effort he shook himself clear and freed his face in order to take a great gulp of air. At the same time, he felt a living shoulder against his own right shoulder. Close to his ear, Francis Bricaud whispered: 'Don't move around like that. Keep your head down. I'm trying to cover Gaston's head. He's not badly hurt.'

Turning a little more to his right, Jef made out Francis'

bare forearm which was noticeably whiter than those of the villagers. Slowly, very slowly, Francis was pushing a sort of ragged, bloody mess with great holes in it: its trousers were full of the bullets of a dead man, the smashed leg of a dead man... Jef felt like he was going to burst into a scream, and he forced his face back into the human mass, looking for contact with a small piece of dry cloth.

Again, Francis pushed his shoulder. Between two shots from a revolver, Jef heard him murmur quite quietly: 'There we go, his head is hidden. If you could...'

A detonation went off close by. Jef was deafened by it. Francis' shoulder jerked violently, so violently that Jef wondered if Francis, losing his cool, was going to get up and try to escape. But the shoulder no longer moved. It became so completely motionless, so heavy, that Jef understood... he had to do all in his power not to promptly pull away. It was not out of disgust, but fear; a new fear. Francis had always seemed to him more frightening than the others because his death seemed impossible, just as it had one minute earlier. Jef did not want to believe it. This presence, this warmth, this reassuring awareness could not have turned into a heap of inert flesh, one more corpse among all the others. But then... then everything was possible. Jef told himself that perhaps he too, without realising it, was in the process of decomposing, in the process of passing into that state of being an unnameable thing.

He did not feel sorry for Francis or the others. He felt nothing beyond this narrow fear, precise and black. He trembled from head to foot and his sole concern was to stop this trembling which was going to draw a killer's pistol in his direction. But he could no more stop the trembling than he could the fear.

The Germans ranged noisily across the barn. Jef could clearly make out the creak of their leather boots. He heard them talking loudly, as if they were encouraging each other. Some were laughing; a big, over-loud laugh. 'If they're laughing, they're madmen. We have no chance of getting out of this, as we've fallen into the hands of madmen.' Madness had always inspired serious terror in him.

With his face pressed against a linen jacket which must have belonged to Julot, the jobbing painter, because it smelled of wallpaper paste, Jef noticed the scratchy rustling of straw over his head. Why are they putting straw on us? Perhaps they were thinking it would be enough to cover up their crime…

The rasp of matches made Jef's skin crawl and he knew what was coming next. He had a choice: be burnt alive or throw himself into a hail of bullets. As soon as he heard close to his ear the cheerful crackling of flames amid the dry straw, Jef tensed his muscles to shake off his burden of corpses. As he was standing up, he saw the bloody but intact face of Gaston Bricard appear. This gave him, not hope, but a curious calm which was close to detachment. He imitated the dull, rapid delivery of Francis to say to him: 'Don't move yet. They'll be leaving.'

However, the fire had caught, and the heat was becoming intolerable. Flames licked Jef's hand, and he quickly retreated under Julot's disembowelled body.

Acrid smoke, combined with the smell of burning flesh, made the air unbreathable… Jef stopped himself coughing violently. This effort made him vomit suddenly. At the same time, his trousers caught fire and a burn to his thigh caused such intense pain that he could not help kicking out. What the hell! He was quitting. He couldn't take any more of this.

He had already got to his knees when a hand grabbed his shoulder and shook with considerable force. That's it. It's over. A *kraut* would deliver the *coup de grâce*... but it was Gaston. Gaston was talking to him in a totally hoarse and broken voice, as if he had been screaming for hours.

'They've just shut the doors. Now's our chance.'

Jef struggled blindly because he was completely suffocating. Gaston had to help him free himself from the arms and legs of the dead who entwined themselves around him with hideous determination. Once on his feet, he staggered and went down on all fours, placing his hands down on guts torn open, on sneering faces with teeth ready to bite. And in spite of his haste, he could not help but recognise those faces that he had once seen smiling. There was Durand, who kept the sweet shop. This little man, who was so self-effacing, so affable, now stared at him with the gaze of the Medusa. And a little further off, that grimace of delirious hatred, those menacing teeth thrust forward like a vampire's failed to completely erase the image of the joyful, light-hearted, mischievous miller, Arlaud... faced with the idea that he might also encounter a macabre imitation of his own father, Jef found sufficient strength to drag himself clear of the sinister embrace. He threw himself headfirst against the little back door of the barn.

'Good idea,' said Gaston rapidly and in a still bizarrely hollow voice. 'Don't make so much noise. There's a path behind, full of nettles. It might not be guarded.'

Gaston had been shot in the left forearm and was bleeding. But he felt no pain and could use his hand.

The two young men tried slowly pushing open the heavy oak door. But it was bolted from the outside. There was a crack in the ancient wood through which they could see the handle of the bolt. Each in turn tried to put their hand through, without success.

'Francis!' Gaston called out. 'You have a go. What are you waiting for? You've got slimmer hands than us. Come on! Oi! Francis!…'

He looked around him blinking and coughing. In panic, Jef put a hand over his mouth.

'Shut up. Didn't you see? Francis can't hear you any more. Don't talk to him.'

Gaston looked at him in fury and lurched towards the pile of bodies which was giving off thicker and thicker smoke, and from which flickers of flame and sparks were shooting. The fire was spreading rapidly through the barn. Jef grabbed Gaston round the waist and dragged him back.

'It's no good. I felt it when they shot him with a revolver.'

Gaston let out a sort of stifled bray. He freed himself with a thrust of the hips, and turned towards Jef, his fists clenched.

'What?'

At that moment the two young men saw a human shape rise from the midst of the dead and rush towards them barking like a terrified dog. They stepped back for a moment, but the man began to roll on the floor of the barn to put out the flames which were beginning to engulf his jacket and linen trousers. Jef and Gaston came to his aid by covering him with an old, discarded sack in a corner.

They then recognised Arnaud, the aged postman who had been talking for so long about his upcoming retirement.

One entire half of his fine white moustache had been torched, exposing his mouth and cheek. He bore not a trace of a bullet. 'I don't know what happened. I didn't see anything. Didn't see anything,' he repeated. As luck would have it, he had fainted at just the right moment.

The fire was everywhere now. In their desperation the three men threw all their weight against the door which did not budge. Then old Arnaud noticed that at the bottom there was a panel which looked less sturdy than the others. A few kicks from the postman's heavy clodhoppers shattered it.

'They must have heard us,' said Gaston. 'Sod it! I'm going first, if you want.'

The little door was not guarded. An embankment invaded with bushes completely hid it. A few seconds later and the three men were sneaking through nettles and burdock on all fours.

Bullets whistled over their heads and the burning barn was not far off collapsing. They had to find another shelter as quickly as possible. Still on all fours, they got as far as the back of Blancard's sheepfolds and thought they could take refuge among the sheep.

They began pushing at the little window where all bar one of the panes had been replaced by planks when from inside they heard: 'Raus! Raus! Chch…' A *kraut* was driving the sheep out.

'Let's get into the loft,' suggested Gaston. 'And hide in the hay.'

They had to hoist old Arnaud up through the ceiling vent. But Gaston and Jef felt a surge of strength. In less than a minute, the three men were buried in a mass of hay which sighed and crackled under their weight.

The relief they felt immediately plunged them into a stupor. All memory was obliterated and they let themselves drift into complete vegetable indifference. The sheer fact of being able to breath easily, to remain still, was an unequalled pleasure.

Suddenly the double doors of the barn were thrown wide open. An SS soldier was climbing the top rungs of a ladder leaning against the wall. He jumped up to where they were. Through the thin curtain of hay with which they had covered themselves, the three men saw him walk in their direction, his machine gun at the ready, and they thought this was the end. The German stopped and stood a matter of centimetres from Jef's leg and still he did not see them. He struck some matches and threw them to the four corners of the pile of fodder, then left in a hurry.

The fire caught extremely quickly. The three men again slipped through the little trapdoor, licked as they went by the flames of a blaze that was already roaring.

At Blanchard's place, the barn was entirely engulfed in flames. Sections of the roof were collapsing noisily onto the piles of bodies below.

The three fugitives, cowering in the ditch, looked around for a new hiding place. To get to a thick hedge which would hide them as far as the cemetery and from there to the edge of the village, they had to cross a wide-open space of about thirty metres.

Old Arnaud declared that he couldn't do it. With a broken bottle, he hollowed out a sort of burrow among the nettles and holed up in it.

Jef and Gaston told him he was wrong. They could not stay where they were. Waiting in extreme danger among the flames and gunshots, they would have lost their minds.

Jef was the one who suggested a tactic.

'We don't both run at the same time. We'll be less visible if we go one at a time. And then, once the first gets through, the next will know he can go.'

In saying this, Jef was overcome with fear. He imagined that as soon as he stood up his well-exposed torso would be riddled with a thousand bullets. However, he had decided to conduct himself well. Besides, in all the stories he had read, he invariably played the finest role.

Furthermore, Gaston did not seem inclined to argue. He muttered between his teeth that even so it'd be better to wait a while, perhaps.

'Right. I'm going,' Jef said suddenly.

Gaston made a vague sign with his head.

Jef set off. He wanted to be invisible so much that at no point did he feel the ground beneath his feet. He reached the hedge and rolled in amongst the strongly-scented elder trees.

He heard the crackle of machine-gun fire, and just had time to stand up and see Gaston, who had set off in turn, double up in mid-stride and fall to the ground.

He fell, collapsing completely like a toy whose spring keeping it in shape had been snapped. His upper body slumped onto itself, his arms and legs whirled in a sort of stunned and dream-like slow motion. There was a faint noise, very faint, of falling. And the seventeen-year old body, in the middle of the square, in the shining dust, among the stones as white as bone, became nothing more than a formless ragged pile.

He did not remain there long. Two SS soldiers grabbed him roughly, one by the shoulders, the other by the feet and carried him towards the burning barn. They never looked towards the hedge. They had only seen Gaston.

Thus, Jef began crawling towards the cemetery. He did not even have to make an effort to forget the horrors he had just seen. He was nothing more than an animal, alive and wary. He listened, sniffed, groped his way. It seemed to him that never again would he rediscover that world, already blurred and distant, where he had friends, a house, a family.

CHAPTER 4

In the church, the women and children were taking longer to die than the men. Only the very weak and those who had already given up hope stayed where they were and were quickly suffocated by the black clouds of smoke.

Old Julie Bricard still lay prostrate. She could not, nor doubtless did she want to, join in the stampeding, shouting mob. First Suzanne Lambert, then Amélie Barnaud shook her and tried to drag her away. In vain. Julie looked up at them with an expression which was less one of fear and more one of immense astonishment and compassion.

Annie, her daughter-in-law, had abandoned her from the outset, probably without realising it. She was sobbing and charged straight in front of her in the direction of where she thought the door was. But she was not cut out for a struggle like this. After a few steps she stumbled and collapsed face down on the ground.

The fallen were immediately covered by a dark mass which now flowed back and forth, now turned on the spot like a raging whirlpool. This crowd blindly overturned pews, smashed chairs to pieces, knocked over the littlest ones and the women who were too feeble or too slow. Without pity, it knocked down anything that did not have the strength to fall in with the rhythm of terror.

Amélie Barnaud was strong. She was used to carrying sacks on her shoulder like a man. Sometimes she even led young, feisty bulls on a rope. So, she had no problem dealing with the craziest of shoving. She kept her cool for quite some time. She was among those who shouted to extinguish the fuse on the infernal device. She wanted to do it herself and she would have managed to, if it were only a matter of pushing aside chests and shoulders. Except that she could not overcome the obstacle of the little children so easily. They grabbed hold of her skirts, they rolled around under her feet. She would have had to wade through these little tearful creatures as if they were thick undergrowth. Amélie did not dare to. And yet, she saw hundreds of women doing just that, their eyes contorted, their mouths twisted into a scream, lifting their knees and thrashing the air, slapping and scratching faces left and right. They no longer knew what they were doing, they were beside themselves, out of their minds. They were wading through the worst quagmire of madness and terror, in a desperate attempt to reach the bank before they went under. But there was no bank to reach. The smoke rose faster and faster. Its black spirals soon reached chest height. This smoke burnt their eyes and rasped their throats. The poor creatures coughed, coughed their lungs up, incessantly.

Amélie tried to keep her two daughters with her. She picked them up and carried them. She barely felt their weight, but the encumbrance prevented her from getting through the crush. She put the little ones down and shouted to them to hang on tight to her skirt. The girls did as they were told, and Amélie set off. Nothing could stand in the way of her thrust forward and the little girls followed in her wake. She was not walking fast, as she was taking care not to tread on the increasing number of women who had been poleaxed by suffocation. But she walked forcefully. She felt she could have walked for longer still, for a very long time. Suzanne Lambert was matching her step-for-step, her arms wrapped tight around her baby. Amélie was reassured by this mark of trust and full of gratitude to the village beauty. She would never have believed that this blonde poppet with such slim ankles and wrists could display such energy. Amélie even noticed that the baby in Suzanne's arms was hiccupping violently, and his eyes were turning white. 'Don't squeeze him so tight,' she shouted in Suzanne's ear. She did not wait around to see if her advice had been heeded; She had just recognised little Mimile bent over a large, dark body; poor Fanny, for sure. Amélie shook Mimile by the shoulder and told him to make for the door.

The child did not hear her; he had grabbed hold of his aunt's arm and was pulling on it with all his strength, trying in vain to lift her. He spoke to her and his voice, his extraordinarily powerful voice, could be heard above the tumult.

'Why?' he repeated vehemently. 'Why? Why don't you help me?'

The question was directed at his aunt, and at all the grown-ups, and perhaps at God. It was certainly the question asked by all those children in the midst of this incomprehensible chaos.

Amélie called Mimile once more. Then she was carried off by a movement of the crowd more forceful than all the rest. Although by now her eyes were burning and full of tears, she could see enough to understand what was happening. The main doors had been half opened and several women had got out. They had been slaughtered on the instant. Now, the others drew back hastily. This backwash was irresistible: Amélie and Suzanne were swept up in it like the others.

This time all hope had disappeared. Horror and panic leapt at the throat of even the bravest. Amélie felt her ribs crack under pressure from the crowd. An apocalyptic shadow now reigned throughout the church. Amélie however still had time to make out the face of Suzanne Lambert. It was distorted and distended. Her mouth, wide open, was being forced even wider. It was becoming an abyss which opened up, slowly wiping out the rest of her features.

Amélie realised that Suzanne was screaming; she could not think about anything else. She had become nothing more than a scream. And at that moment, Amélie realised that she too was screaming at the top of her lungs, with such an effort that it made her body shake from head to toe. She had not noticed up until then because her voice was lost in the massive voice of the others. It was a continual outcry, maintained on the same shrill tone. More than an outcry, it was an elemental, inhuman sound which existed beyond reason. Amélie thought she could see this outcry: in the midst of the billows of black smoke a light was taking shape, too white, too bright for her eyes.

Then, although she thought she was still standing, Amélie lost her footing. From that moment on, she no longer knew what she was doing, nor where she was.

Later, when she came to, it was with the realisation that she was still walking forward. She moved mechanically like this up to a door which suddenly opened in front of her. A little gust of almost breathable air arrived. Amélie recognised this door; it was to the sacristy. She rushed through it, looking neither left nor right, without wondering who these shapeless beings were who continued to push her, bump into her, get in her way. She was no longer in control of her movements, she headed towards the breathable air with crazed speed, as much at the mercy of instinct as a stone is at the mercy of gravity. Whatever stood in her way – a thing or living being – was the enemy; she pushed it aside with all her force, or, if it proved too irresistible, she moved round it. One minute she was shoving past the bodies of other women, the next her hands encountered wood or stone, in which case she ripped the palms of her hands and tore her nails. Sometimes her face, thrust forward, bumped into an obstacle, swelling up and bleeding.

Still taken up in the frenzied mass, she found herself on the point of tumbling down a stone staircase. Then there was a surge of bodies which drove her back up the stairs almost as fast as she had come down them. Down at the bottom, the machine guns had opened fire and the bodies were piling up.

Still Amélie tried to press forward, going down and walking on all fours; she was less afraid of the bullets than the great white scream amid the black smoke. Nothing could be worse than this madness she was moving through. The fear of falling back into that gave her almost supernatural energy. In a series of huge leaps – real wild animal leaps – she felt her leg muscles stretch. Above her head she saw a light shining and threw herself towards it. But it was so high up, dammit! Perched on a narrow ledge she started to climb the wall. She used anything and everything to support herself: a stepladder, a gap between two stones which she had not seen but her hand had somehow found, or a moulding, or the white shoulder of a statue… she was going to make it – she made it – the light was there, within reach. One last effort hoisted her up to the window in the middle of the apse. A head butt, which she had neither intended nor wanted to do, shattered the glass. She had got there, she could see the blue sky, the sun. With her mouth wide open, she took in ferocious great lungfuls of air and filled her chest. Exhilarated, she felt she was about to faint.

A grasping hand which grazed her ankle made her jump. She leaned down, took hold of the wrist and pulled with all her strength, hoisting up a woman… it was Suzanne Lambert who, by some miracle had followed her up here. She was still holding her baby. She had managed to attach it to her chest, partly shoved into her torn shirt, partly hanging round her neck with the aid of a belt. She was suffocating, her strength almost spent. Amélie had to loosen the belt which formed a running knot round her neck.

The black smoke continued to rise and billowed out of the shattered window. Without even looking at the height of the drop, Amélie decided: 'We've got to jump. You jump after me.'

She had already leapt into the void. The church on this side was built on a rocky escarpment. Amélie fell badly, on her side, and felt such a sharp pain in her thigh she thought she was going to faint. It was shouts from Suzanne that caused her to discover a supreme source of energy. She looked up.

'Catch Daniel.' Suzanne said. 'I'll throw him. Catch him.'

Amélie turned round and held out her arms. The little

body hit her in the face and she was so weakened that it was enough to completely stun her. Then the noise of another fall. Suzanne had landed close by her. At once she got to her feet and Amélie handed her the baby: 'Save yourself if you can walk. I can't. I think I've broken a leg.'

In pain, Suzanne took two steps. At that moment a new burst of gunfire rang out and around the two women bullets split the rock. Suzanne got down and curled up as best she could. 'Murderers! Murderers! Murderers!' she kept repeating in a gruff, low voice. But she remained still.

The shooting stopped.

'Are you wounded?' asked Amélie.

'Yes, in the left shoulder. But I can walk.'

Amelie advised her to follow the presbytery as far as the garden where there might be somewhere to hide. She too had felt some violent jolts to her back but, as she had not experienced any very sharp pain, she thought she had just been hit by some splinters of rock.

When Suzanne was some way off, Amélie realised that she was far too visible on this area of the foundations. Very slowly she tried to get on all-fours. Her wounded leg hurt like hell, but she managed to drag herself a few metres further on. She soon came to a low wall that she could not get over. Luckily, she remembered there was a gap where she often used to huddle up when, as a little girl, she was playing with her friends. She found it and made her way into the garden.

A raised bed of runner beans allowed her to stay hidden all the way to the roadside. Then she began dragging herself again. She moved sideways leaning on her two hands and her good leg. She was getting heavier and heavier. It felt like she was wrapped in a very thick blanket or a veritable mattress. She decided to feel her wounds, which she thought were only light. Her hand came back covered in blood. She thought: 'I'm losing all my blood.' She was not afraid but she was loath to die like this, all alone, in the undergrowth flat on the ground like an animal. The Germans must have gone by now. She tried to call for help, but she could not produce anything more than a husky murmur. Only Suzanne would have heard her, if she was still hiding in the garden.

After calling in vain a few times, Amélie finally spotted Suzanne.

She saw her emerge from the other end of the raised bed of beans where she herself had hidden, and run or rather stagger, still holding little Daniel tight to her chest, towards the nearby shed. Then, with a desperate effort Amélie called out again: 'Help.'

Her voice could not be heard: a burst of gunfire had just erupted. Amélie saw Suzanne twist then fall backwards against the wall of the shed, her eyes turned to the sky. Her child rolled over close to her. The Germans fired again, from close range no doubt, because Amélie saw the jerking of the two bodies riddled and raked furiously by bullets.

'Murderers! Murderers!'

Amélie wanted to shout out this word. She no longer thought about hiding, she no longer wanted to live. What's the point, if it meant seeing such things?

She fainted and thought she would die; die face down, exactly the sort of savage death that she dreaded, die alone, desperate, her heart filled with hate.

PART 6

CHAPTER 1

It was past eight on the same evening, and the sun, level with the horizon, was copperplating the heavy storm clouds like lions' manes when the car containing Maître Lambert, father of Philippe and grandfather of young David, left Limoges and drove at speed towards Verrièges.

'We'll be arriving very late,' said M. Perret, his companion, with regret. 'But with the tyres in such poor condition, we couldn't set out without a spare, even for the last few kilometres.'

'Oh,' Maître Lambert protested. 'As I turned up unannounced, it doesn't matter. This really is very good of you.'

He could not have been more pleased to come across this M. Perret who uttered his name with respect and who declared himself greatly honoured to be of service to the famous man: one would have said that of the two men it was M. Perret who was grateful.

For Maître Lambert, a man who felt his sixties approaching faster and faster, train journeys were becoming so arduous that he had not made this journey for many a month.

'They're expecting me even less,' he explained. 'Given that they think I'm in Switzerland. I was meant to leave for there at the beginning of the week. It's quite by chance that I was delayed in Paris. Thanks to you, I won't be leaving without embracing my children, and that's a great comfort to me.'

'On the other hand,' said M. Perret with a smile. 'I'm concerned that my wife doesn't start worrying. Up until now she's got used to my being very punctual and she was expecting me at least three hours ago. As an electrical engineer, I can get assignments quite easily. We're privileged. The Germans need us. They treat us well… but we'll be there soon. From the top of the next rise I think we'll see Verrièges.'

Maître Lambert had just seen a signpost reading 'Verrièges 5km' when the road was blocked by German army lorries and a light tank.

M. Perret immediately got out of the car. With great assurance, he produced his papers and began explaining in German.

But the officer who had jumped into the road was barely listening to him. Very red, his expression was a bit jittery, his movements exaggerated and brusque. like a man who was overstretched and frazzled. He made Maître Lambert and the driver get out of the car, then pushed them roughly until they were standing in the ditch. A soldier guarded them at machine-gun point.

Then began a minute search of the contents of the car, the assignment dossier and identity cards. Finally, the officer became less red. He repeatedly asked if any of the three men were born in Verrièges. M. Perret said no and asked why he was being insistent. As he got no reply, he undertook a long explanation of the purpose of his journey. He had just seen his wife, his daughter, his two little boys…

'Alright, alright,' interrupted the German, looking exasperated. 'I'm not interested. If you're not from Verrièges, go where you want.'

The three men quickly repacked the car with the suitcases which had been scattered on the road. They were silent. The importance the German had attached to the fact that they were not from Verrièges seemed more and more suspicious to them.

And soon, from the top of the rise that M. Perret had announced, they saw…

From this viewpoint, one very much appreciated by photographers, what had been one of the prettiest villages in the province now presented to the eye nothing more than an immense blaze from which rose a column of smoke which darkened the whole countryside.

Maître Lambert saw this and felt very old. So, he had not been wrong! Since 1940 he had been expecting a cataclysm, and there it was, in front of him, almost within reach, this cataclysm.

He was listening to M. Perret who, ever more resolute, was already suggesting an interpretation of the event and putting a plan of action in place.

'They've burnt the village as a reprisal. Obviously. Some senior officer killed by the resistance. They were talking about it in Limoges. We just have to find out where they've rounded up the population. I know the area hereabouts well and I bet

253

the women and children are at Maury, in the big isolation hospital.'

Maître Lambert was listening and nodding in agreement. M. Perret's tone of extreme deference was a great relief to him. It helped him to maintain a certain attitude, to remember that he was *the* Maître Lambert of the 'Rossi Affair', regular defender of the victims of political fanaticism, a man whose statements had formerly carried international significance. He stood up very straight and when he took off his hat to wipe away the sweat of anxiety, he carefully smoothed down the lock of hair which had stubbornly stuck out from his forehead ever since he was a young man. It was white now, but he only remembered this at moments when he was feeling dejected. He did not want to allow himself to feel dejected...

No. He would not give in to this dull voice which told him that all was lost. He would stand his ground, he would fight, he would still defend his own. Moreover, M. Perret may be right in believing they were not directly in danger. The Germans would not find anything against Philippe in this region. He cared too much about the safety of his wife and children to have done anything stupid.

The three men could see the flames clearly and from time to time they heard sections of houses collapse with a dull crash. On the outskirts of the village they were once again stopped by a squad of German soldiers. Under the threat of an automatic rifle, they had to get out of the car with their hands up and allow themselves to be searched.

Still full of self-assurance, M. Perret stated that an officer had given him permission to go as far as Verrièges.

The squad of Germans began a discussion among

themselves. They talked animatedly and seemed a little too jolly, like men returning from a big meal. But it was clear they had not drunk any alcohol. One of them, whom M. Perret took to be a *Feldwebel*, a sergeant, announced he would get his orders from the officers, and went off.

M. Perret's driver was instructed to park the car on the roadside. Then the soldiers led the three men a little further off, to where the departmental tram had just been stopped.

About thirty people were already lined up in the ditch guarded by submachine guns. Despite the ranting and threats of the Germans, women in tears were loudly demanding to know where their children had been put and were insisting that they be taken to them.

The soldiers shook their heads. One of them jabbered constantly.

'*Nicht* women! *Nicht* children! *Kaput*! *Kaput*!'

He said this with an almost joyful lack of concern, and with relief, as if he considered it a tiresome task that was over and done with and in good time.

The unfortunate parents, when they heard this, refused to believe them. Moreover, the soldier did not want to answer any of the questions M. Perret put to him in German.

'Come on now!' the latter exclaimed shrugging his shoulders. 'You won't have me believe that these people would be mindless enough to admit to a monstrous crime in this way. I know the Germans. They become brutes easily enough, but not monsters. Look at them smiling and enjoying themselves!'

Indeed, there were several soldiers who were joking around noisily and looking to tease the young women ranged in the ditch, heedless of their reddened eyes, their features strained by anxiety.

The wait stretched into the night. Suddenly it seemed to Maître Lambert that darkness had descended all at once, like in a nightmare.

Moreover, everything evoked the torturous absurdity of a nightmare: the men in uniform laughing, while all around them everything was just desolation and horror; those women crying who wanted to run and could not move; those nauseating clouds of smoke in a reddening sky: those frenzied escapades of unfettered cattle (the bellowing of the cows was particularly painful. It was the very voice of panic); and those collapses and crashes which for a moment covered up, without interrupting, the chirping of grasshoppers tucked away in the depths of leaves.

However, the surveillance of the Germans was being relaxed. Now only entry into the village was forbidden.

M. Perret planned to follow the paths through the forest to Maury where he still hoped to find his family. He took the driver with him and advised Maître Lambert, who could not hide his fatigue, to stay near the car. Again, he stated his whole-hearted conviction that nobody dared hurt women and children.

Maître Lambert would have liked to accept this view which after all was not unreasonable. Unfortunately, it seemed to him fragile to precisely the same extent that it was reasonable.

CHAPTER 2

For some four years now, Maître Lambert had recognised that the world was obviously at the mercy of madmen. Little by little, madness was permeating each and every soul, gradually taking total possession of it. If Georges, who was six years older than Philippe had not been contaminated in this way, he would not have got himself killed at the head of an irregular force. And his wife!…

His wife had never managed to recover from the grief of losing her child when he was in his twenties. Gripped by a frantic desire for revenge, she had never wanted to settle for what she disdainfully referred to as 'the resistance of symbolic acts.' Despite her age, despite her very delicate health, she had sought out, demanded even, the most dangerous missions. Arrested on a train, her luggage stuffed with political pamphlets, she had been deported, and news of her death reached her husband three months later.

Ever since that date, Maître Lambert had never felt totally alive. He, who had been so often praised for his youthful vigour, was feeling his age, and even older.

He saw the whole world as marked by catastrophic

decrepitude and he had never felt so closely linked to the fate of this world. He was nothing more than a depleted old man lurching forward from day to day at a sleepwalker's pace, waiting for the moment when he would reach the threshold of the final apocalypse.

Here it was! He was getting there. He could see it with his own eyes, and he was astonished to find the spectacle so unsurprising, so strangely close to what he had always imagined. In the appalling dark shadows and the red glow of fire, men were dying, their houses were collapsing, their possessions were going up in smoke, their wives were wandering abroad without roof or consolation. And all this was taking place amid the indifference of nature, under the serene vault of the sky, in the gentle breath of leaves caressed by the breeze. There was even the chuckling mockery of those men who only appeared to be men; of those who had chosen nature over hope, chosen the side of the bestial against the side of the human.

And Maître Lambert could not help but acknowledge the fierce logic of his destiny. He who had always believed in the inevitable victory of man's peaceful goodwill, who had devoted all his energies to it, devoted all the fruitful moments of his life to the struggle in this cause, it was only natural, only normal, that he should be condemned, stripped of everything, humiliated, crushed in this age which sanctified the resounding victory of war. War overcame all. War was everywhere.

It was everywhere because it was here at the heart of this peaceful village; perhaps the most peaceful of villages. Maître Lambert had loved it from the moment he first set foot here. Everything enchanted him: the slow forward march of its inhabitants' history every bit as much as the inexhaustible fertility of its greenery and the limpid waters of its springs.

He had set out totally confident about the fate of Suzanne and her children. He told himself: 'Whatever happens, at least those three will be safe. And down there they will be doubly saved. They will be ignorant of the unforgivable sickness of this world. Maybe they'll remain ignorant of it, maybe they'll never carry the stigmata of a knowledge more evil in itself than the crimes and the remorse, more humiliating and degrading than death.'

He indulged in long daydreams in which Verrièges took on the proportions of a providential refuge. It was a sort of happy isle where a generation capable of new energy and confidence was biding its time. For Maître Lambert the eternal *paysan*, the fundamental man, the 'absolute man' of the historians, was no longer a simple abstraction. He saw him in the features, the appearance and the perspective of a Jean Bricaud. And above all in his quiet courage, his unpretentious pride, his indomitable patience. Also in his subtlety which, although sometimes slow, was unstoppable, and seemed capable, in the long run, of disintegrating the most massive blocks of deceit and pretence which equip man with the weapons of scorn.

Although born into wealth, Maître Lambert had always felt himself to be on the side of the oppressed. From the bottom of his heart he was *for* them, he was *with* them. He recognised them in their approach to things, in their smile. They were the small, the humble, those who dared not scrutinise memorials, and who did not feel they were rich in great moments, and always seemed to owe somebody something. Those who, in the end, did not know their own strength. Because, for him, they were strong, much stronger than the others. Their stuttering language was the only one which still made an effort to speak the truth. They lived as one should: from one minute to the next, from one day to the next. They worked a hundred years to amass a treasure which the imbecile warrior with a single gesture burnt to a crisp. And yet, they were rich; very rich, since they still dared to say 'never' or 'always'. They also said that love overcomes all, and nothing is forbidden when you are in love... 'Alas, my friends, it's all over. The case has been proven: you hadn't understood anything, and I hadn't understood anything. Today, it's not love that is all-powerful. It's hate. An eye for an eye and a tooth for a tooth. Now, we who are still alive will only be even with you who've just died in terror, if we ourselves share your terror. We'll be even with you when, after you and for you, we've shed blood, we've screamed, clawed at stone, stamped our feet, ground our teeth, panted, gasped, crackled in the fire and under torture. Now you have to be avenged, and so the eternal cycle of hatred begins again.'

Thus, Maître Lambert acknowledged his defeat. The great hope which had lit up his whole career had been nothing but a chimera... an agreeable chimera, a delusional construction which was being reduced to nothing at the same time as the village behind him was collapsing, one wall at a time. However, there he was, wandering through the undergrowth, half-blinded by tears, vainly raising his white-haired head to an empty sky – this head which he had always held high such that, despite his modest stature, those who saw him in the courtroom thought he was tall. Now he was walking very upright because he could not walk any other way. But he knew that his proud white head of hair was nothing more than a vain plaything for the nocturnal wind. He was laid low, as crushed as any of the most wretched peasants weeping for their dead. Maybe more so, since he had had the leisure and recklessness to dream a little more often...

CHAPTER 3

The lawyer intended to go back to the car. He must have gone in the wrong direction because he stumbled across a group of Germans who first threatened him with their machine guns, then having shone the beam of their torches in his face and realised he was an old man, they contented themselves with pushing him back brutally, shouting: *Raus! Raus!* One of them even made the effort to jabber: 'Go further back. Quickly. Careful. *Offizier* returns.'

Maître Lambert knew German but preferred to avoid conversation with these brutes whose red mugs and affectation of crude good humour made him want to spit in their faces.

To make himself less visible as he walked, he stuck to the roadside verge under a row of large hazel trees. In this semi-darkness he nearly bumped into a man sitting with his feet in the ditch.

The stranger held his head in his hand and was sobbing. Maître Lambert walked round him. He was ready to continue on his way when he noticed that this man was a German soldier. Judging by the narrowness of his shoulders and the childish way in which he was sobbing, he was very young.

In that moment, Maître Lambert felt a cruel pang of anguish in his heart: if this soldier, this Nazi, was overcome like this, he must have taken part in scenes of unspeakable horror. It proved that the massacre, dismissed by others in such an offhand way that it made their statements scarcely believable, had in fact taken place.

But for Maître Lambert there was nothing really very new in any of this. Deep down he had always believed in the reality of the massacre. Once the world had been given over to the contemptuous man, the 'Blond Teutonic Beast', the possibilities for horror became infinite.

The lawyer's second impulse bore some resemblance to compassion. And he was deeply surprised by that, almost outraged. Faced with anybody who wore the Nazi uniform, there was no other possible emotion than that of hatred and horror. Henceforth, for him hatred was an overriding duty… but at the same time, he understood that this German was also a victim, and the hell that he had just entered was more merciless, more abject, than that of the martyrs.

Maître Lambert heard the drumming of footsteps. Quickly he crossed the ditch and hid himself among the hazels as best he could. Two men approached. They must have been the officers he had been told to beware of.

They stopped close to the crying man.

And suddenly, the older of the two who was tall, thin and with a distinguished look about him, leant quickly over and fired a bullet from his revolver into the back of the neck of the young soldier.

This had happened in such a brutal manner that Maître Lambert had struggled to stifle a cry.

The shorter of the two officers showed not the least surprise but pushed the corpse with his foot and expressed approval.

'Excellent! We don't need these sentimental sissies. Least of all now.'

His voice was youthful – almost the voice of an adolescent – but the tone was so cutting, so harsh, that Maître Lambert could not listen to it without shuddering. This man, about twenty years old, was older than an old man: he was all bitterness and ashes.

This commentary on the atrocious incident was more frightening, infinitely more so, than the act of the murderer.

The latter turned sharply to his companion and spoke straight into his face in a rough voice, as if to an enemy: 'I feel sorry for you, Greven. I feel sorry for you as well. If I killed this soldier, it was out of pity: it was the best solution for the man he'd become today. I know for sure he wouldn't have had the courage to finish it off himself. Or more precisely, he didn't have a sense of what was required. There are those who have it, a lot of them, when it's necessary. But not you... do you dare claim that you'll recognise it, the moment when you'll have to take such action?'

The young officer replied on the instant, with aggressive indifference.

'I certainly won't be taking any such action. Not under any circumstances.'

The other one turned away, and giving up on trying to pursue an impossible conversation, returned to the village. The one called Greven followed him. With a great play of nonchalance, he threw away an almost entire cigarette and lit a new one.

CHAPTER 4

Maître Lambert was walking straight in front of him. He did not remember if he had passed the car or if he was still looking for it.

'Worse than gorillas. There are some humans who are worse than gorillas. Everything is lost.' He did not know if he was still on earth or whether he had begun some great wandering among the clouds and shades of nothingness.

At the top of a small hill, a blinding glow halted him in his tracks, as sudden as a cry. It seemed to him that he had just cried out. He turned to see that it was the church of the little dying town, hurling this sheaf of flame skyward like some final appeal.

The storm that had been slowly gathering during the day held its breath. The motionless leaves in the red glow of the fire seemed sculpted in metal, by turns sulphurous and coppery. Clouds, like fabulous manes, obscured the sky and the convulsions of the dying fires which formerly had been houses created livid chasms, purplish fire-pits, sudden gulfs of dizzying blackness.

The silhouettes of two human beings stood out against

the infernal conflagration: a very old man and a young girl in a meadow had climbed a rocky outcrop. They stood watching, spellbound, leaning slightly forward as if to stop themselves falling to the ground face down.

If he had been able, if the abyss had opened at his feet, Maître Lambert would certainly have leapt in headfirst, for the flames of hell seemed no less dreadful than those he was already living in or living through. Hell was everyday reality at the heart of the twentieth century, at the heart of this world which had no future other than that of violence, delirium, regret and remorse.

In the last few years this village had had a miraculous reprieve which was coming to a sudden end. Verrièges was falling back into the orbit of the modern world. In its turn it was subject to the law: the sadistic law of brutality and passive weakness; the law of humiliated men, violated, treated like objects by other men. And yet, the fields and forest, flowers and foliage still breathed silently and relentlessly. They had no importance. They did not count. There were no more men to see them living their elemental life, to know and state that their life guaranteed and regulated all other lives. Now, the blade of grass whose tip grew towards the blue sky was violated, the eternal balance of the tree swayed by the wind was denied, the harmony between the solid restraint of granite and the gentle nights was forgotten, the wild sensuality and depthless sweltering heat of summer had been scorned.

Humanity was fatally wounded. It would never wholly recover, nor could it let itself be healed by forgetting. To forget would be the unforgivable crime – even more unforgivable than the doziness of the man who let his enemies slowly prepare their plan.

We, all of us, have been to blame at every moment of our lives.

From this night on, death and crime revealed their presence, everywhere. And everywhere they had to be uncovered, tracked down and crushed. What had been forged in the councils of the executioners was simultaneously forged in the veins of those whose carelessness made them accomplices. In the veins and in the guts of all men, threads of vermin were being slowly tied. The strength of the sun itself was gradually diminishing in contact with the crime. It descended in darker and darker rings down to the hideous whirlpools of the souls of the gorillas. The shame of the reflective man was to have sniffed out the crime and not made the earth resound with a howl of alarm. Tomorrow it will be too late, although tomorrow it will be necessary to denounce the massacres promised for future tomorrows. It will be necessary to denounce death in the eyes of children and women, in the rose and in the hyacinth, in the violet and in the poppy. The claw of the Beast, its approaching snout and massive shadow, will haunt the gentlest of gardens and laughter-filled festivities. We have always been to blame. We must not allow ourselves to be so again. Henceforth, it is forbidden to sleep in order to make dreams welcome; forbidden to stretch out on the seabed and let ones breathing correspond with the breath of the swell and the breath of the sea anemones; forbidden to let ourselves be impregnated by the obviousness of the earth and the subtleties of water; forbidden to forget, for the briefest of moments, for the time it takes to smile, that the last shark has not been hunted down to its murky lair, that the last executioner has not been exorcised from the shifting waters of the human conscience…

When a hand shook him by the shoulder, Maître Lambert realised that he was on his knees, sobbing and the nails of his clenched fists had made bloody streaks in his face.

M. Perret this time was much less profligate in his words of comfort. Pale and hunched, he seemed older, harassed.

'I didn't find anything at Maury,' he admitted. 'I don't know what to think any more. In any case, nothing can be done 'til morning.'

He had come across some farmers, the Lavarennes, who lived in the hamlet of Jarissade, where he used to go to get food supplies.

'They're good, decent people. I just asked them for somewhere to stay in the garage, but they insisted on all three of us sleeping in beds. Come.'

Maître Lambert followed him mechanically. He then remembered that Jarissade was precisely where the parents of Francis Bricaud, his son's friend, lived. He had twice been a guest of theirs. How come he hadn't thought of them before? They could certainly provide them with information. And it would be a great comfort to be back in that house.

He told M. Perret who shook his head sadly.

'I'm sorry. There's only the Lavarennes at Jarissade. All the Bricauds went to Verrièges during the day and were kept there. Only Jean's left. He arrived too late to get through the roadblock. But he hasn't been seen for nearly five hours. Nobody knows what's become of him… obviously he could come back at any moment.'

'Yes, yes,' Maître Lambert said keenly. 'He'll come back.'

He needed a scrap of hope like a drowning man needs a

gulp of air.

Just as the two men were about to get in the car, a tremendous crashing din made them jump. It was a shock much more sudden and powerful than the collapse of roofs and walls and out through the dark spread a bronze soundwave – plaintive, hollow and endless.

'It's the church bell,' said M. Perret, turning more and more pale.

He slowly crossed himself. Then he looked at his watch which showed half past ten.

Jean:

Baaang!

What the hell is that – thunderclap – that's going on and on?

I must've fallen among the pigs. If that's all it is, too bad. That's alright by me. Of course, that's all it is. My nose is full of the stale smell of pig shit. If I open my eyes I can see the straw shining, polished by pig fat. This had to happen to me sooner or later. I've always been frightened of these filthy animals. I was deliberately made to fear them when I was little. "You women, you always tell the children what could frighten them. It's so they're more and more buried in your skirts, so they always stay by your side."

Pigs, they're capable of anything. Everything gets stuffed in their mouths. They eat when they're not hungry, just for the pleasure of eating. They even eat men.

'If that's all it is, it's no big deal. But it's odd. When I felt I was nodding off, I held off as much as I could and that was like being stabbed in the shoulder. I don't really know any more. Maybe I'm missing an arm and I fell in among them anyway, through the door… the dividing wall in this pen is too low for men of our size. I've always said this… the straw has been rubbed, polished and polished again by waves of fat, like pebbles on the beach. I roll and sway on a bed of shiny pebbles and I can't feel them under me. I'm floating, I'm weightless.

Something's happened that's taken me to the other side. *I'm on the other side, I can't feel the earth beneath me any more.* Where am I rolling around?

'Help! Help! Help me. Catch hold of me.'

Something's rumbling in my ears like thunder. It's only in my ears. Nothing to worry about. A fever like this, from falling on my shoulder, it's ridiculous! I can't stay here with my nose in the straw. My nose in the straw and in the shit. I've got to get out of here. I don't like pigs. I'm still afraid of them. If they sense I'm afraid, they're capable of anything.

'That's good, Jean. Very good. We'll make something of you yet, if the little pigs don't eat you.'

This was said without malice. M Boiget – of course he couldn't know that it sent a shiver down my spine. He liked to say it so much that I deliberately let others finish a maths problem first before me. That way he stopped congratulating me. He couldn't know, he hadn't heard the horror story of the little boy they'd found asleep in the garden one day when the door had not been shut properly. (These pigs can even get through hedges when their snout ring isn't fixed properly. But that's why I never mess this up). If M. Boiget had known, if this man had been able to guess, he certainly wouldn't have said this. There are some words which open the doors of unhappiness. Yes, totally, like in legends! M. Boiget didn't believe in legends. He wasn't superstitious. He was a good man, a solid decent sort, who said: 'Two and two make four, there's no getting away from that.' The sort of man that's liked in these parts. He knew that pigs were there to be eaten, and not to eat us, and there was no more to be said on the matter. He knew a lot of things. But he didn't know that one day I'd be here in the straw and the shit, unable to get up.

'They can eat me, M. Boiget, these pigs can. They're going to eat me if I stay still, if I can't say a word. Maybe they've already eaten me.'

'Help! Get me out of here. Isn't anybody there?'

Nobody. There wasn't anybody there that evening either, when I cried for help in the yard.

Ha! Here I am, back in the yard. It's starting all over again. I should've suspected I was asleep. It's that bloody dream come back. I'm pulling on the branches of the greengage tree, not far from the fence. Not far at all. If I see the pigs come this way, I'll have time to get clear. It's annoying that I'm only picking the green plums. I've got to pull harder. There, gently does it, so I don't break the branch. If I broke it, the old man'll give me such a hard time…

'What!… whoa!… whoa pigs!… get away, filthy creatures!

They were on me all at once. I had no idea they'd come.

What are they up to? What's going on in their heads? They're drunk on arrogance, today, drunk on their own strength…

What strength! What a stampede! I don't stand a chance

against them. Papa! Papa! Help, Papa! Come quick! Quick!…
it's no good. The old man is cutting maize in the field, he can't
hear me, I'll have to defend myself on my own. I can't, there
are two or three of them, beauties – you can say beauties talking
about pigs too, it's a bit much! – two or three already weighing
a hundred kilos each, as old Grindeau said. Me, I don't weigh
more than thirty-three kilos. They could take me out if I don't
frighten them. I can't move anywhere, they've completely
wedged the gate now, I've got no chance of opening it. I can't
even find the linchpin which acts as a bolt. They've trapped
me. I'm done for. No point shouting any more. I turn round
and look at them… it's extraordinary, they stopped squealing,
they daren't come any closer. What's happening? My father
always said: 'you should never look like you're afraid of an
animal. Look it full in the face. If you manage to get it to
meet your gaze, then it's just unlucky if they do you any harm.
Only, you mustn't wait 'til they get angry.' They're not angry,
they've stopped, they're rubbing up against each other; one of
them is uttering little cries, like it's hurt. But it's all in fun. It's
their way of fondling each other; pig caresses, they say, can't
be trusted.

But they don't mean me any harm at all. They're looking
into my eyes. They raise their heads so that their ears are folded
over, going flap! flap! like the wings of a Breton bonnet. They
push their snouts forward to sniff me, their grunts become
gentle, sometimes even fluty, caressing. And those eyes are not
at all threatening. On the contrary, they're bathed in gentleness.

And then suddenly, snap! One of them takes a big bite at
my clog. Already its neighbour's jaw is open ready to close on
my ankle. I don't say a word, but set about giving them a good

kicking with all my force; first one foot, then the other. I aim at the sort of hollow that forms their snout, trying to hit the spot where the old man has inserted the ring; I know it's the most sensitive part. And above all, I don't stop looking at them.

And it's all over!

Everything went fine: I was able to lift the little latch in time. How well everything went in those days! Everything was green-er, more flowery, more solid than now. There was always some-body there to make me laugh, to help me, to congratulate me.

Those pigs, they were just poor beasts really. That's all. A wave at them, a few kicks and they scatter. But today's pigs have grown huge.

Incredibly!

They've grown much more than me. Much more than men. They crush us now. They're the only ones who count. It's the race of gentle-eyed pigs who've won, who've grown and grown, until now they dominate the world.

'You're lucky.

The German! The soft voice of that German who drove me away… he had the same eyes as that pig that stared at me, that cooed as it approached me, who was just intent on biting me, on eating me. The eyes of a whore, the eyes of a seducer. I knew I'd seen them before.

So here we are: The pigs are our lords and masters from now on. We've always served them. Their appetite ordered everything, like time and the seasons. It's natural. It's the natural order. But now they issue orders for real, they give orders, they threaten us, they can kill us. They're going to kill us. Perhaps they're already killing us…

No! It's not true. The world's not turned upside down. It's just me, just me who's fallen among the pigs. Help me, get me out of here!

Keep quiet. Hold still.

They still talk to me with that cursed gentleness. The pig knows he's master, he's playing with me. All the strength is on his side. He has the numbers, and the weapons...

Now they're lifting me up. None too soon. My nose is full of the smell of pig. I was suffocating from it. All this sweat pouring over my face is enough to drown me. It's thick, salty. Ugh!

Where am I? My feet are still in the shining straw, but I don't see any pigs around me any more. They're still quite big though. Try as I might, I can't open my eyes wide. I can't see a single one of them. Now there's the sound of boots, around me, a little behind me. Pigs in boots carrying me off.

I can see shadows through a sort of whitish haze, against the wall; shadows rising, walking.

I'm already in front of the barn. How come they can carry me so quickly? They've even had time to hook up the cart. It's my low cart – ideal for loading pigs. People come from far and wide to borrow it... the pig cart! They want to load me into the cart which is where *they*'ll be loaded in a few days time.

– Ah! Ah! My pigs! So, you understood me when I said I'd be soon putting you in it? But it's not my fault. Everybody does this. You'll share the fate of all pigs. I wasn't the one who decided this. It's not even me who'll kill you. It's the butcher. He knows his trade. He'll stun you before bleeding you, so you're not made to suffer too much. Then he'll burn off your hairs, split you up the middle and chop you up into pieces, neatly. But what do you care? You don't feel anything, you're just pigs. You live like lords and die like pigs. That's the fate of all pig-lords, the fate of all who put others to a lot of trouble and do nothing for them. Be served, my lords, but don't expect to be spared.

They throw me in the cart. It whines, it jolts, in a clattering of axles. They're going at top speed. Breakneck speed. It's madness. I feel the icy wind on my face.

If only I could move, lift myself up, jump off. No chance: at the slightest effort I get soaked in sweat. My muscles no longer obey me. They're too heavy. And soft at the same time, soft and malleable like lead.

I'm being moved again. Their hands aren't brutal, but they're enormously strong. It feels like I've been put upright. I'm not up on my feet, and yet, I don't fall down. What's going on? I've been put with a heap of other people. I'm wedged on all sides by a thick mass of men, so tightly packed that I can't even turn my head to recognise my neighbours.

I can hear them talking among themselves. I can make out some of their words, but it's odd with the sound of rushing wind in my ears. I don't have time to understand them. I must try.

'Everyone from his household are dead. Yes everyone! He's on his own now.'

I ought to talk to these men and women, however. I feel I know them. I know it. I can't help but know it.

I can't talk any more; I can scarcely catch my breath, with my mouth wide open. My voice is extinguished, forever.

'...Dead. Yes, everyone'

So, they're dead! These men, these women around me, all men and women I knew. And they're dead.

I'm among the dead. I'm on the journey of the dead… so, I must be dead too. I didn't feel myself die. Good! That's how I always wanted to die. But I didn't know, back then, I thought, – I'd been told – that I'll meet up with all the dead I've ever loved. I thought I'd be able to talk to them, to see them. And here I am in the middle of an indifferent crowd, dumb, faceless. They're worse than strangers. I know them and they refuse to know me. They aren't my friends any more. They're my worst enemies: they reject me.

– No!

I don't want to follow them. I want to go away. I want to go back. I don't want a future which is going to devour me.

– I don't want it. I don't want it.

This cart is going too fast. The planks crack under my feet. They fly into splinters. I'm going to fall. I'm falling. That's it, I'm floating gently in the air. It's restful, but I'm ashamed. How ashamed I am to be resting like this!

In the end they let me go. Everything is simple. The hollow road disappears between brambles and rosehips in flower. Ow! I got caught up in the brambles again, and they scratch!… it's nothing. I'm off to school under a full May sun. It's my first year at school. I wallow in the clear, fluffy, infinitely deep thickness of a good, dreamless sleep. I have a whole future ahead of me, I have no future, I don't need them… all I need is sleep.

CHAPTER 5

Maître Lambert had gone to bed out of politeness. He did not want to refuse the offer of a bed from the Lavarennes – such good people – who had deprived themselves of it to be nice to him. He spent the night trying to find a restful position. He did not find it. He was seized by a ceaseless shaking which he could not control and which was like an engine being revved too high. He was unaware of being afraid in any conventional sense. He would have been indifferent to the threat of being shot or killed in a bombardment. It might even have been of some comfort to him to be delivered from these weird tremors in that way. There was something strange within him, beyond his control, an encased mechanism which was forging ahead on its own towards some unimaginable abyss.

At dawn he slipped gradually into a numbness which he pushed back against with all his strength. He tried to cry out, to move his arms and legs, but without success. He had a nightmare, maybe several. Huge stones were falling about him as he lay at the bottom of a hole. And yet he was fine in his black hole, under the rain of stones, and he called himself a coward. All he wanted was to wake up, he did not want the assistance of nightmares…

When young Albert Lavarenne knocked at his door, he welcomed him as a saviour.

'We're going to try and get to Verrièges. Monsieur Perret's determined,' said Albert. 'As it's four o'clock, there's a chance the Germans have left. Obviously, it'd be better for you to stay here and rest. We wanted to let you know anyway.'

'I'm coming, of course.'

The head of the farm, Joseph Lavarenne, had made coffee and put ham and cheese on the table. M. Perret and Maître Lambert could not eat a mouthful, but they forced down a coffee as well as a gulp of *eau-de-vie*.

Léonard, the old retainer, insisted on coming with them. Like all the inhabitants of the villages scattered around Verrièges, he had a number of relatives in the town.

The five men, in espadrilles, made their way towards the town along the country roads, sticking close to the hedges like thieves.

From time to time they took cover and Albert, the nimblest of them, set off on reconnaissance. He crawled towards the Lavaud farm where he knew the Germans had been feasting. He soon returned saying that everything had been torched, but he had seen great piles of empty bottles among the collapsed walls and heaps of ash.

'The bastards didn't even bother to untie the animals. They burnt them alive. The carcasses are all mixed in with the debris of the buildings.'

Joseph Lavarenne clenched his fists. His deep tanned face, under thick tufts of black hair which poked out from his cap, took on the colour of stone.

However, Albert had not seen a single human corpse, which left M. Perret with a shred of hope.

'All the same,' he said. 'They must have taken the people somewhere.'

The three farmers bent their heads in silence. Maître Lambert who was walking at the back suddenly caught sight of the looks that darted between them. They had understood, as he himself had understood from the outset…

Still walking stealthily and coughing from the acrid and weirdly nauseous smoke, they reached the top of the main street. Not one house had been spared. The Café Mazaud, so welcoming with its pergola of greenery and its light grey, newly-painted shutters, had been reduced to a shapeless mound of debris. The outline of the foundations could be barely made out. And yet, among the rubble and twisted iron beds, there was one corner in which lay a large pile of laundry, almost untouched; piles of sheets next to handkerchiefs in little squares carefully arranged according to colour.

Almost everywhere the embers of the fire were still smouldering. The smoke, increasingly thick, hung above the ruins like a storm cloud. The terrible smell made the five men cough and made their eyes stream. Instinctively, they had taken off their hats and were walking on tiptoe.

Here and there whole walls had resisted, such that, from a little way off, it was conceivable that some houses were more or less intact. But the interior had collapsed and the disorder which melded the shattered dishes, the smashed furniture and the charred beams was more heart-breaking than total annihilation.

At Billancourt, Maître Lambert had seen blocks of flats

crushed and ripped apart even more violently by bombs. Never had he been so overcome by a sense of desolation. Here the destroyers had worked by hand, they had destroyed for the sake of destruction, directing their assault with precision. Doors, windows, furniture, crockery, ornaments, everything bore the marks of a hate-filled desire to annihilate. Even in the gardens, the perpetrators had taken the trouble to set fire to any vegetation dry enough to burn. The trunks of fruit trees had begun to burn up to their first branches. In the flower beds, the peas and beans had collapsed around their charred stakes which formed piles of light ash. The climbing plants drew blackish arabesques on the side of walls and along the trellises.

Not even the Lavarennes could recognise the shops in the main street. The gaping facades of the houses everywhere revealed a mass of tiles, rubble and tangled ironwork. All that was left of some cars parked in front of doors was a reddish carcass, buckled and twisted.

'Ah no! Ah no!'

This was all the three *paysans* managed to mumble in a dull voice. Faced with the extent of the cataclysm they had refrained from the curses which they felt were totally inadequate in the circumstances.

M. Perret was weeping silently. He looked straight ahead of him and walked faster and faster.

As for Maître Lambert, tears ran down his cheeks, but he was able to assume they were caused by the smoke and smell of burnt leather which became more and more suffocating. He seemed to be experiencing neither pity, nor terror, nor any sort of known feeling. The shock of so much horror, so overwhelming, carried with it its own antidote: it numbed the senses to the point of anaesthesia.

At the market square they met another group which, like them, was wandering through the smoke and embers which here and there still glowed.

'I recognise Doctor Joly,' said Joseph Lavarenne. 'Maybe he knows something.'

Unfortunately, Dr Joly did not know very much. On the previous day he had been refused entry to the village and had spent the night at the hamlet of Souliac.

When M. Perret asked him if anybody over there had been part of the exodus of villagers, he raised his arms with a look of distress.

'I've no idea. We saw nobody go past. What's surprising is that we see only a few bodies here. Anyway, what I can tell you for my part is I found the bodies of my two grown-up sons. They were murdered in my garden.'

He had found out about the fate of his sons at Souliac from Armand Graetz, the young refugee who had hidden in the thick ivy on top of a wall. Towards daybreak as he could no longer hear the boots and shouts of the killers, Armand had managed to hobble all the way to Souliac despite a leg in plaster.

There was a young woman present who kept repeating in a flat, incessant voice, addressing each one of the men in turn without waiting for their response: 'The Hotel Mazaud. Show me where the Hotel Mazaud is. My husband came to pick up a food parcel from the Hotel Mazaud yesterday… just to pick up a parcel. Nobody's done anything to him. Nobody could've done anything to him; he's not from here. Hotel Mazaud!… you can tell me where it is, Monsieur.'

From time to time, Dr Joly proffered some words of consolation. Not that she understood anything. She would have to be sectioned when there was time to deal with her. In Limoges where she was due to meet her husband, she had heard vague stories about arrests and fighting in the Verrièges area. So, she had walked all night getting lost on a number of occasions on roads and tracks she did not know. As soon as she saw the ruins and breathed the smoke from the fires, she became delirious.

Continuing their sinister pilgrimage, Maître Lambert and his companions passed by a well whose little tiled roof had fallen in. Joseph Lavarenne noticed that the cartwheels, beams, crates, and a lot of by now unrecognisable objects had been piled up and burnt around the edge. Coming up to the well, he noticed that the hole had been blocked up with large stones, earth and roughcast. It would take tools and some serious work to clear that lot out.

What was underneath all those stones? Nobody dared ask this question out loud. They quickly moved away. They were breathing heavily, their faces bathed in sweat.

They arrived at the church. Maître Lambert liked the sober and solid Romanesque construction whose lines seemed so natural in this landscape of granite. All that was left now was a sort of charred jetty. The roof of the nave had fallen in. From the smashed windows there still drifted some smoke which must have been billowing out before, as the wall was black up to the top. The vaulted door of the main entrance was half-blocked by masonry from the neighbouring house which had collapsed in one fell swoop.

Dr Joly learnt from young Graetz that on the previous day

it had been a matter of using the church to shelter the women and children. The sight of the smoking, burnt-out debris drained the colour from his face. However, very calmly, he gestured to the others to wait, and he picked his way through the rubble.

Less than a minute later he re-appeared in haste. Holding his arms wide he barred the way of M. Perret who was also ready to go inside.

'No, please. No. No,' he said hurriedly. 'It's useless. There's nothing we can do. Absolutely nothing.'

His face had taken on an extraordinary pallor and his gaze was wandering. M. Perret thought he was going to lose his balance and he grabbed him by the arm.

'What do you mean, Doctor?' he cried. 'Tell us, quickly. Tell us nobody's in there.'

'No. Nobody... there's nobody. Everything's smashed up. There's nothing we can do. I swear there is absolutely nothing to be done. Let's go.'

Maître Lambert shook his head, walked past the doctor and made his way slowly towards the church. The others followed.

There was blood everywhere. The door, the walls, splinters of burnt chairs – everything was spattered with it. The sanctuary was covered with a huge pile of still burning cinders. As they approached, they gradually made out human shapes half-consumed, then the skeletons of hands, of feet.

Many little hands and many little feet. And most of all, heads. More and more heads. An incredible number of round skulls. Some were picked clean by the fire, while others still retained shreds of scalp, ears, halves of faces. Others, shattered by the impact of bullets and stones, leaked grey matter and the fire had turned it into an almost transparent pulp. Certain bodies had retained their form; they could make out women who were hugging their children, and others who had lifted their little ones above their heads. Tiny skeletons were huddled and entangled in macabre embraces. Some children had grabbed tightly on to the altar rail and their half-consumed hands hung there completely detached from their body. Out of more than a hundred corpses it was not possible to identify more than three or four faces.

Dr Joly was right: there was nothing the men present could do. They could not even bring themselves to tears.

Maître Lambert hesitated, transfixed. He did not want to flee. No. He would not give in to panic. At the same time, he could not stay here.

These children, these women – he had known many of them, he had heard them laugh. Perhaps Suzanne was buried in the thickest part of the tangled magma of skeletons. Perhaps he would recognise her in one of the crushed bodies whose attitude carried all the signs of suffering, despair, insane horror.

Finally, he found himself outside with the others. Entirely void of strength and will, he let himself be led wherever.

And this little group of distraught men trudged on, wandering like lost shadows among the wisps of smoke and ghosts of this day-after of the world. Occasionally they looked at each other and each one recognised in the eyes of the other their own indecision, because now they wanted to deny the evidence. Having understood everything, they were trying to believe that they did not understand, that they could not understand. It was too much, much too much. Human consciousness refused to take on board such a huge burden.

'And yet... and yet...'

M. Perret stammered this out at one point. Such reticence in the speech of a man so clear, so sure of himself, was more dramatic than a lamentation,

'...and yet, you'd have thought they were men.'

Here precisely were the words which he should not have had to utter. At the very moment when they were obliged to remember that 'men' had wanted to create such carnage, that was when the sense of vertigo began.

No!

This 'no' rose from the very depths of being. The whole of humanity should be saying 'no', or else write itself off. Finding a way out, fleeing, was a matter of urgency. To flee back in time, to flee back to the origin of the species. Then, everything would seem simple: one horde came through, annihilating everything, and after it came the formation of another horde, drunk on hatred and vengeance. So, no! Faced with so much absurdity, the outraged mind shied away. It was necessary to flee even further, beyond this nebulous twilight, to bury oneself in the fabled terrors of prehistory. One animal sought its prey amid the shapeless rumble of the forest. An animal always ready to scamper away when confronted by the strong and ready to rush to attack the weak. Thus, unfounded reason had recourse to nothing other than its own collapse.

At certain moments Maître Lambert moved away from the group. He went up to a wall that was still standing and sought to rest his eyes on a few square metres of intact surface. Then the former world, the reasonable, conceivable world, flooded through him with an abundance and speed that made him doubt the very reality of what he had just seen. 'I was mistaken. I'm exasperated. A nervous wreck. It's not possible. There have been some reprisals through burning here, as there have been everywhere, from one end of Europe to the other.' Then he looked up and once again fell headlong into the unimaginable.

The day was brightening, and the ruins seemed blacker and blacker, more and more ghostly. It was not even a village in ruins, but a mass of shapeless and mutilated debris, thrown about at random in the face of a storm-threatening sky, among the shadows of the apocalypse which the heavy black smoke made undulate with funereal slowness, against the background of the pale glow of dawn.

And all at once, Maître Lambert realised that he had started running. Moreover, everybody around him was running. In fact, it was the only thing to do. Maître Lambert was not going far. As soon as he spotted a clump of ferns, he threw himself into it, completely out of breath. His knees gave way and he felt like his heart was going to burst.

Joseph Lavarenne who had followed him, held him up, pushed him towards a bushy hedge and told him why everybody had run off like that: his son Albert had spotted a group of German soldiers, thankfully a long way off.

CHAPTER 6

The first murmurings of this June morning had dragged David out of a deep stupor. He had got up briskly without, as he did on other mornings, stretching or groping around him for the last undulations of sleep. Immediately on the defensive, his hamstrings taut, his head down, he cast an arid look about him, then he set off.

Along the overhung paths it only took him a few minutes to reach the Bricaud's farm at Jarissade.

The door was wide open. He called out, first in a low voice then louder and louder. Familiar names resounded oddly in the clear silence. First it was the women's names (he knew that they were the ones preparing the coffee): 'Mère Julie! Mère Julie!' Then 'Annie!'

If the women were tired then Jean was up and about. Jean was never tired. David shouted for a long time: 'Jean! Jean! Jean!' Then he called the others: 'Gaston!... Francis!... Père Etienne!'

His own voice was alien to him: it resonated too loudly and seemed on the point of breaking.

Suddenly something ran against his legs and he let out

a shout. It was Négrou the dog, whining loudly, low-slung, swaying back and forth with a convulsive wagging of her tail.

Suddenly, she shot straight off towards the far side of the farmyard.

David followed her. As he went, the cows, veal calves and heifers deafened him with their bellowing, to which the sheep responded with their high-pitched bleating. It was enough to drive you crazy…

Négrou was standing in front of the door to the piggery; she was scratching at the handle for all she was worth. David ran forward, opened it quickly and went inside.

Then, by the light of a flickering bulb, he saw Jean.

He saw him lying on the other side of the tip-up dividing wall, huddled up, with his nose in the straw. The pigs, gathered together next to the shutter, turned and looked at David with their sharp eyes, red as embers in the lamplight. There was one, however, a big fat one, which did not look his way. It was very close to Jean and with mechanical regularity, it stuck its snout forward until it got a kick in the nose; then it backed away with a sharp squeal, plaintive and unspeakably sly. It looked like a game, but a frightening game, because the kick that beat back the animal was showing obvious weariness.

David did not hang around. He unlocked and opened wide the door of the piggery which allowed the pigs out. As he had noticed that the animals had already been fed, he left the other door open.

The pigs suffered a moment of agonising uncertainty. Finally, one of them made up its mind. Slowly, stopping and starting many times and looking around warily, it went off, found the food, and immediately began lapping it up noisily.

Within seconds it was joined by all the others and David only had to shut the first door behind them.

Jean did not recognise him. He talked and gesticulated ceaselessly. David unrolled a clean straw mattress near him, did his best to lay him on top of it and ran off to get help.

At the Lavarenne's he only came across the women. They welcomed him warmly, kissed him and informed him that his grandfather had spent the night at their house.

'Ah, good!' David said simply and without the slightest emotion.

He remembered that on the previous day he had resolved never to cry and he thought that some superior power had granted him this wish. He felt his heart was totally dried-up. He gave an account of what he had seen and done.

The woman of the house, robust Maria Lavarenne, decided that Jean should be put in a tipcart and brought to her place so she could look after him, since he had nobody else.

David did not ask for further explanation: nothing could surprise him. He accompanied Maria to the village of Breuil, less than a kilometre away. By an extraordinary stroke of luck, out of the four houses there, only three old women and a fifteen-year-old boy were missing. Two of the men, old Lenoir and his oldest son, immediately ran off to the Bricaud's.

They saw that there was no way Jean could walk. They tied the oxen together and attached them to the low cart which was used to transport pigs. It was more convenient to load a sick man on that than a narrow tipcart with high wheels.

Despite their affectionate words and their urging him to keep calm, Jean struggled and shouted. Maria took hold of the goad and led the oxen while the two Lenoirs and David supported the sick man so as to cushion the jolting.

When they arrived home, the men had returned.

Maître Lambert, sitting on a kitchen bench, did not have the strength to get to his feet and welcome his grandson. But he held him close for a long time. And David noticed that this man whom he had always seen as so calm, so sure of himself, and whom he thought was so strong, was shaking from head to foot. He held him as tight as he could and experienced a great sense of happiness when he felt the trembling die down.

Jean was laid down on young Albert's bed, where Maître Lambert had spent the night. It was impossible to make him understand anything that was said to him. Staring straight ahead, he talked and talked....

Nevertheless, news came in. Joseph Lavarenne had met a man from Souliac who informed him that young Jef Juéry had escaped. He and Arnaud the postman were the only survivors from the barn where Gaston and Francis Bricaud had been.

Joseph looked at Jean with compassion and said that it would've been better for him if he'd succeeded in getting into the village yesterday.

'The whole of his household are dead. He's on his own now.'

Maria went 'ssshhh!' and nodded towards Jean. He had half-risen and fixed Joseph with an unbearably piercing stare. The words poured so fast from his lips, flecked with white foam, that it was impossible to make out their meaning. Moreover, his voice was hoarse to such an extent that it produced nothing more than a raucous splutter.

There was a little morphine in the house which dated back to the final seizure of the now-departed, old Biaise. Maria gave

Jean an injection. His skin was so tough that she twice bent her needle.

'For a man of forty,' she remarked. 'He's got the hide of a boar! He's built to last a hundred years. There's some families like that.'

No sooner had Jean dozed off than a kid on a bike brought some astounding news; among the tiny number of survivors who were turning up one at a time was old Etienne. He had already been taken to Souliac on a stretcher.

To catch his breath, he had laid down a little way from the church by the low wall which bordered the garden of the former tailor, and he had not got up again. Young Robert Leboutet as he was escaping had fallen on top of him with all his weight and almost smothered him. When the old man recovered his voice, he begged Robert not to move.

'Stay there, son, stay there. If you put your head up, you'll get killed, like everybody is getting killed.'

Robert took his advice and he was left undisturbed in his hole. Anybody who went round the side or wanted to try and get past was gunned down. Several had been found hanging on the hedge and two of them lying one on top of the other in a wheelbarrow...

As a result of this, Robert was able to state that he owed his life to Etienne.

Unfortunately, the old man was struggling to cope with so much accumulated emotion and exhaustion. He could not put one foot in front of the other. In addition, although he was still replying in a very sensible manner when somebody spoke to him, he also kept up a tireless conversation with himself asking questions and giving answers.

'What a poor, poor house!' old Maria cried. 'Here are the only two left now and they don't know what they're saying... Ah, but this changes everything. We can't put the both of them here. Go and fetch Etienne. We'll put them in a bed each and I'll stay and look after them for as long as it takes.'

Old Etienne was brought on a cart. No sooner had he arrived at Jarissade than he fell into a deep sleep. They put Jean near him. He was also asleep.

So it was that the father and son returned to their house, a house now empty and silent.

PART 7

CHAPTER 1

On two occasions the Germans returned.

They hounded their victims, they murdered them again, they moved around, they burnt again what they had already burnt.

People assumed that they were hoping to wipe out any trace of their crime, which would have been an undeniable sign of insanity. But they also tried to invent a cover, if not an impossible justification, by scattering around ammunition boxes which came from the English or the Americans.

They themselves understood that these attempts were somewhat ridiculous because in the end they disappeared. Then the emergency teams arrived, with lorries loaded, to clear up the ruins.

Of the women and children, Amélie Bernard was the only one to survive and her injuries would make her an invalid. Out of more than six hundred dead only a few dozen could be identified with any certainty.

From the mass graves there rose a powerful stench which the wind sometimes carried far off across the countryside.

The rescue workers could only carry out their task with the aid of rubber gloves, and their faces covered by a mask soaked in essence of eucalyptus.

The dogs and cats that wandered through the rubble had to be poisoned then burnt. They were buried in a huge ditch alongside the oxen, the cows and the sheep found packed in barns, asphyxiated or burnt alive.

Many families were entirely wiped out, from the oldest great grandparents to babies just a few days old. Most of the dead, moreover, had relatives in the surrounding countryside and towns.

In Germany there were still a few POWs from Verrièges who, when they returned home, found nothing but blackened stones and some names on the marble plaque placed on the common grave.

All the countryfolk wore mourning. They felt it was no ordinary mourning and generally maintained an unaccustomed silence.

Over six hundred dead was a large number, and yet the hole left by their absence in this corner of the country was so great that it was difficult to believe that it was only six hundred. It was an abyss without beginning or end.

In this mass grave, in every mass grave on earth, human flesh was buried. Anonymous and decomposed flesh which had had a name and a shape; a familiar name, a shape acquired over a long time, loved, caressed, envied, protected. This flesh was much more than a mass of flesh: it was life itself, with its essential worries and hopes.

And living flesh suffered still in remembrance of tortured flesh. The memory was in flesh alone, flesh had to give itself up entirely to memory. Let no one enter this world, the world based on torture, if they have no memory of flesh. The countryfolk, with their black stares, carried this dark, overriding and ineluctable memory in the very depths of their being, and it prevented them from fully recovering, from walking as they had before. Here were piled high, brothers, father, mother, the children I had, and those I might have had. Here dwells Man no longer alive.

The greatest innocence and the greatest cruelty had come together in the middle of this century. There, all the innocence and all the crimes of an insane world had known their moment of most acute delirium.

The great glow in the sky above Verrièges, like an abyss, was always there, lurking under the eyelids of those who had seen it. It was not about to be extinguished.

Nor would the great fear be loosening its claw-like grip.

Hatred and fear sustained the fire in the sky. They would sustain it forever.

CHAPTER 2

As soon as Jean had been operated on, it was obvious that his shoulder would heal in a few weeks. He behaved sensibly, not trying to use his arm and keeping in place the bandages the surgeon had applied.

Maria tended to old Etienne and did the housework. Joseph and his son Albert, took it in turns to look after the animals. They also undertook to bring in the hay.

'Don't you do that,' Joseph had said genially to Jean. 'We're here. As you know, we're a big household and half of them have bugger all to do, usually…'

He broke off quickly. He had realised that these were not words to be spoken in Jean's house. From then on, work was the only thing he talked about. He talked about that a great deal. As did Albert.

They had more time to talk than they wanted as Jean never said anything other than 'Yes', 'No' or 'Thanks'.

Maître Lambert, as soon as he had buried his son and daughter-in-law, took young David back to Switzerland with him. Even when it came to goodbyes, and despite the young boy's tears, Jean said nothing. He settled for a smile and a handshake. He found nothing more to say to anyone.

Sometimes his father called for him; he went up to his bed and silently gave him what he was asking for. For his part the old man, having asked several questions which he quickly answered himself, wasted no time in dismissing him.

'I'm too tired. Off you go, my boy. Off you go, I'm going to sleep. You can see how I am: I ask for you and then I tell you to go away. I still need to sleep.'

Etienne's slump was total. The Lavarennes as well as some other farmers from round about who came to see him, left dismayed, saying they could not understand it.

Jean listened to them without saying a word. Not one muscle in his face moved. When he was asked a question, most often he just made some evasive gesture.

'Aren't you surprised,' Joseph asked several times. 'That your father doesn't seem ill, but he spends all day in bed like that?'

He replied: 'Oh! No, no!' And in truth he was not surprised. He did not feel any sort of emotion. He found it very natural that he did not want to get up. At a pinch what might have seemed a bit strange to him was the quiet stubbornness which kept the old man alive.

He walked around and slowly carried out the tasks that were within his capacity as best he could: bringing down the straw for the oxen and cows, preparing the bedding and leading the pigs to their pen.

Late one night, when he was bringing a basketful of clover to the rabbits, he heard Joseph and Maria near the fence, talking about him:

First Maria: 'He can't stay like this. It's not so much that he doesn't talk. Of course, you can understand, after what's happened, he doesn't want to make jokes like before. But he doesn't even listen to what you say. He doesn't listen, he doesn't look, he doesn't pay attention to anything. And... have you ever seen him cry or show any sorrow?'

Joseph shook his head sadly.

'No! No! He shows nothing. Nothing! He hasn't even gone to visit their grave... you'll say that as graves go, it's an odd one. They couldn't identify any of his folk. Ah! God. It's all too much! Too much! I can understand why he tries not to think about it. Even I can't think about it. I don't... Ah! Well!'

In the darkness, Joseph, at a loss for words, made a broad gesture as if he was throwing away with all his might something he could no longer bear holding.

But Maria, hanging her head in that stubborn and astute manner she always adopted to win Joseph over, went on: 'Whatever you say... whatever you say... still, there's something very wrong here, I tell you. (She touched the top of her head). He doesn't even eat; I mean, not like a man should be eating. He stops all of a sudden and let's his bowl of soup go cold in front of him. He doesn't even seem to be thinking of anything. He's just there, neither sad, nor anything. Like a lump. Have you noticed he hasn't smoked a cigarette since?'

'Yes, I noticed. Of course! I'm the one who noticed first. I don't need you to tell me what to notice...'

'I tell you something: if the old man wasn't around, he'd do something nasty... and the old bloke is sinking fast. The doctor told me he probably wouldn't last the week.'

Joseph, arms by his side, shook his head. They looked at each other and said no more. They moved off with a slow, heavy tread.

Jean calmly shared the clover out among the rabbits. These poor creatures would never lack for anything. His mother was the only one who fed them. It was her job and she stuck to it. 'My little ones,' she used to say. 'Here you go.' They would have what they wanted, everything they wanted. As if she was still there.

Suddenly Jean dropped the empty basket. It was made of little strips of wood joined together and resounded mournfully on the stones. Completely motionless, Jean could see the door to the hutch wide open in front of him. He should have closed it, but he did not. He did not want to move, he did not want to know what needed to be done, he did not want to know anything.

'She couldn't keep her mouth shut, could she! She couldn't stay at home.'

He was thinking of Maria with dumb fury. It was because of her that he was there, on the point of suffocating. If she had not said anything, perhaps he could have gone on for a long time doing what he did before.

Now he could not believe that he was still here, on his own, before… he could not even pretend to believe it.

He was suffocating on the spot, unable to sob, unable to go forward or back. There he was, pinned to the present, pierced through and through, nailed to some invisible wooden torture bench. He had seen his mother, actually seen her, making that gesture she always made when putting clover in the rabbits' hutch. She was there with the basket wedged between her hip and the wall. She stood foursquare, upright, chin up, and with her right hand, she spread out the big green bunch while here and there she gave the bolder ones a friendly tap on the nose, the velvety noses which moved up and down like little machines making her laugh. For so many years she had laughed when she looked at them…

Jean could not stop himself seeing her, almost as if she was there. And he could not stop himself knowing, seeing, that she was no longer there and never would be. Never! He could not accept it. It was a lie, since he had just seen her again. No. He had seen her for sure, too clearly. He had definitely seen her. The coming of this mysterious, all-powerful light provided absolute confirmation. It lodged a certainty in his heart – that his mother would never be there again, seen on a daily basis, allowing him to add at leisure another image to so many others which he thought were unimportant.

'Have you ever seen him cry?'

No, he was not crying, he didn't have the slightest desire to cry. If he began remembering, he would do a lot worse than cry… besides, he would soon be able to breathe like he used to. At last, he found his vegetable calm.

Then he went up to the old man's bedroom. And he realised that Maria was telling the truth: his father was going to die.

How had he not noticed it sooner? The old man's breathing was so rapid and laboured that it took all of his little remaining strength to sustain it. Ever since he had been brought back, he left his lamp burning night and day. The pile of books and newspapers that Maria had left within his reach had not been touched. (Up until then he had never lost the habit of reading to send himself to sleep.) He looked in front of him, and his gaze was neither wandering nor vague, but on the contrary, it was very lively and oddly attentive.

This gaze was the reason why, as soon as he stepped into the bedroom, Jean realised that his father was going to die. With a shudder that made his skin crawl, he knew that his father too was aware of this devastating light which, a few minutes ago in the yard, had allowed Jean, in less than a second, to see his mother more completely than at any other time in his life. He wanted to leave on tiptoe without intruding upon a strange dialogue where there was certainly no place for him. However, a sudden tender impulse pushed him towards his father. If this was his last evening… perhaps I'll never see him again. Or rather, he will never see me again.

He went to the foot of the bed. Etienne glanced at him briefly and then went back to staring into the distance over his head. But as usual he immediately started talking.

'You see, my boy, I'm still the same. I know that's dull for you, to see me always the same. You come and see me nonetheless. You're the best of all of them, you are. The others never come. I knew you were the best. I do love the others, as much as I can. But that doesn't stop me from knowing that you're the best. You're the one who works for the others. You're the oldest. I was the oldest too. That's what the real son is. We call him the mother's son around here. But he's also the father's son. Yes. You, François, you're the one I've always counted on first… Oh yes! Oh yes!'

He had said nothing for a while and had glanced towards Jean. And Jean was sure that he was playing games: he did not mistake him for François. He had not made that mistake for real. He was trying to be mistaken. He was deliberately, stubbornly, making himself do this. Jean understood that this was a defence mechanism. He too, until he heard Maria and Joseph talking, had defended himself in the same way. He also understood why his father continued obstinately to talk to all the members of the household as if they were still there. There was no point telling him the truth. He would not hear it. For once and for all, he had refused to hear it.

Jean listened to his wheezing breath which was no shorter or more irregular than on the previous day.

'Goodnight, my boy,' Etienne said quietly. 'I'm tired already. Off you go.'

He had said this with his customary authority. For that, Jean wanted to embrace him. He held back. Since the old man still knew what he wanted, it was much better this way. Jean would certainly not try to thwart him.

'Goodnight, papa.'

He shut the door and heard the latch squeak just like he had heard it squeak for more than thirty years.

'Jean!'

Jean had gone five or six steps down the stairs when he heard his father's voice; it was vibrant and virile, extraordinarily like it had been when Jean, as a little boy, would come running at his call. This voice had the power to give him wings then. It still did, for Jean was back up the stairs in two bounds.

Sitting very stiffly and apparently a lot less breathless, Etienne looked his son in the eye.

'What is it, papa?' asked Jean. And he noticed that he was trying to recapture the tone and the smile of his childhood.

His expression, dark but not at all foggy, on the contrary, shining bright and sharp, examined him with severe sagacity.

'Nothing, Jean son, nothing. You talked to me just now

– good. Me, as you see, I'm done in. But you, take care of yourself, my boy. Go.'

This was his usual piece of advice. He lay back down and Jean left the room noiselessly.

CHAPTER 3

Jean, who ever since the event, dozed or slept almost continuously, felt that on that night sleep would elude him. When he was sure there was no chance of meeting anybody on the road, he walked quickly to Verrièges.

A mist dimmed the moonlight. The contours of the ruins were as blurry as an apparition. Jean walked on tiptoes and his rope espadrilles made no noise. He was a little astonished at feeling so calm. Since he had decided to put an end to it all, since he was certain that he would soon escape the desolation and regret, he took in only fleeting and trivial images. He did not even feel any great curiosity. In the main he felt upset that he no longer recognised his village at all. On either side of the main street, the dilapidated houses no longer looked the same. Some had no walls; others were just a shell with gaping doors and windows. No, the ruins no longer resembled each other, but they scarcely called to mind the houses as they once were. Jean had thought he would find the ghost of the village, and he anticipated this spectacle with fear, but also with a sort of hope: even if they were terrifying, even if they were excruciating in the extreme, memories of a past life would have been precious to him. But death affirmed once and for all that it was to be otherwise.

This cold, powdery light which was the very expression of death, showed him nothing more than the skeleton of a village. An already cleaned-up skeleton, ready for the lab technician who would arrive later to examine it, photograph it, study it. At this thought a terrible anxiety took hold of him and made him tremble all over. He did not want that. He could not accept it. He was there, alive, the bearer of a weight of memories which were capable of detonating and shooting upwards like flames. It was only him and men like him who knew that these houses had been homes, where glances of tenderness and anger shone, where calls and laughter and sobs rang out, where children were born and the old died, where dreams, regrets and projects became entangled... no, it was not right that all that, in one day, was nothing more than a little desert of silent stones, not far from an equally silent mound of bones.

All that was there was the mark and the signature of the madness of those men who called themselves 'wild-men' and who were simply 'pig-men', miserable beasts lagging behind in the evolution of the world, hideous cave-dwellers, incapable of keeping up with the march of life and who exacted crass, ignoble revenge by celebrating the archaic cult of Death. Death was everywhere. The laugh of death danced through the gaps in the walls, in the icy powder of the moonlight. Everywhere death opens its dark maw. Here the men of death had asserted one of their most complete triumphs. Death – easy, sickening and brutish – had triumphed. The living man had been conquered by the bestial man, by the pig-man, who had been allowed to make ignominy into a strength and to call murderers by glorious names.

Death breathed in Jean's face and pushed him back with considerable force.

He knew that he would not resist for long since he had already given up resisting. When he had slipped M. Labarre's large revolver into his pocket, his mind was already made up. But at that moment he was not sure where this irresistible impulse came from. It was simply that he felt drawn to his dead, to the departed who had surrounded him, supported him, maintained him in the world of the living. When they had been alive, he too was alive. Their life was his life, and he could not imagine any other. Everything that constituted his zest for life existed before the massacre and could not exist after it. So, what was left for him to search for in the world?

Here it was different. Here he had to contend with this black squall that lifted him off his feet, with the abominable laughter of the conquerors which still vibrated across the sky, with the memory of those pale eyes in the midst of an expression which was so utterly strange, absolutely scornful.

He had read, he had heard tell, he had already understood – without even realising it, before anger had lit a glow of revelation within him – that for those men he was the supreme Enemy. He, the patient cultivator of life, upright in the face of the rabid worshippers of death. He, the bare-handed provider, standing unarmed in front of the specialist destroyers, the specialist arsonists, the specialist merry-makers, the consumers of unique specialities, the bastards drunk on muddy metaphysics and pride, the swine brought up to supreme power, the Absolute Pigs.

They took hold of the Man of the Earth, they crushed him,

they could trample on him as and when. Having murdered, butchered, hacked and burnt all flesh, all hope, all life which made up his flesh, his hope and his life, it was now considered noble, grandiose even, to push him hither and thither, at the whim of their breath, like a broken puppet, to have him wander, staggering, twisted and breathless until his final gesture of despair.

He was still walking, walking faster and faster, and he was indignant to feel his gait become jerky. Fatigue already. Already the reddening mist of exhaustion in front of his eyes. So, that was what hopelessness felt like: a leap forward in years. Old age at forty. He had not even been working much. He had been sleeping for days and nights, like a very weak, very old man. Like old Etienne! That was the secret of his fatigue: he was imitating papa Etienne because, like him, he could not find the necessary resources to confront this unreasonable expiry date. It was not true sleep that left him prostrate on his bed or in the meadow grass during the long hot afternoons. It was the stupor of denial.

And yet, he knew the monster had been there, that it was still somewhere, that it would always be there as long as pig-men existed and the others, men like himself, would not stand up and fight, immediately and to the death, fight every minute of their lives.

Jean was walking. He tripped over stray stones, he lost his balance and got up again, his hands full of gravel. In this dust which he shook off, perhaps there was dried blood or human ash; the blood and ash of the dead, of his dead, of those who had provided a little of life's sweetness, the only reason for living.

There was nothing he could do on his own. His strength had been sapped by them. His strength had only ever come through them and was for them. As a builder and a farmer, he only worked to construct, to help, to love.

He stopped abruptly in front of a sign; its large letters still very readable.

Bakery.

Below this was the usual jumble of stones, plaster and the debris of charred beams. At the back, Jean could make out the shape of the oven in front of which he sometimes chatted with Paul Pastier the baker. Poor Paul! Where are you, Paul? You won't be telling me any more that I've forgotten to shave and I have five o'clock shadow. You'll not be calling me 'Devil Jean' any more and asking me if I'd really like to sit in the flames of the oven.

A bit further on he also recognised the site of the hotel Mazaud. Shutting his eyes for a moment, he saw in front of him the terrace on public holidays with its wide, blue and orange, striped parasols. Big Felix would pull in his stomach as he moved among the drinkers who would jeer at him from their seats. The bar was lit up by the smile of his wife, that smile which made her look like the porcelain figure of an oriental monk. Régine walked past, slinky and provocative; the same Régine who was such a good dancer and danced with Gaston so often…

His memory, which had been held in check for so long, was suddenly set free with the strength of a passion. With his back to a section of wall, absent-mindedly stroking its intact edge, Jean yielded to the temptation that he had been resisting ever since that grim night because he assumed it would be fatal: he plunged into the past and sank to the very bottom.

A sky filled with June; a June filled with the scent of the perspiring earth. The village fête took place in June. For Jean it lasted all month. He loved the summer tasks, the fervour of living in the sun, and above all the scent-filled nights which the ecstatic song of crickets and the nightingale made as brief and as light as the memory of a dream. Every year he went to the fête. And each fête was a replay of the very first which went back to some forgotten year in his childhood. His brother François took him by the hand. He lifted him up so he could see the clay pipes of the shooting gallery going round, as white as chalk against the black painted background of the stall. François held him to his chest and from time to time his thick moustache tickled him – this terrible moustache was the reason he was known as the Black Man, and also, the Moor. Old Etienne was tossing the rifle from one hand to the other, making it look as light as a cardboard toy, and saying: Hey, my friend, your equipment's a real piece of junk.' His Gallic moustache was thicker and longer than François's but nowhere near as black, nowhere near as menacing. Finally, Etienne raised the rifle to his shoulder and 'crack!' one of the revolving pipes disappeared, shattering into chalk dust. 'Crack!' another... 'Crack!... and another. Jean laughed for all he was worth, threw back his head and wriggled around so much that François shook him, growling: 'Whoa, this isn't a little kid, it's a whole sack of rats, I tell you. Whoa! If you don't keep still, I'll hang you up on the end of my moustache.' And each year the fête began over again. It was the day of total freedom, the day when there was no work, no difficulties of any kind. Later on, Jean still tended to leave things up to the grown-ups on that day. The grown-ups were in possession of inexhaustible powers which could be terrible. But on the day of the fête the gods were on his side. The village was inhabited by easy-going gods, decked out irreproachably in their Sunday best; the baker called himself a *pâtissier* and wore a tie covered with silver stars against his starched white shirt front. The owner of the café – Léonard Mazaud, father of Félix, a colossus of a man – glowed red in the face amid his greying hair, like an ember surrounded with ash. In the shops, the toddler in from the countryside with suntanned cheeks gazed wide-eyed at the ladies and young girls in their dazzling dresses as they approached with a great rustle of silk. A perfumed and powdered face descended on the toddler, the smack of kisses rang out and a warm voice whispered: 'You are the sweetest little thing at the fête! For your trouble, you're going to choose whatever you want and I'll get it for you.' For the children it was their Day of Glory, when they were treated as veritable royalty. The village dressed up for them, it blossomed and frothed everywhere in drifts of ribbons, in endless smiles.

The last time Jean had been there he was already grown up, certainly as fully grown as he was today. He even clearly remembered making quite an effort to take on the role of a grown-up; he was the boss, the head of the family. He was the one who reminded Gaston to tip the excess fine sand out of his sandals. He was the one who wiped Annie's shoes with a cloth he brought for just that purpose; Annie got the giggles and claimed he was tickling her ankles deliberately. Three or four times he had to dust down old Etienne's jacket and straighten his tie. At that time Etienne was jumping over ruts in the road

310

with the disconcerting agility of an old cat. Besides he had always had some cat or other latched onto his shoulders, and maman, indignant, called him Old Tabby. Maman, meanwhile, had not missed a single waltz that year, and without question she was the one who took more turns around the floor than anybody…

Jean opened his eyes. For an instant the vision of the ghost fête persisted. His mother was still dancing, there, in the main room of the Hotel Mazaud. He thought he could make her out in the music and the shouts, beyond the red-necked drinkers, among the sunlit dust, the confetti, the streamers and garlands.

And here there was nothing but the glassy silence of ruins, the void, the infinite and eternal void. Nothing!… but no, not entirely, not yet. Jean clapped a hand to his nose. There, it was that smell again, that smell which had invaded the whole countryside on the evening of the crime, which was so penetrating that it reached into the pigsty where he lay delirious. He refused to recognise it on that evening but he could not escape it. For a long time he had been obsessed by it. The smell of human beings burnt alive was nothing more or less than the smell of grilled pork. There was no denying it.

This was his final memory. This was his ultimate goodbye! And now…

Now Jean knew he could not go on. He had tried to weep but he could not. Just as in a children's story, he told himself that a single tear might have been enough to save him, perhaps. It would have been a sign that he still belonged to life, that he still loved it. But between him and a sense of tenderness there hung, and would always hang, that smell. The smell of an inhuman, unnameable, overwhelming contract.

He would not escape the fate of his kin, which was his fate. His only regret was that he had not disappeared as they had, without leaving a trace. He looked around for a hole in which he could hide.

He had been told – or rather someone had said in front of him – how Francis and Gaston had been burnt in Blanchard's barn. There perhaps he could find a section of wall on the point of collapse under which he could hide. Come on!

However, he had had time to take no more than ten steps in the direction of Blanchard's farm.

His father's voice stopped him dead; this voice which, inexplicably, had retained the strength of youth.

'Take good care, my boy.'

Even more powerfully than his voice, it was old Etienne's expression which held him. This final, hard, severe expression. Why so severe? So, you've guessed what I wanted to do. You don't want your son to be on the side of the weak.

His father had not weakened. He did not believe in fate. If he could live on, he would live on. He would never have agreed to die behind a corner of a wall. His life, his long life, demanded that he die peacefully in his own bed. And he had waited to be carried to his bed. Such a life and such a death were a triumph over Fate.

Without turning his gaze towards the ruins, his head lowered, looking two steps in front of him, Jean set off back towards the house.

CHAPTER 4

When Jean got home, old Etienne was dead. He had not moved, he was still staring straight ahead, without a trace of terror, but with the utmost attention.

Undoubtedly this was the gaze, lucid and wilful, with which he wanted to cross the final threshold. Jean sensed this so strongly that he refused to close the old man's eyes.

He sat as close to his father as he could, and in his company, he waited patiently for daybreak.

Some years passed. Almost all of Jean's land lay fallow; little by little, bracken, brambles, broom and all the coarse, hardy plants by which nature affirms her inexhaustible hostility, stifled the meadow grass.

He only cultivated the enclosures abutting the farm, and out of a herd of eighteen animals, he had only kept the youngest of his milk cows. Although he continued to feed his dogs, he never took them hunting and he let them wander around as they wished.

In the eyes of the other farmers, living in this way was incomprehensible. It represented the worst of scandals. Jean knew this and it tormented him. But a sort of perpetual anger prevented him from explaining himself to them. He would have had to say too many things that he did not know how to say.

First and foremost, he would not have known how to make them understand what had happened on that morning when he had felt that he could no longer work.

He was getting ready to grub up an old plum tree that had not produced any sap in spring. An easy task. Jean had already begun to dig a large hole around the roots. He had brought everything he needed; two axes, rope, the saw, splitting wedges. Then, all at once, while he was shovelling out the area where he was going to cut the tap root, it happened...

The strength had completely drained from his arms and the spade had fallen from his grasp. He had sat down on the edge of the hole and had remained there, motionless, for ages. He was not surprised. Ever since the event, he had not been really working. He was doing what he did before out of habit. He did not feel any need to work. He had lost his faith.

Moreover, it was not this sudden revulsion to work that seemed to him unreasonable, but rather his ancient faith, his dedication to working the land. The more he looked at his former behaviour, the more he judged it absurd and reprehensible, criminal even. To work blindly, for the sake of working, was to resign oneself to becoming simple raw material. Absorbed by labouring in this brutish state, he knew nothing and he thought of nothing. He thought he was working but he was being worked, like a retriever.

No. There was no way he could make the others understand such a thing. Not yet. So, in the meantime, he was content to quickly discourage his questioners. This was why one day he declared to Joseph his neighbour: 'I don't want to work at feeding the pigs any longer. Never again.'

His taciturn manner made his solitude more and more complete, which was exactly how he wanted it. It was via Joseph's wife, the excellent Maria who was ever attentive and incapable of not getting involved in everybody's affairs, that he had learned that the farmers round about had come up with a very simple explanation for his new wildness: 'Up 'til now he was like his mother. Now he's like old Etienne.'

He was happy to just smile, because he knew that these good folk were wrong. In particular they were wrong to believe that Etienne was wild. He was just hard, and he was right to be, since all he could count on was his own efforts and energy. When men in large numbers let themselves go, became soft and easily led, other men – the small number who did not let themselves go – wasted no time in using them for the only game capable of touching their haughty souls: the Massacre game, the true one, the great one, the one which can only be played with much blood, many flames and many ruins.

Jean knew deep down that he was still very much like his mother. Like her he was ready to place himself at the service of the whole world, provided the world agreed to show him a little goodwill. He was not born for hatred.

When he heard about a German employed on a farm about thirty kilometres away whom some claimed they had seen in uniform among the executioners at Verrièges, he went to see him, on the pretext of going for a walk and without telling anybody. What he found was a bloke, not very young, a bit overweight who had lost two front teeth. He was digging,

315

sweat on his brow and old, split clogs on his bare feet. The German spoke a painful, mangled French but he talked about work in such a way that it was immediately obvious he was a labourer. Finally, before he left, Jean made the only gesture which seemed to him natural and useful: he gave him a little of his tobacco.

Very probably those who thought they recognised him were mistaken. And anyway, the fate of this poor sod was beside the point.

The question for Jean was simply one of knowing how to carry on living. He had to do it: living was a necessary protest in itself. If only he had managed to breathe as he did before, opening out his chest confidently, taking pleasure in it, then he would have regained his courage, he would have taken up work again; the proper sort of work, not just scratching at the earth to make money: work in order to understand how the world worked and how to get to understand others. For, most of the other farmers, less tried-and-tested than him, were sinking back into their time-honoured torpor. The great rumblings and the great glow of the cataclysm had only kept them awake for the duration of a nightmare. Since they still had to 'make a living', they settled for that. They had the incredible patience of ants or of those simple men who rebuild on the slopes of a volcano.

Jean was no longer one of them. He saw clearly that men are wrong to behave like ants. But in fact, he sometimes envied them and felt a pang of regret: his previous torpor had its delights. He immediately pushed back against this temptation which all too visibly bore the mark of the devil.

Living simply for the sheer pleasure of living – this was

something he was no longer capable of. Such a way of life would have been a permanent insult to his dead. When such a crime had taken place, the world rocked on its foundations. The stink of crime was suffocating. Those who smelt it continued to choke on it long after the crime.

And yet, he had to go on. His overwhelming dilemma: to resign himself to this perpetual suffocation or accept the sleep of oblivion. Jean would not forget; he was on the side of those who chose to remember. Or rather, he had been chosen, for a long time. Thus, day after day, he dragged himself between two impossibilities: neither capable of living, nor capable of refusing life.

Each morning when he got up, he passed through the bedroom where Gaston had spent his last night, in the light walnut bed which was too short for him, but which he did not want to give up. He had had a happy childhood and he sought to make it last…

Often Jean also went to sit for a moment 'with the old folk'. His place was at the foot of his mother's bed, so close to his father's that a chair would have blocked the gap. This was where he used to come every evening before going to bed to review the day: to discuss the work, ask advice, give details of some project, tell stories, listen to them, dream out loud.

After these silent visits he felt closer, not to an appetite for living which had gone forever, but to a sense of a life which he could forego. It was still an ill-formed, but powerful feeling, radiating deep from within him, like a new instinct. Gaston had not lived in vain, nor had poor little Annie, nor his mother, nor his father. They had been there. They had spoken. They had borne witness. They had acted. And in this, the world had been transformed. Each of them had transmitted an unforgettable, unalterable spark to all those they had come close to. It was an irrefutable, original spark of life, intelligence and sensitivity which had enriched the world, which was and remained necessary to the overall harmony of the world.

This certainty was very useful to Jean. It was enough to keep him alive. But it failed to make use of his strength, which had not diminished. On the contrary, he felt it was more plentiful and effective than before.

Finally, the day came when Jean felt he was going to move forward.

It was a hot July evening. Jean had just had a long discussion with Maître Lambert who had come to spend one or two days with the neighbours, as he often did.

The lawyer had made a very surprising proposal: David, his grandson, had retained such a strong love of the countryside – something he had discovered during the occupation – that it had guided his studies. He had gone to agricultural college and got first class marks.

'He also needs to do a proper apprenticeship,' Maître Lambert said. 'Take him on. He is very fond of you, and I think you like him too. The work here isn't easy. It will be an excellent way to prove himself. We'll see if he's just an amiable dreamer or if he's genuinely good at something.'

Jean made no promises, but he wanted to go for a walk with David through what had been his fields. He did not need to go far to realise that 'the amiable dreamer' was not only sturdy, agile and well-built, but impatient to put to the test his extensive, and by no means fanciful, knowledge.

With this one, he would not be tempted to persist in doing

things the way he used to. Deep down, what Jean had always liked most about his brother Francis (and about Gaston who copied him) was his need to change. He had a horror of all routines, those which he had overcome and those to which he had been subjected.

He headed towards Pré Tort. At the bottom of the valley near old Arlaud's mill ran a babbling stream, as it had for centuries. David used to like this spot surrounded by quickset hedges and thickets. He fished for minnows there and even tried his hand at tickling trout.

Because of the damp no doubt, dealing with the invasion of ferns, broom, thistles and all forms of thick bramble in this place seemed hopeless.

David was not in the slightest bit intimidated. He had already taken out of his pocket a large knife fitted with various accessories and began sawing a juniper bush growing in a spot where previously the grass had been most lush.

Jean stopped him and made him sit down close by.

'There's plenty of time for that,' he said, starting to roll a cigarette.

This was a sign that he agreed to the proposal. The young man's face began to blaze like a sun. Discreetly, Jean turned away and contemplated the lengthening shadows of the great oak trees at the bottom of the valley. They could clearly be seen lengthening; they gathered momentum at the edge of holes and ditches, then leapt over them in one go.

It was twilight; the moment when the sun was disappearing beneath the horizon.

Jean was remembering. He was entering fully into memory with such tranquil assurance that he felt free again.

319

The sun of the elders was sinking for him and would sink again on many days. But it would never again sink for Annie, or for Gaston, or for Félix, of for Francis, or for Pierre, or for hundreds and hundreds of others. They would never grow old. For them, each morning the dawn of youth would appear. For all time they lived in the heart of mother earth, in the heart of those who kept faith, living and radiant, like the sun of youth shining on new faces.

Jean felt a sudden impatience tingling in his hands. He grabbed two big clumps of weeds, tore them up and scattered them some distance.

'Shall we get going?' David asked keenly, already on his feet.

Jean shook his head: 'There's plenty of time, now,' he repeated slowly.